THE RULES OF THE ROAD

C.B. Jones

The characters and events in this book are fictitious. Any similarity to real persons, living or dead, is coincidental and not intended by the author.

THE RULES OF THE ROAD

Copyright © 2021, text by C.B. Jones

All rights reserved, except for brief quotations. No part of this book may be reproduced in any manner without

written permission from the publisher: Ionosphere Press, saintlonesome@gmail.com

Published 2021 by Ionosphere Press

Cover design by Kyle Goldtooth.

Formatting by Alex Wolfgang.

ISBN: 978-1-7374886-0-6

First edition: August 2021

CONTENTS

1. "Station Identification" — 1
2. "Operator" — 10
3. "Carry On Wayward Son" — 24
4. "Alone" — 38
5. "What's Your Name?" — 50
6. "Southern Accents" — 66
7. "Time After Time" — 88
8. "Tuesday's Gone" — 102
9. "Call Me" — 120
10. "Cold as Ice" — 148
11. "Landslide" — 170
12. "Left of the Dial" — 196
13. "Losing My Religion" — 234
14. "Thunder Road" — 272
15. "Greatest Hits" — 288
    Epilogue — 325

    Acknowledgments — 329

For my wife

Many consumer and industrial products and applications make use of some form of electromagnetic energy. One type of electromagnetic energy that is of increasing importance worldwide is radiofrequency energy, including radio waves . . . There are many published reports in the scientific literature concerning possible biological effects resulting from animal or human exposure to radiofrequency energy.

- from "Questions and Answers about Biological Effects and Potential Hazards of Radiofrequency Electromagnetic Fields", FCC OET Bulletin, 1999

1
"STATION IDENTIFICATION"

I was in the middle of the country when I first heard the radio program. The halfway point, more or less.

Later, I'd wonder if it was even real. Like if the whole thing had been some sort of auditory hallucination, the side effects of sleep deprivation and too much caffeine.

Yet miles down the road, fear took hold and I decided there was too much riding on the outcome to blow it off.

I was coming out of North Platte, Nebraska, when I heard it. Driving across barren plains and trying to make Denver before midnight, I was making pretty good time. My destination was my friends' house in Aurora. I hoped to get a good night's rest before we set off for the slopes the next day.

I was listening to a rerun of Car Talk on NPR. I had been on the road for ten hours straight at that point, and the Car Talk guys' thick accents and wheezing laughs were the only thing keeping me awake.

The signal was clear when suddenly there was a wash of static and laughter, a different kind of laughter than the Bostonian cackles of the Magliozzi brothers. It was higher and more feminine, but androgynous at the same time. It almost sounded like it came from within the car itself. Then, the static washed away and some light, tinkly music came on. A voice started talking. It was the voice of a cheery old man with a twangy accent. Below is the transcript as I heard it on that spooky and unsettling night.

HOWDY FOLKS, *I'm Buck Hensley, and these are "The Rules of the Road." Tonight, we come to you with an answer to an age-old question that has perplexed many of y'all out there. Why is it that when you're driving on some highway or busy interstate, you sometimes look out at the shoulder and see a single, solitary shoe? How did it get there? Where is its owner? Why is it only one shoe? We'll try to answer that, but once you learn this rule, you may never look at a single shoe on the side of the road the same way again. In fact, it would be downright deadly not to!*

So, here is tonight's rule: if at any point during your journey you see a single shoe on the side of the road all by its lonesome, then you must pull over immediately. What's that? You say you're in the far lane and spot the shoe and there's a lot of traffic and you can't cross over? Tough titty! You must find a way to that shoe or else, even if you have to turn around.

Once you are pulled over, make sure it is safe for you to exit your vehicle. How tragic and hilarious would it be for you to start out with the good intention of following this vital and important rule, only to be splattered on the interstate by the front tires and bumper of an inattentive driver? How your teeth would scatter on the concrete and glint under the moonlight.

So, you've arrived at the shoe, and the scene is safe and secure? This part is relatively easy. All you need to do is get out and remove one of your socks and place it in the shoe, get back in your car and leave. If you don't have a sock with you, then you better find one. Now, I've made that sound extremely easy and most times it is really that simple, but sometimes the shoe's owner is nearby, and he might give you a good ol' fright.

I can't say that I rightly know this fella's name, but he only has one leg. And I don't mean he's some sort of amputee or anything like that. I mean he is a man of sturdy build and that he has a normal torso and arms and hips, but his pelvis tapers off into just the one leg at the dead center of his body. A thigh as thick as a tree stump. He gets around by hopping on the one leg, and he has a ten or fifteen foot standing broad jump. Sometimes when the leg is tired, he pulls himself along with his arms, dragging his leg behind him. He looks downright dirty and mean, clothes all ragged and worn. You can usually see him at the treeline or in the brush or down in the ditch, waiting for you. He might approach you; it depends on what mood he's in. Just give him a nod, tuck your sock in his shoe, and leave.

Now I hope my folksy demeanor doesn't undermine the gravity of this rule. What happens if you ignore this rule? Well, something bad will happen, that's what. This is not a joke and ignore this at your own peril, but if you don't follow this rule, the next bridge you drive over will collapse either due to a construction failure or some other arbitrary reason, sending you and your vehicle into the water below. This will always result in your untimely death, no matter how good a swimmer you are.

Hope y'all are having a good one out there. Stay

alert. Stay lively. Stay lonely. Once again, I'm Buck Hensley and these are "The Rules of the Road".

FROM THERE A LOUD burst of static occurred, followed by an extremely high-pitched whine, so loud that it was painful, and I had to shut off the stereo. I drove in silence for some time, trying to laugh nervously at the message I had just heard. At first, I thought it was some sort of joke, an audio sketch show recorded by some locals and inserted into the broadcast accidentally or as a goof. It had to be a sketch, right? Some sort of surreal dark comedy or something.

Yet, I found myself slowing down to 60 mph, driving in the right-hand lane and scanning the shoulder for missing shoes. My heart was pounding, and my palms were sweaty on the steering wheel.

What if I missed one?

Were there any bridges between here and Aurora? Any major rivers?

I told myself to quit being ridiculous, but it was no use. I drove 60 mph the whole way to Aurora and added an hour to my total drive time. My eyes were wide and watering, begging for me to shut my lids.

It wasn't until I pulled off the I-225 exit and was coming down the ramp that I calmed down. The fatigue and sleepiness hit me like a freight train and as I made the turn onto 6th, out of the corner of my eye, I saw it: a single shoe, sitting on the side of the road, sole facing up and laces splayed out. I slammed on my brakes.

You're insane, *I told myself.*

It was cold out there. I didn't even bother to put on my coat. The traffic was dead, a bad part of town. A black garbage bag and some trash clung to an overgrown patch of prairie grass and weeds. A car came in the other direction. There was a convenience store off in the distance. I approached the shoe and flipped it over. A basic black canvas low top, a Converse rip-off. I looked around to see if anyone was watching. There was a guy in a heavy brown coat and a low-slung baseball cap sitting against the wall of the convenience store. I couldn't tell how many legs he had. Another car came down the ramp toward me, headlights shining. I probably was going to look crazy, but

I pulled off my right shoe, peeled my sock off and tucked it into the shoe.

From the garbage bag, I heard a rustle and the rattling of aluminum cans. A hand shot out from underneath, buried its fingers into the dirt and pulled a body forward from underneath the garbage bag, a face suddenly appearing and looking at me, yellowed eyes and a mouth full of awful teeth. I screamed and darted back to my car and never looked back.

There were three bridge incidents that year throughout the US. Seventeen deaths. One was an overpass at rush hour, a structural integrity issue. Another incident involved a riverboat barge that crashed into the pylon supporting a hundred-foot interstate bridge and several cars and a semi plunged into the Arkansas River below.

You had to wonder.

I carry a pack of socks with me when I'm out on the road and constantly look for shoes. I always follow the rules to a T and take off the sock I'm wearing, just in case. He hasn't reappeared at any of the shoes I've stopped at.

Everyone thought I was crazy, but nothing bad ever happened to me as long as I followed the rule. I wasn't going to tempt fate and find out what would happen if I didn't.

Have you heard "The Rules of the Road?"

That was the name of the website I started several months after hearing the program. That question with all the words smushed together and a blogspot.com after, or something like that. It's probably still up there if you look hard enough. You know what they say about stuff posted on the internet.

Before the website, hours were spent on the dark corners of the internet. I stalked message boards for paranormal encounters, UFO and bigfoot sightings, cryptids and astral projections. There were emails exchanged with individuals both credible and deceitful, rambling and succinct. Liars and lunatics, skeptics and schizophrenics.

I never claimed to be an expert or journalist, but that's the role I fell into. Two and a half years into college as a journalism major before dropping out, I was a little more prepared than most, maybe a little less amateur. Despite all of that, however, my credentials were little more than a night clerk at 7-11.

I didn't want to end up like any of those weirdoes, though. And despite the steadfast belief in my own experience, I oftentimes viewed myself as above it all, an objective observer.

I must admit that there were various times that I thought I was losing my mind, that I was simply becoming another online conspiracy theorist. Or worse and somehow even more paranoid, that someone out there was orchestrating this whole ruse on me for a big joke.

Through my online investigations, I discovered that others had experienced it too. Common threads between occurrences were that listeners heard the broadcast while driving alone and that it seemed to occur more often on the AM band. Out of everyone that was interviewed, all had followed the instructions that were broadcast on the short program.

If only I had found someone that hadn't.

That blog post was just me putting out a beacon for whoever to find. I had to know I wasn't alone. I needed to know I wasn't the only one.

Well.

I wasn't.

It wasn't long before I discovered there were different versions of the mysterious broadcast. I had initially believed that there was only the strange and singular episode and that it was the same for each listener. However, a new individual contacted me and discussed his experience. It differed completely from what we all had encountered before.

2
"OPERATOR"

B randon was a guy in his twenties who currently lived in Sacramento. He spoke with me over the phone about how he had heard the broadcast and how it had affected him. There were the same common denominators: he was alone in his car, it was late at night, and he had been driving for hours when he encountered the program.

THERE'S NOT REALLY a whole lot of backstory. I was driving home from my buddy's bachelor party in Tahoe, a low-key thing at this swanky cabin he had rented for the weekend. Bunch of us guys, a lot of boozing, a little hiking, some catching up.

Anyways, I was driving home, it was late at night, and I was listening to the radio. Even with all the technology available at our fingertips, I still like to listen to it from time to time. I don't mind the commercials and I like the random nature of it. It seems more real, y'know? That, and my data plan kinda sucks and I'm trying to cut costs where I can.

The good thing about the radio is you can always find a Tom Petty song out there if you look hard enough. That's what I had found, when out of nowhere, there was this burst of static. It was unlike anything I'd ever heard, almost *musical*. It was so mesmerizing that I didn't bother changing the station. Then this voice started talking.

HOWDY FOLKS, Buck Hensley here with more "Rules of the Road". Hope y'all are doing well out there and that you're nice and cozy in your big trucks and SUVs as the cold night whizzes past. I hope your seat warmer starts working again. Nothing like a nice, warm ass on a cold winter's night. I really miss my wife and cuddling up next to hers, how I would call in sick to work some days just to spend those few extra hours in bed with her, how I often wanted to live in that half-awake moment with her forever, but nothing lasts, and I can't get back there . . .

AT THIS POINT, I laughed at the surreal hilarity of the radio program that had preempted the song I was listening to. However, I was a little unnerved by a single detail within the opening monologue: the seat warmer in my Jeep *was* broken. I listened on, transfixed.

WHOOPS! Sorry, got a little off track there. Anyways, on to tonight's rule. If at any point in your journey you get a call from an unknown number, then you must answer your phone. You must take that call. Don't ignore it, don't screen it and don't wait for it to go to voicemail thinking that you might call it back, because you won't be able to. It is imperative that you pick up.
    Now I know what you're thinking, and I know

what you're gonna say. You're gonna say, "Bucky, what if it's another one of them goddang robocallers? I get those all the time and I ignore them and they're just the biggest waste of time and I've been waiting for a callback on an interview, and I've been answering unknown numbers and I get those calls warning me about my vehicle's warranty expiring and it's a scam and they just make me so darn mad I could just scream. Like hell am I gonna answer another one of those calls!"

And to that I say, fair enough. I get why you're so upset. Those calls get me hot under the collar, too. Why do they call them robocallers, anyways? Is there a robot on the other end dialing away with his little metal robot fingers? Bleep-bloop-bleep. But I digress . . .

I WISHED I had a passenger in the car with me. Y'know, someone to exchange confused and amused looks with, someone to ask, "Are you hearing this shit? Google this and see what it is."

So, the first thing you must do is to answer the call. Make sure your phone is on loud. Make sure you hear the ring. Because if you miss it, that is no bueno. Once you answer, you might hear that dead air and clicking you get on your usual telemarketer call. You might hear some strange noises. You might hear something that is downright spooky. Just hang on a second and wait for the voice, a nice pleasing monotone woman's voice asking you your name. I like to call her Carla. She will ask you your name. State your given name. Carla will respond that there has been some unusual activity on your "Card Account" and that she needs the number on your credit or debit card to further research the activity and put a stop to it. This will sound sketchy as hell to you, and you will probably feel the urge to hang up and tell her to "buzz off", but if you do, then you will miss your chance.

Once you give her your card information, do not fret. The folks on the other end of the line ain't gonna clean you out. They are really looking out for you and have your best interest at heart. The most you will see is a dollar or two here and there pulled out of your account every month. It will show up on your bank statements. That's like a cup of coffee a month you're missing out on, but it's totally worth it. What's the value of a dollar? That might be the most valuable dollar of your life!

Okay. So, you say to heck with all of this? Well, let me tell you what will happen. As far as punishments go, with this one you might actually have a fighting chance and it actually makes quite a good PSA for safe driving. From then on, after receiving the call, whether you've answered and didn't give your number or ignored it all together, the next time you pick up your phone while driving it will result in a deadly motor vehicle collision.

It doesn't matter if you're on America's loneliest highway without another vehicle for miles, I'm telling you: DO NOT PICK UP THAT PHONE. Do not text. Do not make a call. Do not adjust your Spotty-fi playlist. Let that hunk of plastic and copper and platinum and gold and terbium lie. Turn it off and throw it in the backseat if you have to.

You will get complacent. You will get comfort-

able, and you will forget. Just a quick buzz and you glance down at the phone, or you take a quick peek at your GPS because you're not sure when your exit is coming up and BLAMMO! That will be all she wrote. A semi from nowhere will appear, a bend in the road that wasn't there before, a sheet of ice on a sultry summer day. The horizon will turn upside down as your vehicle careens across the landscape.

You ever seen what happens to a vehicle that goes underneath a semi-truck's wheels? Think about what happens to the body. I don't even know if you can call it a body at that point. The parts are all there, but they don't seem to add up.

And your face? Think about what will happen to your face. We're wired to see faces, don't you see? Two eyes, a nose, a mouth. Our minds are drawn to them in our environment from birth, seeking that connection. Your mom, your sister, your girlfriend, your boyfriend, they'd do anything to see your face one more time, even if it's lifeless and a little bloated and a little too made up by the mortician. Your family will take seeing that semblance, that mediocre representation of the face they once loved as a means of closure.

But they won't be able to because that thing above your shoulders can not be called a face at that point and all the king's horses and all the king's mortuary men cannot put your broken eggshell runny yolk face back together again and you'll have to have a closed casket. Your loved ones will have to imagine it.

Well, that's all for tonight. Hope y'all have warmed up a bit and got your phones where you can reach 'em. Stay alert out there. Stay lively. Stay

lonely. Once again, I'm Buck Hensley and these are "The Rules of the Road".

I WAS SHAKEN to my core. At first, I felt a little silly getting so spooked by the broadcast, but I *was* on a dark highway all by myself in the middle of the night. I pulled off at the nearest truck stop, went inside a bit, drank some water and returned to my vehicle.

Five miles down the road, my phone rang.

I didn't know what to do. There was the sudden concern that it was all a trick, that if I picked up my phone, I would end up in a deadly car accident. I hesitated. The phone rang again. Making sure I kept my eyes on the road, I reached for my smartphone with a trembling arm and answered.

There was a pause on the other end, followed by a click. Then, a wall of noise. It took me a second to distinguish all the wailing sounds stacked on top of each other.

I had been to funerals before: grandparents and older family members and the funeral of a friend that had died too young, a beloved teacher from my grade school that had gotten cancer. These sounds were the sounds from those funerals, the inexplicable grief that could only be expressed in loud wails and sobs, the cursing of the heavens and the asking of *why? Why? Why?* And they were all happening at once, right there on my phone and in my ear.

I heard the woman's voice suddenly appear on the other line; she cut in through the awful sounds and they faded into the background.

"Please state your name."

I gave her my name.

"We've noticed some unusual activity on your credit card. To verify your identity and investigate this further, we need you to provide the 16-digit credit card number, expiration date, and CVV number. Please provide these now."

I was at a loss. I had the sudden thought that there was a rogue broadcast out there in this part of the country, getting gullible people to listen to the warning and then hitting them with the call. Some sort of scam.

But then I imagined my family in some church, the images and sounds of their grief. I could always cancel the credit card.

I veered toward the shoulder, leaning on my left side to reach the wallet in my back pocket.

"Are you there, Brandon?" the voice asked. "Please provide the numbers now."

I was getting frantic. A patch of gravel forced me into a skid, my car heading off the side of the road. I dropped the phone and gripped the steering wheel, guided myself to safety.

It took me several minutes to find my phone on the floorboards and when I did, the caller had disappeared.

It has been both a blessing and a curse.

I've become something of a Luddite now. I never turn my cell phone on when I'm driving. I actually always place it in the trunk. At first, I thought I could deal with it by just leaving it turned off and in the passenger seat, but during those notorious gridlocked California traffic jams, I feel myself absentmindedly reaching toward it.

I've also stopped carrying it around as much. My attention span seems better now, and I feel more focused. Every time I go out, I can't help but notice how everyone is so glued to their phones, how addicted everyone is.

Sometimes I miss out on some last-minute changes of plans, and I show up to the wrong restaurant. Or there are times when I arrive at friends' apartments when they've already made secondary arrangements for transportation, and they have tried to call me while I was on my way. I have to print out directions for places ahead of time. I've gotten lost on several occasions. Not having my cell phone available has caused several unnecessary fights between me and my girlfriend.

You're the only one I've told about this experience. Nobody else would ever believe me. Even worse, they might try and convince me it was all in my head. I don't want to get too comfortable and deny my experience and forget about what could happen if I don't follow the rule.

I've been going to a cabin an hour outside of Tahoe on any free weekend that I can. It's secluded and remote. Up on the mountain, there's no cell phone service, and I don't get that fear of missing out. I couldn't get a call even if I *wanted* to. When I'm up there, I feel at peace.

I CHECKED *in with Brandon a month later, but he didn't respond to my e-mails. Weeks passed, and I tried calling multiple times. The phone always went straight to voicemail, and he never called me back despite the voice messages.*

I had had some growing concerns about a large wildfire that was in the news over in that area. I wasn't too familiar with the region, but it seemed awfully close to the general whereabouts of his cabin. Through some digging, I got a hold of his girlfriend, Lacy. We spoke on the phone.

"I hate to tell you this, but Brandon's dead."

I was quiet for a while. When he hadn't responded, of course I had had that fear. Hearing it confirmed was still a punch in the gut.

"What happened?" I asked, fearing the cause of death was a car accident.

"It was that damn phone," she said. "He wouldn't pick up. He

was so hard to get a hold of. All the time. I didn't understand why he cared so much about safety all of a sudden. I mean, we all do it, and it is a risk, but he took it to the extreme."

"Lacy, what is it? Did he die in a car wreck?"

"It was the wildfire. He was up at his family's cabin for his decompression time. I wasn't feeling up for it that weekend, and my sister's birthday get-together was going on. It wasn't anything for him to go up there alone. When we saw how bad the fire was getting, we tried and tried to get a hold of him, but of course there was no answer. It was heading straight for him."

"Doesn't the Forest Service or the firefighters order an evacuation and go door to door?"

"Yes, and they did. He finally called us from a landline at the convenience store in town, down the mountain. Said he was heading back, and that it was really getting bad, but that he couldn't contact us from the road. We learned from news updates that the pass he usually took had a shift in winds and the fire was overtaking the road. He would have to take a different route, or he was going to get burned alive. But how could we let him know?"

Her voice cracked. I gave her the time, a knot in my stomach.

"Finally, we got a call from him. He had pulled over and gotten his phone out from the trunk. Told us the pass was awful, walls of flame everywhere, he could feel the heat in the car. He was so scared. I could hear it in his voice."

She was full on crying now.

"Luckily, we could tell him to turn around, to go the other way and take the alternate route. We were both so relieved to get in touch with each other. He said he was going to hang up, that he would be in touch soon."

She sniffled, catching her breath some. She was calming back down.

"A few minutes later, I sent him a message, an 'I love you' text. I just wanted him to know. He never made it home."

There was silence.

"I'm so sorry," I said.

"It's strange. They found his car wedged into this boulder, completely demolished. There wasn't a single burn mark on the vehicle. Somehow the fire had burnt an entire area all around him but didn't even touch his body. I just hope he got my text. I just hope he knew."

I didn't really advertise my blog post. I didn't want to compromise the integrity of my project and be faced with an onslaught of fabricated stories. I figured those that sought me out were genuine.

Let the stories trickle in, I thought.
They will.
And they did.

3
"CARRY ON WAYWARD SON"

An individual named James contacted me with his story. His experience differed from the others in that he was not driving when he heard the mysterious broadcast, and he was also with a small group of people. He and the others all heard the radio program at the same time.

CALL ME A TRAVELER. I don't liken to them other terms anymore, if I ever did in the first place. You may have heard of 'em: the hobos, the vagabonds, the oogles, the trainhoppers, the scumfucks. Although I fraternize and run around with many of them, that lifestyle is a young man's game. Even back then, I was something of a weekend warrior, only committing to the lifestyle exclusively for a few years straight. I would do stints in between oil field jobs until a back injury got me on disability, and I was able to commit to the lifestyle full time.

These days I take it much easier. I don't hop trains. I don't hitchhike. I don't sleep on benches. At risk of sounding like a cliche, I'm too old for that shit.

I've got me a nice little Ford Econoline that I've

converted to my main domicile and source of transportation. Got a mattress in the back. My dog, Leo, is my constant companion. The others may call me a rubber tramp, being as I've got a vehicle and all, but like I said, "call me a traveler."

I don't own a house or rent an apartment, but I'm not homeless in the traditional sense; the road is my home. All the others that I hang out with, you might consider them voluntarily homeless. They chose to live this way. Or maybe it chose them.

We were holed up under a bridge over the Cuyahoga River, somewhere outside of Akron. It was me and four others, Tito, Snoopy, Sleepy-J, and Mudcat. It had been a few days, and I was getting antsy and about ready to move on down the road. I would maybe see these guys again, or maybe not. I liked to travel alone anymore.

But for now, we were having a nice little evening. We had a fire going, a couple cases of Hamm's, and a few joints to pass around. The sun was dipping low over the naked trees that lined the Cuyahoga. Tito and Mudcat had scored eighty bucks from donating plasma and with the spoils had bought the beer as well as some hot dogs from Dollar Tree, and we also had trash bags full of barely stale Kaiser rolls from a bakery's dumpster. Some dented cans of beans and condiments swiped from a 7-11 and we were gonna have a feast. Leo seemed to enjoy it as I slid him some hotdogs and bread.

I had my little boombox sitting out by the fire and the tunes were going. Lynyrd Skynyrd was playing "Free Bird" on a classic rock station, and it appeared to be the album version. You know it's a pretty long song.

"Man, this song has been on forever. Ay Jimbo, change it," Tito said.

"Are you outta your damn head? You never change

"Free Bird". You have to listen to the entire song. It's a rule," I said.

"Whatever, pops."

Just then there was a loud burst of squealing from the stereo. It sounded like a guitar, but I'd heard this song many a time and I knew the solo by heart. It was playing faster and faster and then started sounding weird and out of key, the notes becoming distorted. Then, a blast of static, and that's when we heard the broadcast. A happy sounding voice started speaking.

HIYA FOLKS, Buck Hensley here with another episode of "The Rules of the Road." The smell of spring is in the air and I can feel it in my bones. The doc calls it arthritis, but I told him it was my own bony little barometer, put there by time traveling nanobot viruses from the future. He said, "Nope. Arthritis." I told him I needed a second opinion, and he said, "Well, you're crazy too," so I fired him.

How the smell of his burning flesh and hair filled the waiting room.

"YO, WHAT IS THIS SHIT?" Mudcat asked with a laugh. "Find some more tunes. This is killin' my vibe."

"No, wait. Listen," I said.

The broadcast continued on.

ANYHOW, on to tonight's rule! Alright, turn up your volume knob, cuz you're gonna wanna hear this one. If at any point during your journey you spot a Geo Metro in a Wal-Mart parking lot, then there's your cue. You must approach that vehicle cautiously. On the back window, you must write WASH ME PLEASE in the dust and grime that coat the car. Try to be wary of the car's owner. You don't wanna get in a tussle with her.

I know what you're thinking. You're thinking, "Bucky, I'm 53 goddang years old. I ain't no spring chicken. I don't have time for childish games anymore. I'm too busy reading the paper in the morning and talking about the weather. Sure it was something we did as kids and sometimes we'd even draw a dingaling or a great big ol' pair of bosoms on there, that would really get us laughing, but I don't get the same jollies as I used to. My body aches in the morning and everything's gone sepia toned. I don't feel the same joy like I did. Every day, every hour is that much closer to the end, and it keeps going by faster and faster. I just don't know what I'm going to go or what I'm going to leave behind as I mosey along toward the void."

THE OTHERS all looked at me with knowing smiles. They didn't know my exact age, but the DJ apparently did. They just gave me the smirks you get when a comedian reveals some common truth your friends know you can relate to. As for me, I thought it was a coincidence.

WELL, to that I say, horse pucky! Age is just a number, and I was never that good at math. I know I have to get up three times a night to take a piss, and I still feel as young as I once did. Why, I still get out once a month to play mailbox baseball. Sometimes pedestrian baseball too! Them's worth fifty points.

But if you insist that this is too childish of an endeavor for you, then you must pay the viper. Should you heed this warning, then you must never sleep in the same place twice, for if you do, then the car's owner will find you and then ...well, it certainly won't be pretty is all I can say.

Hope y'all are having a good one out there and I hope that the spring comes soon to wake us up out of this god-awful winter. It has been far too long and the gray days seem to stretch on forever. Stay alert. Stay lively. Stay lonely. Once again, I'm Buck Hensley and these are "The Rules of the Road".

THE BROADCAST CUT off with a jerk and returned to another classic rock song.

Mudcat threw an empty beer can at the stereo.

"Fuck that. We could teach that old bastard about the real rules of the road. Like double wrap it with anyone you meet in Ybor," he said with a laugh.

"Was that kinda creepy to anyone else?" asked Sleepy-J.

We all shrugged and continued drinking. Mudcat, so named because of his supposed ability as a catfisherman, claimed that he could catch a catfish by hand. He assured us it was too cold on this late February evening and that the catfish were out hibernating. Later on, as the night wore on and the beers were almost gone, I was beginning to doze off in my lawn chair when there was a splash followed by loud laughter. The other three except for Mudcat returned to the campfire in hysterics. Mudcat soon followed, dripping and shivering.

Leo and I passed out soon after.

I awoke at noon the next day and was itching to go. Snoopy and Sleepy J were gonna hang out for a while and then hitch on somewhere else, but Tito and Mudcat asked for a ride and I obliged. I needed to hit up Wal-Mart for a couple supplies, use their bathroom, and regroup. I was thinking of going South and greeting the spring, maybe hit up New Orleans.

By the time we made it to the Wal-Mart after I had to run Mudcat around all over Akron so he could score, it was getting dark. As I came back to my van from the store I noticed that Tito and Mudcat had smirks on their faces.

"What is it?" I asked.

"We found one of them cars, from the broadcast y'know? It's a Geo Metro. It's shaped like a bubble, and it is *really* dirty," Tito said.

"Looks like some damn hoarder's ride, packed full of shit," Mudcat added.

"Well, y'all know the rules," I said with a smile. Leo barked.

"Are you serious?"

"I dunno," I shrugged.

Leo's hair bristled and he started to let out a low growl. I suddenly got nervous and anxious and thought of the broadcast. I took it as a warning that should be heeded.

"Where's the car?" I asked.

The car was parked under a parking lot lamp, all by itself at the edge of the lot. For whatever reason, I felt a sense of dread as I approached it. It was turquoise blue and boxy and through the back windows I could see piles of boxes and newspapers and several baby doll arms sticking out through the piles of clutter, glass bottles against one window. There was no one in the driver's seat and the passenger seat was full of clutter as well. Paperback books filled the crevice between the dashboard and windshield.

There was a fine layer of yellow dust over the entire vehicle and coating the back window especially. I looked around. No driver or owner in sight. Leo stood at my side, whining. I approached the back window, licked the tip of my finger, pressed it to the glass, and began to trace in the dirt: WASH ME PLEA—

Suddenly, from over my right shoulder something big and heavy moved past me in a whoosh. The back windshield shattered right next to me, and I jumped back and looked behind me. It was Mudcat.

"What the fuck, man?"

"We're the ones that write the rules of the road. Not no crazy-ass broadcast," he said.

"There's cameras everywhere here. What are you thinkin'?"

He looked jittery, like he may have used recently.

"I'm getting the hell outta here. See y'all down the road. They can track my plates," I said as I jogged toward my van.

There was a figure standing near my van. Heavy and almost as tall as me, wearing clothing that covered its entire body. I stopped dead in my tracks. The figure looked at me and started walking slowly toward Leo and I. Gray sweatpants and a hoodie drawn down tight and nothing but darkness where its face should be. It had the body of a heavy woman with wide hips and large pendulous breasts and she (was it a she?) sauntered ever closer. There was nobody else around.

Leo and I turned and ran, but as soon as I did, I ran straight into a thick, unyielding wall that had been draped in fabric. It was her, somehow behind me now. She reached for my neck, and I tripped backwards. Leo started barking and she towered over me. I scooted back on my ass and jumped up, my bad back screaming and shooting lightning down my legs. I went to shove her back so that I could get away, but she gripped my wrist tight. Oh, so tight. She leaned her head toward me and I could smell rot and decay and garbage. I went to unzip the front of her sweat suit and beneath was a cluster of baby doll heads, pink and shiny little faces.

Looking at her hand, I realized it was part newsprint and used Band-Aids and dental floss and yarn that had somehow been wound tightly to form the shape of a hand. I shoved my fingers into the gap of the hoody where a face should be, and they sunk into wilted lettuce and something gritty.

Leo—God bless him—came to my rescue. He sprung forward and clamped his jaws down on her thigh and started jerking his head. The fabric of her pants tore, and bottle caps and buttons and silverware clattered to the asphalt. She let go of me and I sprinted to my van, Leo right on my heels. We started up the vehicle and peeled out of that parking lot and never looked back.

To this day, we still haven't looked back. I wasn't superstitious before the broadcast, but after spotting the car so soon after hearing the show and the attack in the parking lot, I sure as hell am now. My only regret is that I couldn't get a hold of Tito or Mudcat after my attack to warn them how true the thing actually was.

I didn't hear anything from them for a long while. That's the way life can be out there on the road. You go months without seeing folks, sometimes even years. You hear rumors about how they're in rehab or not doing so well or got in trouble with the law and then you think you might not ever see them again, but then one day at a bonfire in Slab City or in downtown Portland there they are, smiling like nothing's happened. But in Tito and Mudcat's case, I didn't ever see them again.

I first heard about Mudcat. The way I hear it is that he did heed the warning for a period of time. People said that he was always super paranoid and skittish and liked to move around a lot, but they chalked it all up to the drugs. But then they said he met up with this gal in Birmingham and his mom wired him a bunch of money. They scored some dope and holed up in a motel room. The first night, nothing happened.

The cops answered a call of a hysterical woman at a Rodeway Inn, said her boyfriend had been buried alive. They found his body lying in the motel bed under hundreds of pounds of garbage that had somehow been transported into the room. It was just pure garbage: rotting food, paper plates, tissue paper, aluminum cans. His mouth and airway were obstructed with hundreds of little balls of foil gum wrapper and q-tips.

Tito, I later heard was arrested for a breaking and entering charge and was serving some time in county before his sentencing. He must've heard about Mudcat, and he must've known how dire his situation was. He must've believed. He spent the first week in county, begging fellow inmates to allow him to switch bunks with him. The way it was set up is that there was a row of cells that opened up to a small common area with a table where they could sit and wile away the day.

This worked out for the first seven nights, but then he ran into an inmate that didn't want to give his bunk up, refused to. Tito tried to get in there late at night and an altercation ensued. In the end he died from blunt force trauma to the head.

As for me, I suppose my fate could've been worse. I was built for the lifestyle, y'know. I could've had a home and family and a job and then I would have truly been screwed.

I often wonder how different it could've all been. If only I had finished those last two letters, I could've continued to live my life the way I had previously, without a care in the world. But now, I'm much more regimented and planned out. It's funny, I chose the road because of the limitless freedom it offered, but now I couldn't choose anything else even if I wanted to.

Back when I used to travel, it often felt like I was running toward something, some sort of clarity or deeper discovery of the self. But now, it feels like I'm running *from* something. Because, well, I am. If I think too hard about it, though, I'm not sure there's really any difference.

That's the end of my story. I've gotta get off here now and find a place to park for the evening. I'll keep traveling for now, keep hitting the road and never sleeping in the same place twice. The math works out and I've got many places to hide. America's full of 'em. If I run out, I'll head north to Canada, always on the move, never waking in the same place twice.

The broadcast had been growing stronger and with more range and means of attack. No longer would a listener be required to only be listening to the radio in order to pick it up. Some listeners began to report that they had been listening to podcast streams or Spotify or Apple Music when the mysterious program suddenly appeared.

4
"ALONE"

I *received a call from Leslie, a young woman in her early 20s who had experienced Buck Hensley's down-home delivery and dire warning sometime last June.*
This is her story.

"YOU KNOW it's not very safe for a girl out there alone and on the road."
 This is something that I heard all the time, no matter the journey, no matter the situation, and no matter my history of traveling alone as a female without incident.
 I rolled my eyes in response to Jamie's words of caution.
 "It's just something I've never really had to think about, like as a guy, you know? Need to go down to the store by myself late at night? I do it without thinking. Drink at a bar alone? Check. I can do it without getting creeped on. I mean, I guess I could get robbed, but they might be less apt to jump a 180 lb guy vs. whatever you're checking in at these days," Jamie said.
 "Bitch, do you wanna go? I will get you on the ground

and have you tapping out in 5 seconds." Although it had been a few months, I had taken some Brazilian jiu-jitsu classes and had grappled my brother into submission many a time. He said he was going to go to a class so he could beat me, but he never did.

"Haha, no thanks. I know how that will end. Seriously, Les, just be careful out there. As your older brother, I'm obligated to tell you these things. If you could just wait a couple weeks until I get my time off, I could go with you."

"Can't wait. The mountains are calling, and I must go. I've got a schedule to work around too y'know," I said.

"You got your taser? The pepper spray? Knife?"

"Yeah, yeah, yeah."

"Fine, fine. Well, I'll see you down there in a few weeks. And update me on your itinerary as you go. I don't need mom freaking out while you're off the grid."

"Will do, Brocephus."

My older brother Jamie and I were close, about as close as a pair of siblings could get. Sometimes I could almost consider him my best friend. In fact, based on our long-shared history and his loyalty and consistency throughout our lives, he was probably "best friend runner up".

I had planned this trip for a while now. Graduating from the University of Michigan this past spring, I was taking a long summer trip before grad school in the fall. It was going to be an epic cross-country trip, and I would be solo for big portions of it. Starting at Zion and Arches in Utah, I would then wind over to Yosemite and up toward the Pacific Northwest. I was meeting a guy from school down for some rock climbing and would meet with other various friends along the way. My brother was planning on meeting me in Yosemite. I was looking forward to the adventure.

And so, with my bags packed and plenty of snacks and

water, a Spotify playlist I had labored over for the past week, I set off on the road. I didn't get out as early as I had wanted—the bed just seemed too cozy—but by ten o'clock I was heading west.

I was just outside of Omaha by eleven and found a La Quinta Inn. After a mediocre continental breakfast, I was back on the road. My plan was to take a more scenic route in my approach to Zion, cut through the northern part of Colorado, making my way down. After a flight of beers at a brewery pit stop in Ft. Collins, I was on the road once again and the night was all around me.

My road trip playlist was getting old, and my mind was numb and loopy. I was just about to turn it off and drive in sweet silence for a while when the song I was playing suddenly sped up and sounded like Alvin and the Chipmunks. I laughed at how it sounded while the speed devolved into a high-pitched whine. A thumping followed and a voice emerged from the speakers.

HIYA FOLKS, Buck Hensley here with another episode of "The Rules of the Road". I interrupt your Spottyfi playlist tonight with a special message from our sponsors. I'd like to tell you about a little product I have available known as Buck's Sassy Sarsaparilla.

Feelin' a little down? A sip of Buck's Sassy Sarsaparilla will perk ya right up. Feelin' a little too "up" and on edge? A sip of Buck's will calm you right down. Feelin' a little too constrained by the linear progression of time and causal events? A sip of Buck's will get you all shook up and allow you to experience everything all at once, forever.

It's available in all stores near you, provided you know who to ask and you know the secret password. Just wink at the clerk, give him a thumbs up,

and say, "I'm looking for that sassy sweetness."
They'll know what to do.

WHAT WAS THIS? Hadn't I paid for Premium with no ads? I listened on as I found it humorous, and I *had* needed something besides music, anyways.

YOU KNOW *it's not very safe for a girl out there alone and on the road.*

A SHIVER DOWN MY SPINE. Those familiar words.

IT'S NOT VERY *safe for a boy out there on the road either. Or a non-binary person, for that matter. And it sure as hell ain't that safe for a genderless individual who has transcended their corporeal body. The road is just a plain, dangerous place. Wouldn't it be nice to have a little protection out there? Someone looking out for you? Well, follow tonight's "Rule of the Road" if you desire a little more security and reassurance.*

It is extremely simple. If at any point during your journey, you come across a panhandler with a cardboard sign and a dog at his side, toss him a couple bucks. He's been on the road for a long time and his dog is hungry and he is oh so tired. Look closely. The panhandler is tall and imposing, and something is not right about the dog. Why, the dog has its own little coat on and a hood pulled over its head. Isn't that funny?

You seem skeptical, and I get that. I know what

you're gonna say. You're gonna say, "Buck, it's twenty-dang-twenty. Nobody carries cash anymore. I'm lucky if I have fifty cents in my ashtray. Why just the other day I blew through a toll station and the alarms went off and I thought I was a goner and I pulled off at a long-term parking lot and changed my license plates so they wouldn't find me. I use Venbo and Gooble Pay and all these other fancy bells and whistle appa-la-cations on my smartphone."

And to that I say, *"fair enough."* But you better have some cash on you when you take a long journey. Why, it's just plain common sense. What if you run into a toll road? What if you find the world's best taco truck and they only accept cash? What if you pull over at a rest stop and they have a soda machine and it's serving Buck's Sassy Sarsaparilla? All of those things would be a huge inconvenience and things you could avoid if you had some scratch on hand.

But if you don't have the cash or you just straight up ignore the warning, then this is what will happen: absolutely nothing! Yep, that's right. Nothing will happen. You can just go on your merry little way and have a good ol' time out there on your journey. But you must remember, the road is not a safe place. Wouldn't you like to have a little protection? I know I would.

Welp, that's all for tonight. I bid you adieu. May the road rise up to meet you and not ask you if you have met your savior. May it rise up to meet you and not ask if you would like to learn about a brand new and exciting business opportunity. May it simply rise up to meet you and say, "sup?"

Stay alert. Stay lively. Stay lonely. Once again,

I'm Buck Hensley and these are "The Rules of the Road".

THE MONOLOGUE SHUT OFF INSTANTLY. My playlist returned. I turned it off and drove in silence. That advertisement or whatever it was had perturbed me a little. I was thinking about emailing a complaint to Spotify. Being a premium subscriber and all, I wasn't supposed to receive ads. But besides the annoyance, I didn't like how it had echoed what my brother had said prior to my departure—his very own words. It had to be coincidence; it was a common sentiment, after all.

    I got creeped out and paranoid, especially driving on the dark roads through the mountains while the night got later and later. Why had I planned it this way? Why was I in such a rush? I was missing all the pretty mountains by driving through them at night. I should've stayed the night in Ft. Collins. I barreled on ahead.

    I was going to need gas soon, and I figured I could make it to Steamboat Springs. I was 25 miles to empty when I saw the signs for town, and I pulled off toward the first gas station that I saw.

    It was off the highway behind some trees and the lights were bright. The station looked empty. As I was pulling into the station, I could see a tall figure walking down a sidewalk. He had a dog with him. They were both wearing coats, and the figure had a ball cap slung down low over his face. In his other hand, he clutched a piece of cardboard to his side.

    I pulled next to the pump and looked back at the man and his dog. They walked across the parking lot and sat down on a large decorative boulder in a flowerbed with a yucca. The dog had a literal hoodie on, and it was pulled over his head. Aside from the four legs and the wagging tail, you wouldn't be able to tell what it was. It was a medium-sized dog, and the hood seemed to cover a rather large head. I thought of approaching them. I had cash on me. I knew it was important. That was something Buck Hensley didn't have to tell me.

Was I really going to give money to every panhandler I saw with a dog from here on out for the next two months?

I pumped my gas, keeping a wary eye on the man and his dog. They were about a hundred feet away. The man reached in his backpack and pull something out to feed his dog.

"Excuse me, miss?"

I turned around. I hadn't even heard him come up behind me. He was a wiry man with wild eyes, a tear tattooed on his face. His arms were ropes of muscle, dark with the sleeves of faded tattoos.

Instinctively, I reached for the knife in my pocket, but before I could even do so, there was a blinding flash in my eyes and pain across the bridge of my nose that almost brought me to my knees. I could feel pain and a heavy feeling across my face and I cried out, but that was met with a rough and calloused hand across my mouth. It tasted dirty and gagged me, and I felt cold steel on my throat. He whispered in my ear as I struggled against him.

"Shh. Shh. Shh. Don't scream, or I'll slit your fucking throat, bitch. You got that?"

I nodded. My nose ached, and his hand pressed against it only made it worse. Warm blood and tears ran down my face and over my lips and into his hand. He gripped my face tightly, reached into my pocket and got my knife.

I liked to think that in the face of such a thing that I would go down fighting. That I would put up more of a fight than I did, that I would escape. Maybe all those victims out there had thought the same. But I did nothing like that. I went into a sort of autopilot and in that initial moment, if he had told me to walk off a cliff or into traffic, I probably would have complied. As it is, he told me to get into the trunk of an old-looking sedan and I did so.

I lay in the trunk, claustrophobic panic rising within me, trying to stay calm. It all had happened so fast. Surely someone had seen this happen? Someone had to have called the cops. The guy with his dog, did he see?

My nose was still bleeding, so I pulled the front of my shirt up and put gentle pressure on it. I thought of screaming and kicking the trunk door, but I was afraid to anger my captor and what he would do to silence me if I did.

I focused on my breath and took stock of my surroundings, feeling with my hands until my eyes adjusted to the dark. There were several objects of smooth plastic with liquid in them. Containers of motor oil or antifreeze. Then there were several metal cylinders, cans of some type of spray. One can had a big plastic nozzle in the shape of a trumpet. I couldn't feel anything else and was hoping for a tire iron or something else as a makeshift weapon. The warm glow of streetlamps shone in through a rusted-out hole in the lid of the trunk while the car's tires hummed on the road.

The car slowed and the texture of the road changed into something crunchy. There was no more illumination. We had left the highway and were now going down some back road. The roads were winding, and the car leaned into steep curves while I steadied myself against the trunk walls to keep from rolling around. I feared the worst. We were going out in the wilderness far from everyone, and he was going to have his way with me. I would not let him, and I vowed I would go down fighting.

Finally, the car stopped. The engine turned off. Silence. I could hear his footsteps crunching on gravel outside, see his shadow cross the rust holes. I rolled onto my stomach, face down, a can of spray in my hands.

The trunk creaked open; the hinges bounced.

"Get out," he commanded.

I didn't answer.

"Get *out*," he hissed.

I lay still, playing possum.

"Get up. Get up. Get up," he said and slapped my ass, hard. I still didn't move. He kneeled into the trunk, grabbed me by the shoulder and rolled me over.

I saw his face and was ready. Since he had to kneel in to reach me, he was at close range. I hit him directly in the face and eyes with a full blast of wasp spray.

"Gah!" he said and staggered back. I leapt out of the trunk as fast as I could, the metal latch of the trunk hitting the back of my scalp and then digging into my back and gashing me as I flew.

He was rubbing his eyes, coughing and spitting, hunched over. At his beltline was a large sheath with a knife handle sticking out. In my frantic rage I sidestepped him as he gagged and sputtered, gripped the knife handle, yanked backwards. The blade came free, and I hammered it down into the small of his back again and again. I managed three deep stabs in quick succession before he jerked up quickly, swinging his arm backwards, striking me in the face.

I held steady while he stumbled and windmilled like a dazed and unskilled boxer. He swung at me again. I had the knife blade up and it raked across his forearm. He screamed and gripped the fresh wound. Seeing that he was distracted for the briefest instant, I swung the blade at his face and other arm, then darted away.

He staggered around drunkenly and tried to rush me, but I was too far away and dodged him easily. Whimpering, he fell to his knees, crawled toward his vehicle, and collapsed. I stood watching him, panting. I could feel my blood running down my back and head from the gashes I had suffered jumping out of the trunk.

Out of nowhere, from behind me, a voice spoke.

"Excuse me, miss. Do you have a couple bucks I could borrow?"

I almost jumped out of my skin and whirled around and held out the knife in a defensive posture.

"My dog and I are starving. We've been on the road a long, long time."

It was the man and the dog I had seen at the gas station. He was tall and with a dark complexion, and he looked clean. I looked down at the dog and saw he was still wearing that dog hoodie. His owner reached down and pulled the hood back. My mind couldn't quite comprehend what I saw. The dog looked like a pit bull mix of some sort, its fur a mixture of white and gray, but the remarkable thing about the dog was that it had *two* separate heads, each one panting with a pink tongue hanging out.

"I . . . I . . ." I stammered. There was so much going on at once. I had just been kidnapped, had stabbed a guy multiple times, and now a man and his two-headed pit bull were asking me for money. And I didn't even have money on me. It was back at my car.

"I'll make it worth your while," the man said.

I went over to my bleeding captor, held my knife at him. He was on his stomach, inching toward his car. I stepped on the back of his thigh, and he groaned. In the back pocket of his blue jeans was the bulge of a wallet. I bent over and plucked it out.

"Here you go," I said and handed it to the man with the dog. "Take as much as you want."

He smiled at me. "I'll take care of this from here. Your car's at the end of this gravel road. Did you need anything else?"

"I think I can manage," I said.

I set off down the road. Behind me, the other man's screams echoed into the night.

I checked the papers for Steamboat Springs all summer and there was never any mention of a dead body or vehicle found. My guess is that there was nothing left of the body and the vehicle simply disappeared.

I still see him sometimes when I'm out there, standing on highway exit ramps or outside gas stations. He always gives me a little wave. I feel like he shows up like this as a reminder.

The near-death episode hasn't knocked me down. I still have that zest for travel. Do I still travel alone? Yes, but only because I've had a little extra protection ever since that summer night in northern Colorado.

They may be right about traveling alone. While I certainly had gotten out of the situation on my own, it could've ended so much differently. I still have the occasional nightmare and flashback and sick feeling when I think back on how I could've been raped and murdered. Take special precautions if you're out there by yourself, no matter who you are. Check in with people frequently and let them know your location. Practice situational awareness and have some means of self-defense.

And if you see a panhandler on the side of the road with his dog, toss him a couple bucks. What have you got to lose? You really can't be too careful.

"What newspaper did you say you work for again?"
"It's not a newspaper. It's an online blog."
"Oh."
"I'm investigating a mysterious radio broadcast."
"Like on a car radio?"
"Yes."
"Where did this happen? What frequency did it appear on? These stations are required to give their call signs."
"It's been all over the country. It's even popped up on non-radio channels. Streaming services."
"Look, I dunno. I've been retired for a while now. Maybe file a complaint with the FCC."
"I can't entirely prove it, but there's been deadly consequences. I think this broadcast is killing people."
"I see. I think we're done here."

5
"WHAT'S YOUR NAME?"

Sasha contacted me via email, and we later had a meeting on Skype. She was a young woman in her early twenties and had heard the broadcast while road tripping in California with her friend, Greta. In her email, she was assured and driven. It was important for her to share her story, she said. But as I got her on the screen, as she sat at a desk in a pleasant home office with stark white walls and plenty of natural sunlight, she was tentative and shy at first. She read from a stack of papers in a shaky voice. However, the longer she spoke, the more her voice shed the insecurity and a sly, confident young woman emerged.
  This is her story.

THEY SAY that behind every great man is a great woman. What they don't tell you is behind that great woman is me, taking a picture of that great woman's behind, making sure that I perfectly frame it in the shot as she stands before some grand vista or gorgeous natural landscape. I'm there to capture the natural beauty of both the scenery and her ass, a perfect upside-down heart that's squeezed into whatever activewear she's promoting, her thick blonde mane of hair cascading down her back like the many waterfalls she's posed in front of.

Greta was an Instagrammer, an influencer, and I was the one standing behind her, responsible for much of her success as her photographer and caption writer and social media manager. For several years I considered her my best friend.

Before I go further, I'd like to preface all of this by saying that my relationship with Greta has always been kind of . . . complicated. And by complicated, I mean borderline exploitative. I believe that in any relationship there are givers and there are takers. Greta was not a giver.

Not that she was some awful, soul-sucking bitch. In fact, I did have genuine warm feelings toward her and still do to this day. In any abusive relationship, there is some sort of love there, something that drew us to that person initially. That's what keeps us coming back: the belief that maybe they will change back into the person we revered in the beginning.

We met back east in college in Comp II. She approached me regarding an essay that she needed help with, and the friendship blossomed from there. She was charismatic and full of a crackling energy that instantly drew me in, and her taking an interest in me was flattering. Sure, it seemed like it was a relationship that was started solely on her needing something, my assistance with her various writing assignments, but she offered much in return and genuinely liked me.

What did she offer? Adventure and excitement. She talked me into using marijuana for the first time, late nights out in the city with crazy experiences, concerts and Broadway shows, meeting all sorts of new people, my first shot of absinthe, and the travel—oh, the travel. I wouldn't have seen many parts of the world if it wasn't for her.

She came from a rich family, and I was on scholarship

and had federal work-study to get by. I simply couldn't afford the lavish trips and restaurants that she took me to. It was always hard to simply turn her down when she invited me out to eat or to a concert or show, and I would have to politely decline without giving the real reasons, but she saw through that.

"Whatever dude, I'm buying," she would say, and off we would go.

The response was the same when she came with the bright idea that we should fly to Paris on summer break.

"Do you know how much homework you've helped me with this semester? It's the least I can do. I don't wanna go alone. You're my PIC. I'll get your airfare, you just get the meals and maybe buy some wine here and there."

And so, we went. It was here that she developed her passion for her Instagram page, even more so than your average college girl. She already had a sizable following of over three thousand followers, and I took cute pictures of her all over the city and came up with clever captions. By the time we returned to the states, she had doubled the followers and was discussing it constantly.

"You know, we may be onto something here. There's like these people that do this full time, just fly around and travel and get sponsors and shit. They pay for everything. How cool is that?"

The rest of the summer was filled with adventures and shenanigans, me the ever tag-along, taking photos of her and validating her every move: long weekends at the Hamptons, cocktails at rooftop bars in NYC, fashion galas, and a hike in the Adirondacks so she "wouldn't appear too metropolitan."

IT WAS HERE that Sasha paused in her story and stared off into space. Reflecting, perhaps? How was this story going to end? What broadcast did Buck Hensley present to them? What rule was obeyed or ignored?

"*Sasha?*"

"*Oh, sorry.*" *She continued.*

I COULDN'T REALLY KEEP up with her financially, but she paid for lots of amenities: meals, hotels, transportation. "Don't worry about it," she would say. "You're like my publicist. We're growing followers all the time. I really think this will work. We need to think bigger. You consider yourself the manager. It's our brand, I'm just the face of it."

Despite whatever support I received, it still would clean me out—pride kept me from outright begging every time—and I lived constantly on the verge of overdraft from my checking account. I didn't want to miss out on all the fun and excitement though; she had me addicted. But I often wished she would take it easy and we could just relax and do more low-key activities, activities that I would suggest and that she would shoot down.

She didn't have a boyfriend and never strived for anything long term.

"I don't need no man," she would say. "They'll only keep me from reaching my full potential. Once I reach that, I'll reconsider."

This is not to say that she didn't enjoy male attention—she very much did—and she was prone to random hookups and casual flings. I, on the other hand, didn't like these types of relationships and the particularly sleazy douchebag guys who flocked to her at the different bars we would frequent. Greta often left me to fend for myself with the friends of whichever guy she was flirting with. Most of the time, I could fight them off, but alcohol and exhaustion and boredom led to too many mornings where I would awaken in a strange location and a depressing subway ride home, hating myself and the night I could barely remember. It was times like these where I felt like Greta was dragging me down.

Ultimately, I knew I was an adult and made my own decisions, but I wished she did a better job of looking out for me sometimes. I was losing myself in her, remaking myself into a person I wasn't, and I couldn't get off the carousel that was continuing to spin faster and faster and out of control.

Greta broke 100k followers by the fall semester and had gained several sponsors, getting her first checks and free products. She gave me the hand-me-down products, the items she didn't want. I also received a cut of the profits for taking the pictures and writing the captions. She never revealed how much she got paid and I never worried if I was getting a fair share. There were never any thoughts about getting a lawyer or drawing up contracts. It was just a casual affair, and frankly I was just happy to be getting any money.

Greta continued to gain followers. We got busier and busier. My grades slipped that semester, and I think Greta's did as well. She dropped classes and wasn't even carrying a full course load. Whenever I expressed reservations about the workload and falling behind in classes, she would come with the convenient exciting news that we had received another payment and cut me a check. This was usually enough to appease me.

By the time that summer rolled around and I had graduated, Greta had reached 750k followers and I was tired. So, so tired. I felt like a shell of myself and desperately in need of a break. I had gotten a coveted internship at a magazine for the summer, and I was thankful for the opportunity to not have to live in Greta's shadow, taking her pictures and bolstering her fame. She was not too pleased with my decision, and it led to a dramatic confrontation at my apartment after my graduation.

"I can't believe you're gonna be gone all summer. Leaving me high and dry right when we're about to break a million," she said as she sipped her wine.

"*Greta*," I said in a pleading tone. "This internship really means a lot to me. This is big time. It can really open a lot of doors."

"Fine, fine," she said. She pulled out a joint for us.

We zoned out to TV and soon I noticed that the bottle of wine was empty and could hear her banging around in the kitchen. She returned to the couch with a glass of bourbon.

"You know what, fuck your magazine and fuck your internship. How much are they paying you, anyways?"

"It's not about the money."

"Well, what's it about? You getting tired of me? That's how it always ends. I thought you were different." I could see tears at the corners of her eyes.

"Greta."

"No, it's fine. I just thought we were in this together. I totally understand." Her voice broke.

"I'm just so, so tired of the fast-paced life. I can't keep up with you anymore."

"But this is gonna be totally different. It's more travel, more road trips. Cross-country. It would be like one last trip before we have to enter the world of adulthood. It will be totally epic and totally laid back at the same time. More outdoorsy."

I said nothing.

"I can pay you. How much are you supposed to make over there? I'll pay all your room and board, plus a weekly rate." She was sounding frantic, spouting stuff off, anything to get me to change my mind. Before I knew it, the glass of liquor was empty. Her words were slurring.

"My dad has some connections with The New Yorker. He could land you an editing job, I swear. *Do* this for me. We're so close. I *need* you. You're like a sister."

I could only wince and shake my head. The words were caught in my throat.

"Fine!" she cried and stormed off back into the kitchen and I heard glass breaking and she soon emerged, standing at the threshold of the kitchen, a stream of blood running down her forearm and onto the floor.

"I'm so sorry," she sobbed repeatedly while I held a dishrag over her wound to stop the bleeding. I held her as she cried into my shoulder.

I ended up withdrawing from my internship and going on the road trip. The self-inflicted scar on her forearm: we took an artsy black-and-white photo of it and made an Instagram post about how all of us had struggles and the importance of self-care and taking care of your mental health. It got 500 thousand likes.

SASHA STOPPED AGAIN *and didn't speak for a while. I was beginning to wonder if she had somehow mistakenly contacted me. Her story, while riveting in a millennial sort of way, didn't seem to have anything to do with Buck Hensley.*

"Sasha, did you have an experience with the broadcast on your road trip?"

She looked up at me, confused.

"Buck Hensley and 'The Rules of the Road?'" I asked.

"Oh, right. Yes, we heard it in California."

WE HAD JUST LEFT Joshua Tree and had taken a plethora of photos. I was sunburned and tired and cranky, and the sun was coming down. I had come up with a caption for a photo of Greta hanging off a tree, something like: *If you're cool enough, he'll let you hang on his branches and call him Josh.* Not my best work, but it was something. Greta looked stunning as usual and she rode in the passenger seat, posting the pic and hashtags and "fended off the haters and tended to the horny boys" in the comments of the post.

I tuned Greta out while she talked to herself and read comments out loud until she suddenly turned to me, a serious expression on her face. "Sasha. Some publisher found my Insta feed and wants a book deal. One of the big ones. They want photos and stories of my adventures on the road."

"That's great!" I said. "I can help with the writing. I've done all the captions. I mean, I can help you portray your vision. Our vision."

"Um, yeah, that's the thing. They have a team they wanna use. Like a ghostwriter and publicist and editor and everything. I've already been in contact with all of them."

"Oh."

The news was a sledgehammer to the gut, knocking the air out of me. Maybe the whole car, too, because a whole hour passed without either of us saying a word, me fighting back tears the whole time. I was so goddamn angry, and it took all I had not to explode on her. I was done. Next chance I got, I was out of here. She had her publishing team. She didn't need me. I had given her everything and then some.

I turned on the radio, some Top 40 BS. I wasn't even listening. Rage coursed through me. She could sense I was upset and knew well enough not to talk. I turned up the volume of the radio and the drum machine beats of the dance music transformed into the sound of a heartbeat, a heartbeat that throbbed right in my ears and then into my throat. There was an abrupt silence and then a voice started talking.

This is what it said:

. . .

GOOD EVENING FOLKS, Burke Hensley here with yet another episode of "The Rules of the Road." Hope y'all are doing just dandy out there tonight on that highway known as life on that planet known as Earth. Why do they call it Earth, anyways? Who named it? Is that what's on the birth certificate out there after it shot out of a supernova's hoo-ha? If you asked me, Earth's parents dropped it on its head a few too many times. That's why she's so weird and wonky and cruel.

Speaking of names, what's in a name (besides letters, that is)? I don't rightly know, but I do know that names are important. Since the dawn of written and oral history, folks have had names. Even the Elder Gods that have existed long before us had names. You just can't pronounce them! By golly, names are important, or my name ain't Bud Henson!

So, that brings us to tonight's "Rule of the Road." It has to do with names, your names in particular. If at any point in your journey you stop at a gift shop or truck stop and they have them personalized souvenir key chains, then you must purchase the one with your name on it. I'm partial to the ones with the state license plates on 'em myself.

I know what you're thinking. You're thinking, "Buckley, my parents were a bunch of chuckleheads and they named me Stephanie with a 'fun' in the middle: Stefunee and that is anything but 'funee' to me. Or you're thinking they named me Chris with two z's and two t's and they screw it up at Starbucks all the time. There ain't no way in hell *they're gonna have my correct name at no gift shop."*

And to that I say, fair enough. But look closer. You might be surprised at what you find.

So, what happens if you ignore this rule? Well, it might seem like a simple thing at first. How often do you really think about your own name? How important is it to you? I bet you overlook it, take it for granted. What if you lost it? If you ignore this rule, you might come to find what it's like to lose your very own name. Do so at your own peril.

Welp, that's all I got for tonight. Thoughts and prayers to whomever may be listening up there that you arrive at your destination safely. But remember, these prayers are just a courtesy. It is already written, and they already know and we are doomed to stay on the same predetermined path until the end, no choice and no say in the matter. Stay alert. Stay lively. Stay lonely. Stay lucid. I'm Buck Hornswallow and these are "The Rules of the Road."

AT THE TIME, I was too mad to think much of the broadcast. It may have lightened my mood a bit, and Greta gave a few nervous laughs. But that was it.

I drove on and pulled off at a hotel near Bakersfield and got a room for the night.

I HAD SPOKEN a little more to Greta, the bare minimum. In my mind, I was planning on getting to Sacramento and flying back home and trying to pick up the pieces. I hadn't revealed this information to her yet. We were low on gas and had stopped at a large truck stop. It was like a miniature grocery store in there. Rows and rows of snacks and souvenir T-shirts and trucker equipment and books on CD and DVDs and sunglasses.

"Hey, look," Greta called over to me. She was standing at one of those little spinning display racks. It was full of souvenir keychains with names on them, little Route 66 themed ones.

"Oh yeah, like that weird radio show we heard," I said.

"Think they'll have our names on them? Not the most common. If they do, we better get them, just in case."

"It would suck to lose your name after all the fame you've got."

"Wow, they've got 'em." She held up two key chains, Greta and Sasha.

SASHA PAUSED and shuffled the papers. That strange look on her face again. Was she about to reveal what I suspected?

"NICE. I'm gonna get some water and I'll buy these," I said. "My treat."

She went back to the car and at the checkout I paid for one bottled water and one keychain with my name on it. The other one, I left behind.

SASHA LOOKED down at her stack of papers for a long time, most likely processing the weight of what she had done back in Bakersfield. She had no way of knowing that the rules were real and that they could be deadly. What had been the consequence? Death? Was there a gravestone out there over Greta's body, no name etched into the granite?

She shuffled the papers and squinted at the words and then began again, her voice now monotone.

. . .

It was subtle at first, occurring over weeks and the rest of the summer. First, I would have to repeat myself a lot of times to get her attention, like she wasn't hearing her name. She would get a confused look on her face and kind of snap back into it and laugh and say something about a "brain fart" or "being hungover."

Then, she would freeze up when trying to sign credit card receipts, staring blankly for an awkward amount of time. I would have to sign for her. We couldn't rely on her to make any reservations, she would never know what name to put it under. This would come and go, at strange and random times. Sometimes it was like nothing had ever happened and she would seem completely normal, her old self. She could remember her name and who she was and all of our prior adventures.

Other times she put on a good front and could conceal just how confused she really was. It was only in talking to her that she would say something outrageous about her past —that she was a supermodel from Australia or that her name was Ashley—and you would realize she was in one of her states.

Meeting new people was a problem. She could only smile awkwardly during the introduction, and I would have to say her name for her. She talked much less when she was like this, only smiled and nodded. You could ask her a question directly and she would answer, but not in a way that made sense. She seemed lost in her own apartment, frequently opening the wrong drawers and cabinets and asking me where the bathroom was.

She let go of her hygiene. Her hair looked matted and greasy, and I would notice her wearing the same clothes for days at a time. Dishes piled up in her sink, dirty clothes all over her house.

She had gotten lost several times, and I received calls from strangers in a bar to pick her up. One time her parents had to pick her up from an emergency room. The police had found her in an alley behind a Dunkin Donuts, lost and confused, clothing and hair disheveled. She had been missing for almost 24 hours.

They got her an ID bracelet with contact information, but we all kept a closer eye on her. It was hard to go out in public, because she could appear very normal, and we never knew when she would suddenly "turn" and might wander off.

Her parents took her to a neurologist, and she underwent a battery of tests. All the tests were normal, and they couldn't find anything conclusive. Maybe it was psychological, they suggested? I offered to take care of her and let her stay with me during the day. Had I done this to her? Was the broadcast's warning real? At the time, I thought it was just a goof. If I had known this was to happen, I wouldn't have done it. I wouldn't wish this on anyone.

Either way, I felt responsible and watching her during the day was the least I could do. It worked out pretty well. I could still go out at night and during the day I was working on my book deal stuff.

BOOK DEAL? Had Sasha taken over the book deal after Greta's mind started to go?

I'VE NOTICED other weird things lately. Sometimes I call her the wrong name, just a few letters off or something similar. She doesn't notice, of course. She doesn't even respond if I call her by the right name. I've noticed her parents doing it too. They call her Natasha or Sharon or Shannon or Shelly. The thing is, they don't notice it. It's really weird.

. . .

WHAT? *Didn't she mean names similar to Greta? Sasha spaced out again. She didn't talk for a long time.*

"Sasha?" *I asked.*

She didn't respond.

"Are you ok? You couldn't have known the rules were real. I know you feel awfully guilty."

She looked at me through the screen and then to the right and to the left, picked up the papers she was reading from, and that's when I noticed it: a silver bracelet on her left wrist. A medical ID bracelet.

I heard a voice shouting from the other room. It grew louder. Sasha turned toward the door, the voice. The door burst open and in burst a radiant and glamorous blonde.

"There you are," she said. "What are you doing up here?"

"I'm just..." she trailed off and gestured toward the computer screen.

"Oh, who have you called up? Is this that journalist guy you were talking about? Hope you didn't tell him anything too bad about me," the blonde said with a wink at the camera. She looked at me and spoke. "The psychiatrist recommended her keeping a journal, write things down when she remembered. He thinks it might help some. I guess she contacted you when she was lucid?"

"Yes. You must be Greta."

"Sure am."

"Can you tell me what's going on?" I asked.

Greta sat down at the desk and patted Sasha on the back. "She's been stable for a while. Has some really good days." She turned to Sasha and said in a babyish voice, "We have to get you to your parents soon. Mommy has a big date tonight." She turned to look at me. "Are you two done here? I've got a book release party this evening and lots of getting ready to do."

"But, I thought that . . ." I started.

Greta looked down at the stack of papers. "What are these doing here?" she asked. "Have you been getting into my stuff again? You got part of yours mixed up with mine, ya big goof."

Sasha looked down like a scolded child.

"I'm going to release a memoir about taking care of a friend with a mentally debilitating disease," Greta said. "It's going to be my sophomore publication. These are some notes for the ghostwriter. Well, it was nice to meet you. Say bye, Natasha."

Sasha only looked at me with a flat expression as everything I had just learned was turned upside down. As Greta reached to turn off the computer and hang up the call, I could see in her hand she held her keys. From the keys hung a little Route 66 souvenir keychain with a name etched on it: Greta.

"Hey man, think you might make it up this season? Supposed to be some good snow this year."

"Maybe. I'll have to see. I don't know if I have enough PTO."

"Seriously? You get that at 7-11?"

"Well, not really, but they're shorthanded."

"Is this about that time you got spooked driving out?"

"Not at all."

"You could totally fly. It's gonna be baller. Brad's got the hookup on this sweet condo at Breck."

"I'll see."

6

"SOUTHERN ACCENTS"

Trevor heard the broadcast while driving in the southeastern United States, heading east from Birmingham toward Atlanta. He spilled his story out to me in a venomous diatribe against the South, and I wasn't sure what his vendetta against the region was. I knew it had its problems and troubled history just like any other place in America, but he viewed it with a personal contempt that was jarring.

This is how he began.

THE GODDAMN SOUTH.

Why, oh why, did my best friend have to move here?

I guess these things are bound to happen, eventually. You know someone all of your life: through kindergarten and junior high and high school and even end up at the same college together. But the real world comes along and so starts the job hunt and all the offers and for some reason he accepts a job in Birmingham Freaking Alabama. There's a big signing bonus and relocation fees, and if you commit to three years at the company, you get another huge bonus. They're practically bribing anyone with a STEM degree to come to these shitty little flyover states. I mean, we were from an almost flyover state in Pennsylvania, and both of us had gone to college at Stanford where I thought we had seen the light. The goal was to not end up in one of these places. The least he could've done was to go back to Pittsburgh. It's really come a long way.

For Tyler to move to a *red* state after all this time feels like a betrayal of all of our values and morals. I guess there really is a price tag on everything. We got really political together during our college years in Stanford. It was hard not to be. It was in the air and water down there, and it was a great way to make friends and meet chicks. When 2016 happened, the first presidential election we could vote in, the politicking hit a fever pitch.

First, when our boy Bernie didn't get the nomination through some shadiness from the DNC, and then when Trump won, hoo-boy! We were full on in the whole resistance movement. It felt like we were part of something, you know? We even went to a couple of protests in Berkeley that got a little out of hand.

So, after graduation, when he told me the news, it was a huge kick in the nuts. What was I gonna do without Tyler? We were brothers in arms. Since kindergarten, we hadn't gone a full three weeks without seeing each other. Like hell was I going to follow him to that godforsaken hell hole. Alabama?

It is *possible* that he moved there because of that gal he started talking to on the internet. From what little he talked of her, she was from somewhere down south. I thought it was just a one-off thing, a line of communication to someone on the front lines of the resistance, but maybe not. He didn't confirm either way when he called me and told me that things were getting serious and that he really wanted me to come meet her. The worst part of it was that he wanted me to come there. I offered to host them at my place in Portland, but he deferred my offer.

"So, I guess this is it, huh? You're some kind of *Southerner*?" I said.

"C'mon, man. It's not that bad," he replied.

"Why didn't you at least take a job in Austin if you wanted to go to the South so badly? Austin, I could vibe with."

"Austin isn't in the South, though, it's Texas."

"Whatever. How is it living in a third world country?"

"It's Alabama. Not Mississippi," he said.

"You think you're gonna fulfill your contract and get the hell out as soon as you can?"

"I dunno. I'm actually starting to like it here. It's laid back."

"Yeah, if you're white," I said.

"It's not what you think. Just come on down here and see for yourself. I haven't seen you in a while and it would be good to hang. Things are getting really serious between me and Diane. I think she might be the one. I'd love for you to meet her and have your blessing. Make sure I'm not making a rash decision."

"Fine," I sighed. "I'll visit The Goddamn South with its n-word using, gay bashing, illiterate, immigrant fearing, inbred hicks."

"Hey man, cut the shit. You're completely off base. You've never even *been* here. Do you even know how many immigrants we've got here? You know you're really in your own little bubble out there. Cut off from reality. I didn't see it until I moved out here, how out of touch we could be. You're talking like some kinda 'coastal elite.' How's that diversity thing working out for y'all in Portland?"

Coastal elite? Y'all? It was really worse than I had feared. They were converting him. I knew I had to visit, and soon. Not for a visit to catch up on old times and give him my blessing, but for an intervention.

I apologized to him over the phone, and instantly made arrangements for my visit. Hopefully, I could save him.

Securing some time off from work, my plan was set in motion. I can't get into the specifics just yet, but I was a programmer at a startup for a new app that was going to involve car repairs and hopefully disrupt that industry. They were cool with giving me a full week off. I had never seen New Orleans and always kind of wanted to go, so my plan was to stay a night there and then drive up and over to Birmingham.

I roamed up and down Bourbon Street alone and listened to some jazz and drank Sazeracs and hurricanes and almost puked in an alleyway as I hear is tradition in New Orleans. Later, I got some beignets at Café Du Monde, and it sobered me up enough to get an Uber back to my hotel safely.

A late start the next morning on account of my hangover, I took I-59 North. I was a half day early for my meetup with Tyler, so I figured I would drive over to Montgomery and check out this new memorial they had there.

The interstate was a corridor with walls of tall skinny pines lining the sides. The pines bordered extensive fields of brown, tufts of white popping out like snow. Cotton. The air was thick and hot and my AC was blasting. Large green vines crawled and completely covered low-lying ravines and anything in their path. The shapes of trees were visible under the green mass that had swallowed them. I would later learn that this vine was called kudzu.

Billboards appeared now and then, advertising and sharing their messages. CHOOSE LIFE, one said, and had a picture of a baby on it. HOW WILL YOU SPEND ETERNITY? Asked another. Later, I would see one that read "GO TO CHURCH OR THE DEVIL'S GONNA GET YOU" and it featured a large red Satan holding a scythe.

I pulled off at a large truck stop near a city called Meridian in Mississippi where I milled about for a while, looking for Southern artifacts. There was a small area that sold T-shirts and keychains that had Mississippi flags on them. These looked like Confederate flags to me. On a table sat a couple of metal canisters with ladles sticking out of them. A sign read "Boiled Peanuts." *Boiled peanuts?* That was a first for me. Peeking inside, I found the canister was full of slimy looking peanuts with the shells still on them, simmering in a brown liquid. Yuck.

There was a fast-food restaurant connected to the truck stop and the day-after post-drunken binge cravings were hitting me hard, so I ordered a greasy cheeseburger and fries. I sat toward the back of the restaurant. Maybe it was the hangover effects or maybe it was because I was in the South, but I was feeling paranoid and anxious.

A big burly guy in a plaid shirt and a trucker's cap shuffled into the fast-food area, carrying a Styrofoam cup full of the boiled peanuts and a plastic bag. His neck was thick and stubbled, and his gut rested up against the table as he sat in a booth. He sat the peanuts down and looked at them for a long time. From the bag he pulled out a box of Benadryl and ripped it open, punching every single little pink pill out of the blister packet and onto the table. Soon, he had a small pile of pink pills as he swept the trash from the packaging aside. Next, he got two plastic cylinders from the plastic sack and sat them next to the pills.

I watched in bewilderment as he picked at the boiled soft peanut husks with his stubby fingers and squeezed out the nuts within. He placed these back in the Styrofoam cup and tossed the desiccated shells onto the table. I watched this bizarre ritual for a while until he had shelled the entire container.

The Goddamn South, I thought, shaking my head. *What a freak.*

He pinched a handful of the Benadryl tablets and dry swallowed them. His Adam's apple bobbing as he stared up at the ceiling with his eyes closed. He looked back down at the peanuts for a long time, psyching himself up. Sliding his fingers in, he pulled out some peanuts, and then shoveled them into his mouth. This action was repeated until his mouth was full, his jaw working and working.

What in the Dixieland fuck?

He got the first mouthful down, gasped for air, and then shoved another handful into his mouth. At the top of his hairy chest, I could see pink splotches spreading upwards and across his neck like expanding enemy territories on a map. Putting another cache of nuts into his mouth, he picked up one of the plastic cylinders off the table, flicked off a cap, and shoved it right into his arm. Through his shirt and everything.

An EpiPen. Holy shit, this guy's allergic! What is he thinking?

The invading splotches on his skin had advanced across the stubbled territory of his neck and over the crest of his jawline. His lips had begun to swell, and bits of chewed peanut flecked his cheeks and chin, yet he still continued eating and eating. He jabbed another EpiPen into his arm while he could still see, for his eyes were now almost swollen shut, the sockets inflated with fleshy bags that formed cracks where his eyes should be.

He was huffing and puffing for air, a loud whistling wheeze that could be heard from across the room. Drool ran down his chin and neck and his eyes watered. Yet still he chewed. Still, he consumed. Still, he swallowed.

"Hey man, whatchoo doing?" a bystander asked him. "You's havin' a reaction to them." The bystander reached for the peanuts, but the anaphylactic man swatted him away, his face a bloated and hideous mask with slits for eyes.

He tipped the Styrofoam cup back toward his swollen head and dumped the remaining peanuts down his desperate maw, chewed and collapsed onto the floor.

"Aye yo, somebody call an ambulance!" The bystander yelled.

I could still hear the man's whistling wheeze, his fat stomach rising and falling, and I thought *I have got to get the hell outta here.*

I HAD TO ASK TREVOR, did the guy die? He told me he didn't know for sure, that he watched paramedics arrive and successfully intubate the man with the anaphylactic reaction and haul him away. He continued with his story.

I ARRIVED in Birmingham without further incident. That whole episode had frightened and disgusted me, and I kept replaying it in my mind for the rest of my journey. I wasn't used to seeing that sort of shit. Were Southerners so dumb they thought they could just eat something they were allergic to and not suffer any repercussions?

Tyler lived in a revitalized urban area near downtown Birmingham. It seemed like an area that was an imitation of the trends that had started in bigger and hipper cities. There were hipster bars with craft cocktails, microbreweries, cool little restaurants, murals, and public art. All of this actually surprised me.

"You made it!" he said when he answered the door. His apartment was nice and spacious. His girlfriend, Diane, had yet to arrive.

"Barely." I responded.

We sat for a while, drinking IPAs from cans, catching up.

"So, I guess this little neighborhood is pretty cool," I said. "Didn't know they had anything like that down here."

"Yeah, it's really up and coming. This is a local beer."

He seemed impressed by this, and it was kind of depressing. We had more local microbreweries out on the coast per capita than just about anywhere. I spent weekends trying to discover them all, from Seattle to Bend, Oregon. In a couple years, he'd be telling me excitedly about the local dispensaries that they had down here.

I cleared my throat. I figured now was the time to talk some sense into him, while Diane wasn't around. "Is it like really racist here? How do you deal with it all? I mean, I've been on Twitter a lot, reading the political headlines, and I'm starting to think we should just expel this entire southeastern region. They're dragging us down, man. All our tax dollars on the coasts helps these people and their hate out."

"Trevor, it's like any other place. Do you know Oregon drafted a state constitution banning black people? I'm sure there's racists and stuff around here, but I don't really see any of it. As far as the red state stuff goes, do you understand gerrymandering? Voter suppression? The southeast has a large black population, more cities that are majority African American than anywhere. Are you just gonna expel them, too? I don't know about you, but that sounds a little racist."

"I dunno man, driving up here, it's like the buckle of the bible belt. I think I'm going to hell now, by the way."

"Just relax with all this political stuff. Quit trying to be so woke and right the world's wrongs from your phone while you're not really doing much else. Unplug from social media and Twitter and all of that. Start living in the real world for a change. Let's have some fun this week. Miss ya bud," he said and gave my shoulder a stiff squeeze.

"I've been off social media for a bit. There's this thing the tech dudes are all doing called a dopamine fast. It involves getting off of that stuff periodically so your reward centers in your brain can reset and recharge. I haven't seen pictures of you and Diane, yet by the way, because of the fast."

"Welp, she should be up here shortly."

She arrived and I must say that he had done well for himself. She was stunning and had a laid-back personality and made me relaxed. I only had one main concern, and it had to do with where he lived and who she was. She was Black.

I ASKED Trevor why that bothered him. He responded he was "worried about prejudice and stuff" and that Tyler had "never dated anyone like that before." Anyone like what? "You know, like a person of color, or whatever." When I asked him if he could expound further on these concerns, he really couldn't. He continued on.

THE VISIT WENT WELL for the next few days. Tyler and Diane were gracious hosts, and I learned a little about Southern hospitality from Diane, who had been born and raised in Atlanta. They showed me the sights of Birmingham and we ate a lot of that good southern cooking. Everyone in town seemed really friendly, too. I must admit that I was reversing my stance on the South a little. It didn't seem like a half-bad place, after all.

But then I would scroll through news stories in the morning about the sad state of affairs our country was in, and I couldn't help but blame the legislators and senators in this part of the country and the people that voted for them. This feeling that I was in the wrong place would fall over me and I would feel the urge to get the hell out of here.

Tyler and I had a bit of a guy's night out on what was to be my last night in town. We went to a neighborhood called Five Points South and spent the night hopping from bar to bar. If you didn't focus too much, you could be anywhere. Only thing different was the accents, and even those weren't too bad.

As the night wore on, we were feeling better and better and having more and more of a good time. We snuck into a back alley, behind this dumpster, where Tyler magically produced a spliff.

"Look at you! Where did you get that?" I asked with drunken glee.

"I have my ways."

He lit it and we took turns taking hits. It was such a good night. A sudden melancholy fell over me. These nights were no longer the norm. Going forward, we'd be seeing each other less and less and less. Grief and anger welled up from somewhere deep within me. Tyler was laughing at something he had just said and this contradiction to how I was feeling angered me.

"Man, what a night, eh? Too bad these are gonna be few and far between from here on out. It was nice knowing ya," I said.

"Aw man, we'll still see each other. How about Diane and I fly out and visit you in Portland?"

"It won't be the same," I mumbled. I was quiet for a while—we both were—and stared at the dirty ground, lit orange by streetlights. I started getting more upset. "We're never gonna be able to just fuck off and go to Thailand or whatever. Burning Man. You're gonna be down here, getting all established with your job and your girlfriend, and next thing you know you're married to your token black girlfriend and having little half-and—"

An impact flashed across my jaw, jerking my head and forcing me to stumble. I would feel the pain later, but right now I was sinking. I hit the ground and lay there, dizzy and everything out of focus.

"Fuck you," I heard Tyler say from somewhere above me.

I didn't get up.

I stayed on the ground for a long time, feeling sorry for myself. Why not just stay down here forever? No one would care. I got bored after a while and got up and brushed myself off and realized my phone was completely dead. I staggered out into the street. Maybe I could borrow someone's phone and hail an Uber. I had a bit of cash.

Out on the sidewalk a group of Black guys were walking my way, talking loudly and laughing it up. I got a bad vibe from them, so I quickly hurried across the street and headed in the opposite direction. I didn't want to add being mugged to the night's insults.

I found a late-night donut shop where I ordered some coffee and charged my phone. Between the joint, the coffee, the water and being punched in the face by my best friend, I was feeling more sober than I ever had in my life. I decided to leave after my phone charged enough. I hailed an Uber to my hotel, got my things and hit the road. I was heading east to Atlanta, where I had a direct flight back to Portland.

I was heading east on I-20. It was about 4:15 in the morning. I was letting my phone charge and the XM Radio was barely audible. A voice spoke with utmost clarity, almost like someone was sitting in the passenger seat talking to me. It was the radio, the broadcast that people have been telling you about.

Gooooood mornin' folks! I'm Buck Hensley and I'm here with another episode of "The Rules of the Road." Oh, I wish I was in the land of cotton, old

times there are not forgotten, look away! Look away.

I don't remember how the rest of that dang song goes, but boy do I wish I was in the land of cotton. Carla and I took a little tour of the region back in the day. That southern heat sure was sultry, and the windows were down while our sweaty legs stuck to the vinyl seats as we cruised down gravel roads past fields of cotton. The ubiquitous chirping of cicadas filled the air, soon to be joined by a chorus of frogs in the waning evening light. It was just downright beautiful. But a kind of sad beauty, you know? Carla must've thought so too as the tears streamed down her face all the while she kept smiling and smiling. I asked her what was wrong, but she didn't have to tell me. We both knew.

Speaking of that dixie song, did y'all know it was from minstrel shows? A bunch of white folk dressed up as black people, wearing blackface and everything. It was even one of Abraham Lincoln's favorite songs. Ain't that something?

Speaking of blackface, I feel like I'm wearing a type of face myself these days . . . human face . . . and a pale imitation at that. I may have to go fetch me a new one. This one's getting a little torn around the edges. But I digress.

Alrighty, on to tonight's rule, if at any point during your journey you pull over at a gas station or convenience store or vegetable stand or whatever and you see that they have boiled peanuts for sale, then you must buy them. Ladle up a big ol' heapin' cup or bowl full of them delicious goobers, pay for 'em, and eat them right there on sight. I promise I won't be too jealous.

. . .

TREVOR TOLD me that this was a sudden revelation to him, and he thought of the man he had seen at the truck stop. An eerie feeling came over him. He continued listening.

BEFORE YOU GO *off in a tizzy, I know what you're gonna say. You're gonna say, "Buck! I ain't eatin' no dang roadside boiled peanuts. I like my peanuts honey roasted and floatin' in my Coke bottle. Who ever heard of boiling peanuts? Nuts are supposed to be hot and roasted and saltier than my girlfriend's attitude. My mama made me chicken strips and hot dogs every night of my life, and I'm afraid to try any sort of new food. I'm afraid it might come up and bite me or taste yucky."*

And to that I say, "Fair enough." But you might wanna pinch your nose and go ahead and swallow those tasty legumes down. For if you don't follow this rule of the road, then you are in for a rude awakening. A slow and creepy crawling terror might just befall you. Watch your back and don't get too settled for too long, because it might just slowly choke you out.

Welp, that's all I've got for tonight. The sun's about to come up and I've gotta get a move on. I've got so many other faces to meet and places to see and folks to inform. y'all stay safe out there. Stay alert. Stay lively. Stay lonely. I'm Buck Hensley, and these are "The Rules of the Road."

"THAT WAS WEIRD," I said to myself. Did that trucker back in Mississippi hear this broadcast? He must have. Why else would he have done that to himself, knowing that he had a nut allergy? How gullible and stupid could you get? The warning seemed vague. Even if he did believe it, wouldn't he have much rather taken his chances?

The rental car needed a full tank before I returned it. Sure enough, at the first gas station I stopped at they had boiled peanuts for sale. The broadcast and the rule I was given weighed on my mind. There was no reason for me to believe it, but a little good luck couldn't hurt. I opened a Crockpot full of peanuts and ladled one into a napkin. I wanted to try it first. I peeled it out of its shell and popped them in my mouth.

Yuck. It tasted like some sort of bean. I spit it out.

"Fuck the South," I muttered to myself and left the gas station.

THEY CANCELED my flight out of Atlanta. Something mechanical. The airline comped me a room. Before I left the boarding area, I overheard some flight attendants and a pilot talking about the issue.

"Really? That's the strangest thing."

"Yeah, it was wrapped all up in both engines. And that's not the strangest part. It was all over the landing gear, climbing up the side and *into* the engine. Must be some sort of sabotage, I guess. How else can you explain it?"

I looked out the window at the plane I was supposed to board, but I couldn't make out what they were talking about, just something green hanging from the jet engine.

So YEAH, I'm holed up in this shitty hotel, killing time and waiting for my flight. It leaves out tomorrow afternoon. I got to Googling "The Rules of the Road" and to see if it was some sort of regional radio program or what, and that's where I found your website and your call for those that encountered the broadcast. That's really all I have. I didn't follow the rules. I must admit that it made me a little paranoid reading about the encounters on your website, haha. So, you're behind this whole thing, huh?

I TOLD TREVOR THAT NO, I'm not behind it. I don't know if he believed it. He asked me if this was some sort of ARG game, what company I worked for. I told him that as far as I knew, the rules were very, very true. I then asked him if he was pulling one over on me.

He asked, are they going to make a movie about this?

We asked each other more similar questions and then ended the call. I was a little worried about him. He may have been a douchebag and a hypocrite, prone to a strange overcompensation, but I didn't want him to meet his demise. The rules don't fuck around.

Do douchebags realize that they're douchebags? Are they aware of their behavior and its negativity? Maybe not in the moment, but after a period of self-reflection do they ever look back with regret? Can they change?

HE CALLED THE NEXT MORNING, *frantic.*

"Okay, so this is all a big joke, right? The cameras are gonna burst in at any moment and we're all gonna have a big laugh. Did Tyler put you up to this? To teach me a lesson?"

I was groggy. "Is this Trevor? What's going on?"

"QUIT FUCKING WITH ME, MAN!"

"Trevor, just calm down. Tell me what's happening."

"I woke up and there were all these, like, vines. They were covering my entire body, my legs and arms and round my neck and everything. One was going down my throat."

"I had nothing to do with this, Trevor. It's the goddamn rules. They are real. I follow the ones I've heard. Where are you now?"

"I'm in the motel bathroom. I managed to yank most of them off of me, but one is still around my ankle, and it's on there really tight. They're *moving* under the door. Oh shit, oh shit, oh shit."

"*Can you, like, call 911? Give them your location? If I was a prank show, I swear I wouldn't have you do that.*"

I heard him take a deep breath.

"Okay, okay, okay."

I continued to reassure him. I told him I would have my phone by me and for him to please call me back. After a very long five minutes, my phone rang.

"They say they're on their way. They didn't sound like they believed me. So, I told them I had killed somebody in my room and that I was going to kill more. *That* got their attention. Fuck, I'm so scared."

His voice was growing higher in pitch, manic.

"SHIT! My fucking ankle's bleeding! Holy shit, I can see the bone!"

"*Trevor! Stay with me!*"

"Oh God, there's so many vines in here. It's kudzu. That's what it is. It takes over!" *He began to laugh hysterically and hyperventilate.*

I could hear the clang of a toilet tank lid. I could imagine him standing on it, the vine wrapped tight around his ankle, blood running down the porcelain, greenery advancing upon him and wrapping around whatever limb or part of his body it could find.

"The shower rod! Whack them with the shower rod!"

Over the phone, I could hear rustling and clanging and him hollering and screaming.

"Oh God, they're up my leg! Call Buck Hensley! I'm begging you. Please, please, please."

"*Trevor, I can't. Just . . .*"

I didn't know what to say.

The rustling grew louder, and I could only hear him mumbling to himself, prayers and apologies to gods and people unknown. Then, there was a sudden scream, a loud bang, and nothing. I called his name again and again, but there was no response. Silence.

"WE FOUND HIM OUT BACK, by the dumpster. In the brush and weeds. Deceased."

The authorities had found Trevor's cellphone in the hotel room and had contacted the last number that was called.

"Detective, can you tell me how he died? You can be blunt," I said.

"Right now, I only have a couple of ideas. The victim's right leg was missing below the knee, just torn off real messily, but it's weird. It didn't look like he bled out from that, because whoever did this had wrapped a tourniquet on that thigh, a tourniquet made of vines. It prevented the massive blood loss that would normally cause shock in that situation, so despite losing a limb, bleeding out wasn't the cause of death."

"Hmm," was all I could say.

"So, that's a possibility. But he had ligature marks around his neck, all made with vines. So, he may have died from strangulation. But there were also vines in his mouth, down his throat, and in his abdominal cavity. One of the strangest things I ever saw. His whole body, just covered with vines, the silhouette of a person just out there in the landscape like a goddamn art project."

"I . . . I don't . . ." I could only stammer.

"Where did you say you were from?"

I told her.

"Well, we'll be in touch. Right now, we suspect some type of sicko ritual murder. The killer called us from his phone, so he likely had his time with Trevor all night before the call. We haven't even found the leg. So, our best guess is that the killer had his way with this poor guy, wrapped him up in vines, shoved them in every possible place he could, *and then presented him. Maybe it was this Buck Hensley fella. Whatever it is, it was like they were trying to make some kind of statement."*

I told her I would help them in any way that I could.

But I knew that there was nothing they could uncover that would make sense of this whole awful mess. Not unless the Atlanta PD had some sort of supernatural connection.

"It's a weird coincidence. They grounded a plane out at Hartsfield just yesterday. Had vines all wrapped up in the landing gear and both engines. Kudzu. They'd never seen anything like it."

"So, you're telling me radio waves are everywhere?"
   "Yes. They're simply part of the electromagnetic spectrum."
   "Like light waves and stuff?"
   "Yeah. How did you think radios worked?"
   "Just signals, I guess? It always seemed like magic to me."
   "I mean, it kind of is."

7

"TIME AFTER TIME"

Reuben, an early retiree in his fifties, contacted me by phone with his story. He had actually recorded the broadcast and during our conversation he played it back to me over the phone. I hadn't heard Buck's voice since my own encounter with him on the night everything changed. It was a dizzying and rattling experience to hear him again. I got flashbacks and was filled with a paranoia that sent me looking out the windows and the sky above my apartment, a sudden sensation that he could see me as he spoke.

Reuben told me he would send the file to me when he had a chance. He was on the road and didn't have any sort of internet coverage and was actually driving as we spoke. I never got the file, but I got his story.

Here it is.

I GUESS I wasn't made for companionship. Lord knows I've tried. But after three wives and a couple kids that don't ever even keep in touch, I'm through with finding the crooked lid to *this* crooked pot.

Some cookware's just beyond pairing, I guess.

I'm not gonna bore you with the details of my failed

relationships. Just know that I live alone and I'm a retired insurance salesman whose last wife actually paid *me* off to make the divorce quick and painless. I'd caught her in bed with one of her co-workers—one much younger than the both of us—and that was basically the end of my attempts to forge a lifelong connection with any sort of romantic partner.

Even when I caught her cheating, I didn't feel the rush of jealousy and anger like I should have. I just stood in the bedroom doorway with a kind of blank expression, thinking, had I met this guy before? Weren't we introduced at the company Christmas party, Will or Bill, or something? Was he the one who told me about hang gliding and fly fishing and hunting elk? Or was that a different guy? Was this the guy that could get us scuba certified? Why did he look so familiar?

"Look, buddy. I don't want there to be any trouble on this. She said that you two were going through some rough times," the guy in bed with my wife had said.

They had remained under the bedspread, my wife not even bothering to cover up her breasts. No guilt or shame, more annoyed than anything.

"Well, aren't you going to say anything? I mean, this is part of the reason that I'm even doing this right now. You couldn't even muster up any feeling when we were together and you can't even muster up any feeling when you catch your wife fucking some other guy," she said.

Then it hit me. "Phil! That's it. We ran into you at the summer concert series down by the river. Lori introduced us. You said you had your pilot's license."

My third wife shook her head, made a face like one of her molars was hurting.

"Hey man, any time you and Lori wanna go up in the clouds, be my guest," Phil said.

"Goddammit, Reuben," Lori said.

And "Goddammit Reuben" was right. Why keep the charade up any longer? I suppose I entered these situations —wives and jobs and kids—because I felt like I had to. While standing there with my cheating wife—her angrier than me—mundane thoughts seeped into my brain. What was bubbling in the Crockpot and filling the house with its smell? Were we still going to eat it? Would we be able to wrap this up in time so that I wouldn't miss my favorite TV show? I came to the revelation that she was right, that I was wasting everyone's time.

Even when I was here by my family's side, I wasn't ever really present. I was off somewhere else, daydreaming, never existing in the moment I was actually in, but miles away in my head.

Looking back, my absent-mindedness had always been a problem. My careful attention and adoration were present during the early stages of a relationship—the so-called infatuation phase—but a distance within would encroach as the days turned into months and the months into years.

My kids weren't spared the affliction of my aloofness either. And like I said, they seldom call and seldom return my calls.

Sometimes it takes fifty-six years of living to truly know yourself. I know it did for me. Better late than never, I guess. What I found was that I was better off alone, that solitude was my natural and preferred state of being.

So, when Lori divorced me and left a hefty amount of funds in our joint account (she never even bothered or asked about it, that's how badly she wanted to be done with me), I did a full assessment of my savings. Lori had left me with an even bigger benefit, with some investment and stock recommendations early in the marriage. With everything I had, I could retire early and comfortably.

And that's what I did.

The first order of business was to get a proper rig. I

found a Ford panel van with not too many miles on it and bought it, fixed the back up with a little mattress and kitchenette. My goal was to travel the country. I was—and still am—a huge American history buff and I had long daydreamed of the freedom of exploring all the nooks and crannies this great country offered. We spent our first family vacations chasing after Goofy and Mickey or on a beach crowded with sunburnt and bloated tourists. I spent these trips in a sour mood, begging to stop off at a historical site here and there, but the kids' complaints and my wives' boredom kept me from enjoying even these slight excursions.

Now there was nobody that I needed to accommodate on my journey, nobody that I had to talk to and entertain, nobody that would complain about my choice of music on the stereo. It was just me.

It was actually early on during my complete run-through of Route 66, from Chicago to Barstow, when I heard the broadcast. I was just listening to NPR or something when it came on, some sort of talk radio, I can't really remember. It was late; I was in Missouri, and I was trying to make Lebanon at a decent hour.

There was this ticking that interrupted the broadcast. First, it started off quiet and dim, and soon grew incessant and insistent, like someone had thrown a bag of old-school wind-up clocks in my backseat, all ticking at different beats. Then there was a voice.

"Earth to Reuben, Earth to Reuben," it said, and it sounded exactly like my second wife, Pamela.

My first thought was, *Man, this is pretty strange and spooky,* and my second thought was, *I better record this.* So, I pulled out my phone and hit the record button on my voice recorder. I got the entire monologue recorded. Here, let me play it for you.

. . .

Gooooood evening my little nighttime travelers, Buck Hensley here with a friendly reminder that the present state is only an illusion, and that this episode is already over.

Y'know they say that all we have is now. But even now isn't really now. By the time we perceive now in our big dumb brains, now has already passed into the next instant. The sounds we hear, the light we see, already gone and evaporated into that all-encompassing abyss of the past, never to be experienced again until the next cycle.

And boy howdy I am not looking forward to the next cycle. I didn't much care for this ride the first time. Lucky for me I found an exit ramp, ha!

Anyhow, all of this talk about time has me thinking of tonight's "Rule of the Road." Them boys and girls with their white coats and pocket protectors and glasses have determined that speed is equal to the distance traveled divided by—yep, you guessed it! —time. That's how we get those lovely speed limit signs, miles per hour. Nice and convenient, don'tcha think? Much easier than feet per second or inches per minute. I mean they only have so much space on the sign.

So that's where tonight's rule comes in. Turn your volume knobs up, 'cause you don't wanna miss this one. If at any point during your journey, you see a speed limit sign with a bizarre value, something that's outside of your ordinary numerals of five—say, for instance, a limit reading 67 miles per hour—then you must maintain that rate of speed. Do not go faster. Do not go slower. You must go 67 miles per hour and you must stay at 67 miles per hour until you see another normal sign.

Now I know what you're gonna say, you're

gonna say "Buck, my foot is chock full of lead. I keep that puppy pedal to the metal all the time. In fact, my podiatrist recommends it, otherwise I get cramps in my little toesies. I've got a need for speed and gasoline in my veins, I can't putter around at no 67 miles per hour. I'll go insane!"

Or you might say, "I don't know Buck. What do I look like, some kind of NASCAR racer? I keep my hands at ten and two and always drive five miles under the speed limit. I make the blue-hairs look like Dale Earnhardt. Why, just the other day I was passed by a bumper car."

And to that I say, "Fair enough." Do what you must, but if you don't follow the rule, you may find the consequence most appropriate for your rate of travel.

Welp, that's all I got for tonight. Stay safe. Stay lively. Stay lonely. I'm Buck Hensley and these are "The Rules of the Road." I told you the episode was already over.

So, I just played that for you from the audio file on my cell phone, but I'm talking to you on a *satellite* phone. I got one of these to avoid any dead areas as I travelled. I haven't had cell service for quite some time now, being out in the middle of nowhere and all.

Let me back up to explain my predicament. I thought that the Buck Hensley broadcast was creepy and all, especially with the preamble with the ticking clocks and what sounded like my second wife, and for the time being, I certainly kept my eyes peeled for any strange speed-limit signs. However, I ultimately thought it was just an audio sketch or something and thought little about it the next day. I only Googled "The Rules of the Road" at a diner one morning when it came back to me and that's where I found your site and saved your number in my phone.

I honestly thought I might call you from the road sometime later and have a chat. Even though I have this predilection for being alone most of the time, I still get lonely on occasion. Less so than I did back when I was younger, but it's still there.

Anyways, to cut to the chase, certain circumstances have spurred me to call you much sooner than I had expected. I finished the Route 66 trip with no issues. There were no bizarre speed limit signs, no more broadcasts. After staying in California for a couple of weeks, I decided to check out America's Loneliest Highway, US Route 50 through Nevada.

Let me tell you, they weren't kidding about this highway. It's desolate as hell out here, just miles and miles of nothing, little towns scattered sparsely along the way.

I was coming out of Austin, Nevada when I saw it. I almost missed it, zoning out and numb from the endless nothingness, but sure enough, it was there: a sign that read "Speed Limit 67".

So, what do you think I should do? I set the cruise control as soon as I could and I've been driving for miles, all the while going 67 miles per hour. Thank God you answered your phone.

"Thank God you took the rule seriously. You did the right thing by following the rule. You just have to wait until you see a regular speed limit sign and then you're off the hook," I told him.

Is there anything you can offer me? Anything you can do to reassure me?

"I've heard of the consequences of people who failed to follow certain rules. I don't have an inside line to Buck Hensley, if that's what you're asking. I can only recommend that you follow the rule. From what I've seen, sometimes outside forces affect your ability to follow the

rule, but you must do your best to follow it. I mean, what have you got to lose? Just drive 67 miles an hour for a bit."

I guess, but have you ever been on this road? It's flat and straight and empty as hell. That speed feels like walking way out here. Can I ask you something and you be straight with me?

"Sure."

Is this legit? Like are you for real? I'm not sure I believe all this stuff. I think I saw the speed limit sign, but what if I just imagined it? What if this is all a—Holy shit, dude. Get off my ass.

I could hear him talking to someone off the call. "Reuben?" *I asked.*

It's nothing, there's just this prick riding my ass. A big ol' semi. First vehicle I've seen in miles. Go around, go around. There's plenty of room.

A bit of dread simmered in my stomach. "Just maintain your current speed. Don't let him mess with you."

Goddammit, he's getting really close.

"Can you veer onto the shoulder, the other lane? What's the terrain like?"

Oh, just great, there's a car up ahead, 300 yards or so. I'm going to get sandwiched here if this yahoo keeps this up.

Over the phone, I could hear the loud blare and honk of a semi horn followed by Reuben yelling more obscenities. I thought I heard a bang, and then Reuben spoke into the phone.

Look, I've done what I could. I'm gunning it.

I felt my stomach drop. I was hoping he could finish the rule to completion. He could have been so close. Still, the way these things went, it might have been just as well. He may have been driving the correct rate until he ran out of gas and was forced to stop or until there was a sharp curve in the road causing him to crash.

I could hear the roar of the accelerator over the phone.

Oh, God. Oh, God. Oh, shit. Oh, shiiiit.

"*Reuben? Talk to me, buddy. What's going on?*"

I'm pulling over. Slow it down. It's all moving too fast. Why are you talking like that?

He talked slowly and slurred, like he was drunk or on opiates.

"*What is it? Can you give me an idea of your location? Do you need help?*"

Woah, dude. I can't barely catch what you're saying. It's like a little sped up chipmunk voice. Can you talk slower?

But he didn't respond when I asked if he needed help. His voice sounded distant as if he had set the phone down and I could hear him talking to himself, saying, "why's the sun moving like that?"

I CONTACTED the Nevada Highway Patrol. I told them I had been talking with a friend on the phone and had concerns that he had been run off the road on US Highway 50 outside of Austin. They told me they would look into it, but they never called me back.

I HEARD nothing about Reuben for the next several months. This was how these things usually went. I was low on the list of priorities of people to contact when these tragedies occurred, and most of the time it was only dumb luck that they would contact me at all.

Sometimes, if I was vigilant and had been left with other points of contact, I could speed the process along. I didn't even have Reuben's last name, so there was nowhere for me to track him down.

His daughter finally contacted me. They had found my name and number in some of his personal effects once he was transferred from Reno, NV, to a facility in the Pacific Northwest. She had just found the time to go through it.

"I don't really have much to say. Dad and I haven't really been close these past few years, and I can't even remember the last time we spoke. You said that you were a journalist?"

"Sort of. I've been talking with people that have encountered a specific radio program, a strange broadcast. Your father told me he had heard it and I was talking with him about it on the phone when . . . something happened."

"Hmm. Well, I don't know about any sort of broadcast, and as far as what happened, I can send you an article that was written by one of the doctors that was treating him. Other than that, I'm washing my hands of the guy. He never was there for me. Why should I be there for him?"

A Patient on a Different Clock
Dr. Percy Sutherland

I was called in for the assessment and evaluation of Mr. Reuben, a 56-year-old man, who had been found wandering outside his vehicle on US Highway 50 in a near catatonic state in what was essentially the middle of nowhere. He was conscious and would walk and eat with assistance but would otherwise remain practically frozen in place. He would not respond to verbal questions and only stare blankly, his eyes darting back and forth with bouts of severe nystagmus. Occasionally, his lips would tremble in an effort to speak, a guttural groan emanating from within.

An organic cause to Mr. Reuben's condition was ruled out; all of his lab work and imaging studies were completely normal. He had been on no medications as best as we could tell, and for all intents and purposes it had seemed that he was afflicted by this new condition while driving, yet there were no signs of a significant stroke, hemorrhage, or tumor.

I took the time to observe him over several days and noted two startling patterns. First, if I sat in the corner of the room for hours at a time, he would acknowledge my presence by glancing my way (I discovered this pattern incidentally while being preoccupied with the writing of another article in his room.) I repeated this instance on numerous occasions and would witness him focusing on me.

The second pattern I observed was his attempt to write in a notebook that sat on his bedside tray while he was fed his meals. Reuben would stare at the page, only making the slightest of marks with his pen. He moved so slowly that he resembled a statue holding a writing utensil. He would make little headway with his writing, however; he was often interrupted. This would be for meals or physical therapy or group therapy or yard time. He had come to the completion of some letters. I could see the beginning of a sentence: "E-v-e-r . . ."

I ordered the staff to hold any physical therapy activities and to always make sure Mr. Reuben had his notebook and pen close at hand. They were free to take him outside, as long as they did so in a wheelchair with a tray and the notebook. I would see him out there, being pushed around the grounds as he continued to hold the pen and write, slowly but surely.

Finally, he had finished writing his first sentence.

"Everything is happening so quickly—make it STOP!"

An explanation formed in my mind, but my hypothesis required more data. I scribbled my name and job title on a whiteboard and placed it at the foot of Reuben's bed. Then I added, "Can you read this? Please respond if you can," and left it there for days.

Mr. Reuben's eyes locked onto the whiteboard, and he started writing in the notebook. It took him three days to write out the three letters of his response. "Yes," he wrote.

The whiteboard was a static object, and Mr. Reuben only noticed me after I had sat in the same spot for a while, effectively becoming momentarily stationary and within his view. I came to the startling and disturbing conclusion that Mr. Reuben was *experiencing* time at a rapidly accelerated pace.

To fully explore the depths of time and its perception is beyond the limits of this simple article and quite frankly beyond my expertise. Just know that there is a perception of time *and* a real time. One subjective, the other objective. Our perception of time influences how we experience the world.

We've all heard the phrase "time flies when you're having fun" and we've all experienced the tediousness of watching the clock count down on a slow workday. We've also heard our elders report about time speeding up as they age, how the years pass by so quickly. Also noteworthy: the speed at which the elderly drive and their diminished reaction time. This is partially because their perception of time is speeding up, the cars on the highway appear to move much faster than they are in reality.

Mr. Reuben was experiencing everything much quicker than a typical elderly patient, from what I could observe. Much, *much* quicker. By his perception, the staff were no doubt flitting like hummingbirds in and out of his room, talking at an imperceptible speed, his only recourse being able to see something stationary.

I've often wondered what it looks like from his perspective. Is he witnessing our world as if he pressed the fast forward button on a VCR remote? Or is it the more likely scenario of his life being a reel of film with a series of jump cuts formed by gaps of amnesia? Either way, his life is going by much faster than the rest of ours in a way that I have yet been able to quantify.

As for Mr. Reuben, he was eventually transferred from my care to a facility in the Pacific Northwest. (Perhaps he would benefit from their euthanasia laws; Though, I don't think Mr. Reuben will have time to contend with this dilemma; his life will pass him by before he knows it. I may visit Mr. Reuben someday, years down the road, to see how long it's felt for him. It could be seen as a variation of Einstein's clocks, one moving at a different pace the further it gets away from the other, the difference only known when they meet up again.

Will years have passed for him in the matter of hours? Weeks in a day? Decades? The possibilities are staggering and haunting if one dwells on them for long. I am reminded of a quote that came to me from some poem I read long ago, or perhaps from some half-remembered dream: *Which as tomorrow seems to you and me, decades will have passed for he.*

You may be wondering, "I've followed none of these rules and have been fine, but now that I am aware of them, does that mean I have to abide?"

Well, fear not, dear reader. At a certain point I established that the rules only applied to an individual if they had heard the rule broadcast specifically to them. It wasn't a virus that could transcend through different media. It would be irresponsible for me to share these if I knew I could pass it along in such a manner.

So, don't worry too much about not following any rules after reading these.

Still, if you do find yourself following some, I suppose it couldn't hurt.

8
"TUESDAY'S GONE"

I received a call from a real estate investor from the greater Los Angeles area. His name was Ethan Finley, and he had heard "The Rules of the Road" broadcast while stuck in traffic. Due to the sprawling layout of Los Angeles and its reliance on car culture, his odds of experiencing an opportunity to follow the provided rule were higher than most.

Perhaps he would have been better off in New York City.

This is his story.

I LOVE MY PORSCHE.

I know it's such a cliché: the hotshot real estate guy from Los Angeles, wearing his sunglasses and whipping his little red sports car into the parking spot—and even better if it's a parallel job—and jumping out to make a deal. I get that. The looks on their faces, their body language. I know what they're thinking. It's not like I'm not totally oblivious.

They're thinking, *this uppity douchebag. This total freakin' tool in his Armani suit and his sunglasses and his Porsche. I can just see the slime glistening on him all the way from over here.*

But then they see the smile. They feel the handshake.

The warmth. The sincerity. They think about how I'm going to make them some money and then they're all mine.

Why start at a disadvantage though? Couldn't I come off as more trustworthy from the get-go if I wasn't pulling up in the flashy little car? Maybe so. But then I wouldn't be getting to drive a Porsche around, which—let me tell you, bro— is a reward in and of itself. When you're whipping in and out of traffic on the 405, sliding in and out of impossible spaces, leaving everyone else to choke on your dust, you could give two shits about looking like a walking and talking cliché.

I started out flipping residential properties. That's where I learned I had the knack for this sort of thing. After a run of success with that, I transitioned into real estate development. Had some big wins right from the get-go with some properties turned into offices for a few tech firms.

So yeah, I'm a developer. I like to think of it as speculations with a long view. I'm the guy who can turn blank into bank. Just give me the eyes. Lately I've been doing a lot of consulting work with some firms out of China. They want my input on what they should buy and need help to get through the red tape. They pay handsomely.

You'd be surprised by how much American real estate is owned by China and other foreign investors. Meanwhile, there's people that can't afford their rent and a homelessness crisis going on, rows of tents along the streets and parking lots full of people living out of their cars. Yet the rules allow for it and *somebody* keeps buying these places, so I keep making money. I can't help it if I'm lucky.

Other folks, maybe not so much. I don't look inward much; I never had the need. But after all this started, I can't help but wonder if this whole thing is a sort of payback for the part I've played in the city's gentrification. With the cheaper housing that was knocked down to make way for expensive new condos and businesses, how many people had my deals displaced? How much history and character had I incidentally destroyed?

At the time I had considered it progress and justified it by a steadfast belief in the rule that everything changes, and nothing can stay the same.

IN THIS CITY, it's all about who you know. It's this whole culture of, "what can you do for me?" People know this, absorb this, embrace this. Luckily, I'm at the point where I don't have to worry about that anymore. Everyone else, they're the ones coming to me. They come with their hands out and their smiles and their attentive ears, hanging onto my every word. They wouldn't want to miss a crucial detail to pull out so they can impress me.

The other thing about this city is that everyone's coming out here to make it big. Whether it's show biz or something else, there is constantly a new influx of people. These new people, they recognize me as a gatekeeper, they can see it in me, and when I go out, they want to get to know me. There is no shortage of places for me to meet up with these new arrivals: cocktail mixers and parties and premieres; I rub elbows with a lot of show business types.

Basically, what I'm trying to get at, is that I get lots of pussy and lots of *different* pussy. It's a constant rotation of the new and there have been no signs of it slowing down. Even as I've gotten older and a little grayer, I'm still pulling down gals the same age as when I was younger.

We have fun. They know the name of the game and I'd say they get their money's worth. We have a whirlwind of fun for a couple of weeks: courtside Lakers tickets, movie premieres, weekends at Catalina. But that's about all I can stand. I can't sit still for too long with the same girl. I've been divorced once, and it took me years to get built back up to where I was. Won't fall for *that* again.

I'm not trying to brag about my love life or my cool car or anything like that. Like I said, I'm acutely aware of the optics, especially now. I just wanted to paint the picture of what my life was like before I heard that cursed radio broadcast. I was on top of the world. Not the King of LA, but maybe like an Earl or a Duke. Something like that.

And then I found out about Buck Hensley.

IT WAS a bitch of a traffic jam on the 405. My Waze said there was a ten-car pileup five miles ahead. The exits were all congested. It was start, stop, start, stop. Rinse, repeat. The sun was beating down, and the glare from other windshields was cutting through my sunglasses. I had a property to survey in Venice, the next up-and-coming place. I was going to be late and the caffeine from the double espresso I'd had earlier was racing through my veins like the Indy 500, making me frustrated and antsy.

Stuck behind a semi-trailer, the podcast I was listening to grew tiresome. I was about to flick it off when out of nowhere, Joe Rogan said over my speakers:

"Hey, Jamie, pull up the video of this guy, Ethan Finley. He's a real estate developer, and he's currently stuck in traffic. Yup. A Porsche Cayman. Oh, he's got the Amaranth Red. That's a sweet fucking car."

A feathery sensation crept down my spine and I got goosebumps. I looked around frantically. Life appeared normal in the surrounding cars. People stared at the road or at their phones. A girl picked her nose surreptitiously. No one was looking at me or filming me.

I rolled down the window and looked up at the sky. A helicopter, perhaps? Nothing.

Rogan continued, "Remember when his dad got drunk in the evenings? Hell, he'd come home already half-sauced, drink more, yell at the wife, slap Ethan, and fall asleep in the recliner. One time, Ethan tried to stand up to him. He should've waited until he was a little bigger. Do some pushups, son! Pull that up, Jamie. Look at—watch this. So, Dad's passed out in the recliner. Ethan comes up behind him, goes for the rear naked choke, and boom! Dad body slams Ethan. Holy fuck. Look at *that*. See how his head dents the sheetrock?"

"Shut up!" I yelled, looking around frantically. My heart pounded. Tears had welled up at the corners of my eyes. The scene that had just been described came back to me in vivid detail, all of those years of hell with my dad growing up. It was as if they were watching a video of it and commentating on it.

I stopped the podcast on my phone, but there was still sound coming out of the speakers, a bunch of chimpanzees screaming. It got louder and louder and louder and stayed even when I turned the volume down and kicked the stereo. There was a burst of static and *he* began to talk.

Howdy, folks. How y'all doing on this bright and sunny morning? Does it feel like you're rooted in place? Stuck at a standstill? Like your feet are in concrete and it's about to dry? Well, unless you're a movie star down at The Chinese Theatre, you best be keeping your appendages out of the wet cement.

Whenever I find myself at a place like this, when time is standing still and all forward momentum has ceased, I just use that stillness to take a moment of quiet reflection. I reflect back on all the things I've done and all the things that I've undone. Could I undo the things I've done or redo the things I've undone? Or was I stuck doing those things at every point and time? I know I don't do things like I used to do, but I still undo things like I did before I stopped doing the things the way I did. What is it that you do the way you did? Or do you not do that anymore?

I WAS PANTING, still stuck in place, cornered on all sides by traffic. I wanted to just jump out of my car and run, leave it abandoned here on the interstate, keys in it and everything. Let someone else take this cursed thing and its speakers playing this demonic drivel.

I was a boat stuck on a frozen lake though. Couldn't even move while dozens of suppressed memories of my father surfaced from some tucked-away corner of my brain.

ANYHOW, where was I? Ah yes, I was talking about the importance of standing still on this special early morning edition of "The Rules of the Road." Them good ol' boys down south knew the importance of stopping and smelling the roses. They knew you had to slow down every once in a while and take your time. That's why they never got in a hurry with the song "Free Bird." You know it's a very long song.

Why yes, I am talking about the Southern rock band Lynyrd Skynyrd. Good bunch of guys. They give me a personal show every now and then and haven't missed a beat (even though the fella in charge of refueling their plane did). That's where today's "Rule of the Road" comes in. If at any point during your journey, you hear the song "Free Bird", you must listen to it in its entirety. It is imperative that you do so—the whole thing—I'm talking guitar solo and outro and everything until fade out.

I know what you're thinking. You're thinking, "Buck, I'm a very busy man and my schedule is packed, and I mean packed to the gills. I gotta work my 9-5, but before that I gotta get up at 6 in the morning, so I can practice my Bulgarian throat singing and milk the goats, and then I have to get my case assignment finished in time so Jenkins doesn't jump all over my hiney, the little twerp. After working my fingers to blood and pulp at the grindstone, I gotta take little Timmy to soccer practice and then have dinner with the family and then massage the little miss's footsies. My, how those things have looked gnarly lately, and I mean rougher than sandpaper, but I don't know how to tell her. And then I gotta hit the hay, out like a light, only to wake up and do it all over again. I don't have time to listen to no song that has a three-minute guitar solo. Time is money and three minutes might as well be a thousand smackers."

And to that I say, "Fair enough." If you don't have time to finish "Free Bird," then you won't have time to finish anything else. You'll never finish another deal again. Ignore this rule at your own peril.

Welp, that's all I got for this morning. I hope the coffee is hitting you just right, and the sun is shining bright and that California dreaming doesn't turn into any sort of California nightmare. y'all have a good one now. Stay safe. Stay lively. Stay lonely. I'm Buck Hensley, and these are "The Rules of the Road."

The stereo shut off and silence filled my car, soon to be followed by honking from behind me. I'd been staring at the passenger seat floorboards and when I looked up, the traffic before me was moving steadily.

I took the next exit and called to cancel my appointment, went home and took a couple Valiums and nursed gin and tonics until I passed out.

LIFE CARRIED on for the next few weeks without a hitch. Work consumed and distracted me, mostly.

I called my mom. It had been months. The weird stuff had brought her to my mind. She had landed well after the death of my dead, had remarried and was retired and living her best life with my stepdad in Florida.

I checked the Joe Rogan Podcast episode list and saw nothing untoward. I thought about listening to the most recent episode again to see if he said anything about me, but when I heard his voice I got sick to my stomach.

I got to thinking about what I had heard that day in the car and chalked it up to suppressed memories from my unresolved childhood trauma.

I asked some of my friends and colleagues about their go-to shrinks and got a laundry list of names and recommendations, doctors who would prescribe the best drugs, spiritual gurus who would align my chakras, marijuana dispensaries that sold healing strains, and a gal in West Hollywood who could perform what was known as a "trauma colonic."

THE WEEKS PASSED WITHOUT INCIDENT. I buried myself in work. I made conference calls, attended business lunches, scoped out properties, and sealed a few deals.

Maybe this was all a midlife crisis, a sort of sign that I should reassess my place in the universe and how I was living. How long could

I go on like this, making money hand over fist, a new girl every few weeks? Wasn't there a sort of emptiness to it all?

These thoughts usually evaporated pretty easily when I hugged the curves of Mulholland in my beloved Porsche. Nothing like 350 horsepower to throw you back into your seat and erase all your self-doubt.

So, in lieu of a trauma colonic or talking about my childhood to some stranger, I got in my Porsche and took off. The windows were down, and the air was clear. I drove past rows of palms and strip malls and parking lots and little Mexican grocery stores and fast-food restaurants and homeless encampments, all the while keeping my eye out for places that would appreciate in value. The next big thing.

I took Fairfax north and turned west on Hollywood, heading toward Laurel Canyon, with its winding roads and seclusion and where hippies once lived and partied and recorded some fine music. Now it was full of million-dollar homes, all thanks to the likes of people like yours truly.

I was feeling good, and I absentmindedly turned the satellite radio on. It had been a while since I drove out this way and I wanted to match the scene with that 70s Laurel Canyon sound. That's when I heard it, that familiar opening.

It starts with a Hammond B3 organ, these pleasant-sounding drones. Then the drums kick in and shortly after the slide guitar comes roaring out in front of the mix playing that telltale riff. This is followed shortly by those opening lines about the hypothetical leaving.

I mean, we all know the song, and if you don't, then I suppose I envy you for getting to experience this American masterpiece for the first time with fresh ears. It's been overplayed for the rest of us.

I instantly thought of "The Rules of the Road" when I heard it coming on and I cranked up the volume. It had been a long time since I had paid attention and actually listened to the song in its entirety. I vowed to finish the whole thing. What did I have to lose?

For the briefest instant, I closed my eyes during the guitar solo and played a little air guitar on my steering wheel. Eyes open or not, it wouldn't have changed what happened next. It would have only allowed me an extra nanosecond to flinch at the inevitable collision with the truck that had pulled out in front of me as I topped the hill.

THE PORSCHE WAS TOTALED, and I was rattled and whiplashed, but not severely injured. I took a few days off to rest and recover and allow my black eye and swollen face to look more presentable. A contract I was close to closing on got Hoovered up by a competing firm with a better offer. Even though I would spend the next couple months trying to work and function and get back to the peak of what I was, that was the closest I would ever get to finishing a deal again.

THERE WAS something different about her. She wasn't a model or an aspiring actress. She had already made it, was a producer for Universal Studios. In a way, she was into speculations like me, weighing risks and rewards for the maximum payoff for the studios. She was responsible for finding the right projects for the studio, turning blank into bank.

We hit it off, and it was clear from the start that this was going to differ from any of my other more recent flings. We took things slowly, and that was fine with me. I enjoyed her company and actually having conversations and dinner and drinks with her. It was fun to let the sexual tension just build for once, send each other flirtatious texts throughout the day. I had missed this kind of relationship, one that was more than sex.

Everything built to a crescendo after a dinner at Spago (which in hindsight, I didn't finish) and winding up back at her place. The little black dress she wore, the straps over her shoulders, the kissing in the foyer, the curve of her calf as she bent her leg and pulled her heels off, our clothes littering the hallway to her bedroom. There we were, on her bed. She was topless and on her knees while I lay back and admired her. The way her hair cascaded over her breasts, her hips flaring out like the bottom of a vase, her thighs touching and the line between them leading to the V of her mound. I was raring to go, and her visage in the lamplight was like nothing I had ever seen.

She reached toward me and I blasted all over the inside of my boxers, trying to hide the spasms and contractions of my body during my severely premature orgasm. The bewildered look on her face slowly giving way to disappointment is one I can still see to this very day, even after everything I've gone through.

Being a little older and more mature, she was understanding. I only had to swallow my pride and know what she was really thinking of, despite her reassurances. I still feared that I was going to be a story she would tell the gals over lunch—the rich, hotshot real estate guy with premature ejaculation issues—but she gave me more chances.

We continued to date, and the next attempt was the complete opposite of my problem before. Pounding and pounding into her, I just could not finish. My dick felt like it was a million miles away. Numb or something, like it was somebody else's. I pretended I had orgasmed into the condom I wore and snuck off into the bathroom to douse my junk under cold water.

Sure, she came during this session, but it only bought me

a little more time regarding our relationship as the next few times we attempted sex were complete busts. I was limp dicked and unable to perform, a problem I had never had before. She started pulling away from what had been a blossoming little relationship, slowly and surely. She texted less and less and eventually quit responding, what the kids nowadays call ghosting.

I felt the closest thing to heartbreak that I had experienced in many years. It was raw and painful, and I realized that not only did I never finish having sex with her, I never felt the closure of something like a breakup. The relationship itself never felt finished, man.

AS FAILURES and falling outs mounted at work, I noticed other things. I seldom finished meals. At my favorite lounge, I left drinks half empty on the bar after I had ordered them. I couldn't finish a movie or TV show. Even if I vowed to concentrate and see it through to the end—which most times I failed at, anyways—some outside force would cause it to stop prematurely.

For instance, I went out with some colleagues to a premiere and there was a power outage at the theater and they issued us rain checks. I went to see one of my favorite bands live at The Troubadour, and a freaking fire broke out in the middle of the opening number.

WITH EACH PASSING DAY, it only seems to worsen. I find myself unable to finish sentences. Conversations lull into an awkward standstill as I zone out.

"Ethan? Ethan, are you with us?" they ask.

"Oh," I say.

"Sorry," I say. "What was that?"

Forget finishing a book. I can't even finish an e-mail or a memo. I try to dial numbers and have to be sure and take a break halfway through.

I can't finish my order at the coffee shop or at the restaurants. I carry a handwritten note for episodes such as these and go to the same few places.

Oh, sure, I can finish some things now and then, but it's almost like it's just enough for basic function, just enough to piss you off. I'm *surviving* and all, but I wouldn't call it living.

I mean, every time I take a shit, I feel like I don't get it all out.

I HAVEN'T REPLACED the Porsche. All the insurance paperwork after the accident, everything you need to do in order to buy a new car, I just haven't been able to *finish* it. I've hired a personal assistant, and we're going to chip away at some of this stuff.

Sometimes I just can't believe it. I'm forty-one years old and already an invalid, basically requiring personal care like I've got dementia or something. I can no longer do what I was put here on this earth to do you see? Sometimes I feel like this curse or whatever would've affected my body's vital processes and allowed me to just die, unable to take a full breath or pump a complete heart chamber of blood.

I've started and stopped this story so many times. In fact, I'm not even on the phone with you right now. This is a recording that I've been working on piece by piece for three goddamn weeks. I've no doubt left the room by now, off to start some activity I won't complete or even hope to finish.

So yeah, I've just come back to record this last part and you're gonna have to hang up at this point and call me back. Oh, there was one other thing I was going to . . .

. . .

FROM THERE, the recording stopped and started playing again from the beginning. I hung up the phone and called Ethan back. There was no answer. I called back several times to no avail, found his information on LinkedIn and tried to contact him through there with no success. It was several days before I heard anything.

I received a call from a personal assistant. She had found my number amongst some of Ethan's personal effects, with the instructions to call me if anything had happened and something had *happened.*

Ethan had attempted suicide.

He had put a revolver to his temple and pulled the trigger. A utility worker had been in the area at the time and had heard the gunshot and called the police. They got him to the hospital in time, where he was now on life support.

Even in suicide, he could not complete the deed.

They had extubated him and he was breathing on his own, but he was unresponsive to any stimuli.

There he was in that hospital bed, lying in a persistent vegetative state from a death he couldn't achieve, dreaming dreams he would never finish.

"Still working on your project? Those rules or whatever?"

"Yeah. I don't have to go in tomorrow until 7, so I think it's gonna be a late one."

Sighs. "Okayyyy."

"Look, I think I'm really in the zone right now and focused. I gotta strike while the iron's hot."

"It's just that last night you didn't come to bed until late."

"Well, maybe I could take a break here soon."

"We could . . . y'know . . . I mean I don't want to distract you or anything."

"Oh. Right. Sure. Just let me finish this up real quick. I'll be up in a bit."

9
"CALL ME"

A *23-year-old college student named Yuvisela contacted me with her account of hearing the broadcast. She and her boyfriend had encountered the broadcast while driving one sultry summer afternoon from Austin, TX.*

So, I have this thing with waterfalls. I'm a little obsessed with them. In my free time and when I'm not paying attention in lecture, I like to look on the internet at pictures of them and daydream that I'm there: the roar of the splashing water, the white foamy spray, my bare toes dipped into the icy spring. I've got a Pinterest page with hundreds of falls that I would like to visit one day. Niagara, Havasu, Victoria Falls, Gullfoss, Iguazu; they're all on there. I keep them all catalogued for my bucket list.

Yet, how many people go to the grave with their bucket list hardly finished? I bet a lot.

My boyfriend, Gabriel, likes to mess with me about my obsession. He'll come up behind me while I'm on my computer or look over my shoulder at my phone and see that I'm looking at waterfalls.

He'll start singing this old song he knows when he catches me, some line about chasing waterfalls by a group called TLC. He's about six years older than me. I'll joke with him to leave me alone and quit singing that old-ass music, ask him if he used to listen to that on an 8-track or something.

"No, my older sister listened to it on CD. You know CDs? Those little plastic things with the holes in them? That little slot in your car's stereo, a *CD* goes in there. They don't make 'em in the new cars anymore."

We've had a variation of this same conversation a bunch of times. It's kind of a running joke between the two of us—him poking fun at my waterfall obsession and me making fun of how old he is—and while he thinks the waterfall thing is a cute little quirk of mine, he also has been supportive of my passion. That's why he surprised me with the trip that summer. He knew I was yearning to see some of these places. He knew he wanted to make me happy. He knew my resources were limited. He knew we weren't getting any younger; I was 23 and still had a semester to go.

But he also knew that we weren't getting any richer, either. At least not soon. I know I'm a bit older for a college student, but it's taken me longer on account of having to work and stuff. I can't take a full load every semester. Money's always tight. I work full time and barely stay ahead, even sending some of my money to help my mom out. Gabriel offered to help me out some and we'd even talked about moving in together, but we had only been together a year at that point, and I wasn't quite ready.

Before my dad had passed, I'd promised him I was going to get my college degree, and I wanted to do it all on my own. While I loved Gabriel and could see myself marrying him, I didn't want to deal with a transition like that so close to the finish line. Besides, we were getting along so well as it was. Why mess with a good thing?

And it *was* a good thing that kept getting better. Just when I thought I couldn't love Gabriel more, on my birthday he surprised me with the best present I've ever gotten. It was a little black notebook with this kind of leathery cover. While the notebook itself was nice, it was what was inside that was the true present. At some point, he logged on to my Pinterest page and wrote page after page of waterfalls, organizing them by country and state. He put little squares beside them, boxes to check off. The last two pages were Texas and Oklahoma. He left a note there. It read:

"Let's start now . . ."
-Gabriel

THE TRIP HAD BEEN A BLAST. We had started out in Abilene, where we both lived and where I attended college. From there, we went to a place called Gorman Falls at this state park. It was one of the tallest waterfalls in the state and all the surrounding vegetation was lush and green. For a while, if I crossed my eyes just right, it was like I wasn't even in Texas.

We couldn't hit all the sites in a day. It was a road trip with multiple nights in hotels. After Gorman Falls and staying at a hotel, we headed toward Austin and stopped off at Hamilton Pool Preserve. The waterfall wasn't as tall as Gorman, but I have to say I liked it better. The water formed a curtain as it poured off of a rocky shelf and into this sunken grotto of blue green water.

We stayed at this magical place for hours, swimming in

the water and soaking up the sun. I could've stayed longer, but it was getting crowded, so we headed to Austin for a night on the town on 6th Street.

The next day we slept in and got a late start on the road. Lunch was at a Whataburger outside Waco. We sat and ate our food and looked at our phones. I browsed Instagram and my eyes skimmed over a gorgeous site. Yep, another waterfall. I slid my phone over to Gabriel.

"Look!" I said.

"Am I supposed to be looking at the butt or the waterfall?" he asked. An Instagram model was standing with her back to the camera, gazing in awe at the water.

"The waterfall, silly."

"Seriously, that skinny white girl ain't got nothing on you. Better let me take a look, just to be sure."

I stood and twirled around quickly, teasing him. "Ok, so back to the waterfall. Did you look at it?"

"Yeah, it's beautiful, babe. Where was this one?"

"Iceland," I sighed.

"Oh, right."

"It's not looking good for the time being. Maybe in a few years, yeah?"

"Just gotta see how the election goes. I ain't holding my breath."

See, neither of us were US citizens. We were DACA recipients. Both of us had wound up in America via illegal means on behalf of our parents, back when we were kids. This was when we were too young to have any say in the matter. I can hardly remember my life before, my life back in Mexico. I grew up here, went to school here. Texas and America are the only home I've ever known. Gabriel, he was originally from Guatemala. His situation is more or less the same.

If we were to leave the country, then we might risk not being able to get back in. You could apply for eligibility to travel if you had special circumstances, but they didn't allow travel for leisure. We didn't even have passports. Until then, our dreams of traveling—something we both wanted to do—were just that: dreams.

There was a little light at the end of the tunnel. Obama and that DREAM Act, I'm sure you've heard of it. You know, the *Dreamers* or whatever? That's what they call us. I guess they call it that because it's just a freaking fantasy that disappears at the slightest thing—the sunrise, your phone alarm—out of your grasp as soon as you start your day.

Anyways, I applied for DACA recipiency, but it hasn't been a guarantee. We're all stuck in a sort of limbo, waiting for the people in Washington to figure out what the hell to do with us, using us as a bargaining chip.

Not Gabriel, though. He didn't apply for the act. Part of it was that he was bad about procrastinating. The other part was that he was paranoid about signing up. I told him he was an idiot and if he blew his chance to become a legal permanent resident, then I wouldn't follow him to Guatemala if he got deported. He told me he didn't trust the program, that once they had you in the system, they could track you easier, keep tabs on you. Said he knew a guy who got deported this way. I told him the guy must've gotten into some legal trouble, a DUI or something, to have been deported.

"We're all just one slip up from some legal trouble. Hell, some people consider us illegal right now," he had said.

It was hard to argue against that, I guess. At least he knew where he stood, didn't have that false hope. Sometimes, I think it's the hope that gets you, makes things worse.

Gabriel frowned and handed the phone back to me, looked out the window and took a sip of his Coke. I suddenly felt bad and ungrateful. Here was this amazing man that had planned out an awesome road trip just for me and I was busy looking at other far off adventures, not appreciating what I had right in front of me, the moment I was living in right now.

I leaned forward and kissed him. "I don't care where I'm at as long as you're with me," I said, and he smiled.

What I told him just then *was* true. That didn't mean I was going to grow complacent and quit dreaming.

They called us Dreamers, after all.

IT WAS one of those giant truck stops, the kind that was a little smaller than a Wal-Mart or Target, but just barely. We filled up and paced around inside and looked at the aisles and aisles of candy, the funny toys and souvenirs, and the tacky t-shirts.

"Hey Yuvi, whaddaya say? It's your size." Gabriel asked, holding up a black t-shirt with glittery letters. "PROUD TRUCKER WIFE," it read.

"Only if you get that one," I said, pointing at a T-shirt with a semi-truck on it that read "I JUST DROPPED A LOAD."

"Eww," Gabriel said, laughing.

We both wandered around on our own. They had a huge candy section, and I was looking to see if they had any Vero Elotes candy. I had just found a bag on a bottom shelf when Gabriel came skipping up.

"We are so getting this," he said, holding up a plastic CD case.

"What is it?"

"Best of the '90s. It's got your song on there, see? 'Don't Go Chasing Waterfalls.' Can we get it? It's only 3.99."

"Ha, ok. But only if you buy me this," I said, handing him the candy.

. . .

THERE WAS traffic from hell just south of Denton on account of construction and a car wreck or two. We were stop-and-go for what seemed like an hour. I was passenger side while Gabriel idled along.

"Okay. I think now's the time to break out this bad boy," Gabriel said as he started tearing at the plastic wrap around the CD case.

"I think this is the first time I've even used the CD player in this car."

"Aw, hell yeah," Gabriel said as the first song started playing. "Gettin' Jiggy Wit It."

"Getting what, now?"

"It's your boy, Will Smith. Y'know the Fresh Prince? Betcha didn't know he had a little music career."

"That guy from *I Am Legend* and *Aladdin*?"

Gabriel rolled his eyes. "I *guess*. His older work is much better."

"Well, I don't know. You act like you're this old and wise millennial. You're not *that* much older than me, y'know."

"I'm telling ya, my Gen-X sister raised me on all of this stuff. I *think* she was Gen-X. I don't know the damn cutoffs. Anyways, she babysat me a lot growing up while Mama was working and stuff. She *cultured* my little ass. Ooh, here it is!"

A new song started playing. I couldn't help but laugh at how it started. "It sounds like porn music!"

"Nah, shhh. Shhh." Gabriel bobbed his head along to the beat.

The chorus wormed its way into my head. The song was okay, I guess. I still can't really listen to it to this day.

"You gotta listen to this dope rap coming up," Gabriel said.

There was the sound of hissing and popping, wet logs burning in a fire. Whispers intermingled with the sound effects. One voice rose above the others and said, "Listen!" harshly in Spanish, you know, "Escuchen! Escuchen!"

We both looked at each other with wide eyes. The traffic crept forward slowly and Gabriel kept his hands on the wheel while I kept mine in my lap, and that's when *he* started to talk. It was this happy sounding older guy, talking right there on my car's speakers.

*G*OOOOD AFTERNOON FOLKS, *Buck Hensley here with a special rush hour edition of "The Rules of the Road". Hope y'all are doing alright out there while you're idling on the clogged arteries of America's highways and byways, breathing in those delicious exhaust fumes. I know that good ol' Mother Earth likes to take a big fat rip of that stuff from time to time, although as of late she seems to be getting quite a contact high from that delicious Co2 and starting to feel the effects just a little too much.*

And yet you all keep puff-puffing and passing, never slowing down. What with your jet planes and your driving and your travel and your never ending consumption and your cow farts and whatnot. All I'm saying is that you folks might wanna slow down a bit on that stuff, because I've seen the end results and all I can say is that they are hilarious. But I understand if you wanna keep on keeping on and having a good time. All I can say is smoke 'em if you got 'em.

Speaking of good times, that reminds me of today's special "Rule of the Road." You're gonna want to listen to this one as it's all about good times. Why, that was Carla's favorite sitcom for a spell there, Good Times. She'd watch reruns on into the night, the TV casting a pale glow that was kinda comforting across the bed, and I'd wake up to live studio laughter and her snoring softly beside me, the serene look of slumber on her face and the years I'd wasted.

GABRIEL and I both looked at each other. He shrugged and reached for the stereo. I shooed his hand away. I wanted to listen to it. The voice continued.

BUT I DIGRESS ... Well, now, on to today's "Rule of the Road." If at any point during your journey you stop off for a pit stop or a potty break and you enter a public restroom to do your business, take note of the writing on the stalls. You might notice some graffiti that reads, "For a Good Time, Call" and then a phone number listed after it. If you notice this, then take the number down for later use. Whenever you are in dire need of a good time, then give that number a call.

Now before you go off with a bee in your bonnet and tell me how you ain't gonna call no sketchy phone number taken off a lady's or men's room wall, let me just tell you that this will be worth it. You can trust me. When has old Bucky ever let ya down?

I know what you're gonna say next though, you're gonna say, "Buck, I don't ever call no numbers on my phone. I'm deathly afraid of voices on the other line. If I can't text and send little emojis and the like, then forget it. If I can't use an app to order Thai food or a pizza, then I go hungry that night. I haven't even made an appointment with a doctor since I've lived with my parents. What if since we can't see each other's faces we start talking at the same time and we talk over each other and then say, 'oops sorry, no you go ahead' and then we both say it again at the same time and then we both start trying to talk again and then get stuck in some sort of infinite loop?"

And to that I say, *"fair enough."* Don't use the phone. The consequences of not following this rule are a little less dire than previous rules you may have heard. If you don't follow this rule, then you will simply miss out on a good time. That's it. But you wouldn't want to miss out on anything, would ya?

Welp. That's all I've got on this fine late afternoon. May the wind be always at your back, your picnic basket full of snacks, and your cheese ever be pepper jack. Y'all stay sane out there. Stay symbiotic. Stay lonely. I'm Buck Hensley and these are "The Rules of the Road."

THE VOICE INSTANTLY STOPPED, and the song resumed. Gabriel had a dumbfounded look on his face.

"What the hell?" he said and tried to rewind the CD.

"Umm, was that part of the song? Maybe a different version?"

"No way," he said, and kept rewinding and playing the song over. The little skit that we heard never returned.

"Weird," I said.

"Beats the heck out of me."

"Maybe the CD is haunted. That was pretty spooky, y'know? That voice telling us to listen?" I said.

"Maybe it was like a hidden track or something, yeah? They used to put those on CD's back in the day. And this CD was pretty cheap and has all these songs on it. Could've been like a pirated deal."

The recorded message or whatever the heck it was didn't

really scare us at the time. More than anything, it just left us confused. It was only looking back that we saw the importance of what we had heard, how from there our path seemed to be led a certain way. At the time it was just this weird little thing, a funny little mystery that was forgettable for the time being.

We crept along for a while without incident, the traffic slowly gaining momentum. The music on the CD played on as usual and we heard no extra voices. The songs played like they were supposed to. Everything was fine.

Of course, outside of Gainesville, it hit me. I had been trying to ignore it and power through until we stopped for the night, but I had the sudden urge to pee. All that slow traffic and iced tea and a bottle of water must've caught up with me. This was intense. Usually, I could hold it pretty good, but I had to get Gabriel to stop at the first exit we saw.

It was this gas station kind of off by itself and it was all dingy and old and faded and didn't look the cleanest. Gabriel parked and my lower stomach and bladder ached as soon as I stood up and got out of the car. I burst into the place and made a beeline toward the restroom, over in the corner past the ATM and the glass fridges down a hall with burnt out fluorescent lights.

They were singles you could lock, one for men and one for women. The floor was sticky and paper towels piled out of a trash can, and a strip of toilet paper floated in a pool of standing water. A condom dispensing machine was on the wall opposite the toilet.

It wasn't the worst public restroom I'd ever used, but I didn't have many options; I was literally about to pee myself. I would have to do the hover move over the toilet. No seat covers in a joint like this and I didn't have time to prep it with toilet paper or anything.

So, I was doing my business, thighs burning from the squat, and kind of laughing to myself at the condom dispenser machine with its brands like the "FRENCH TICKLER" That's when I saw it, the graffiti written in Sharpie, right there on the vending machine. It said, "For A Good Time, Call 9xx-XXX-XXXX *[Redacted]*".

After I finished and had washed my hands, I snapped a pic of the graffiti. I figured Gabriel would get a kick out of it.

"You're supposed to call it. That's the rule," Gabriel said when I showed him.

"I'm too nervous. You call. You heard it, too."

"Chicken."

"Yep."

"How many of those things do you even see? I've seen them all the time. I bet it's just dudes pranking each other or fucking with their ex-girlfriends," Gabriel said

"Well, I found it in the ladies' room, so hopefully it wasn't dudes," I replied.

"Okay, you enter it in your phone, and I'll dial. I'll try to do a caller ID block or something. Let's just see what happens."

"Are you sure?" I asked.

"Eh, come on. Maybe it's fate."

The Texas travel center appeared on the southbound side of the interstate, and we were soon crossing the Red River and on into Oklahoma as I transcribed the numbers from the picture to the keypad on my dialer.

A large casino came into view. It was ginormous with this sort of facade of all these famous buildings on its outside. I could see Big Ben and that Roman coliseum and all these other world architecture things. The casino just stretched on and on.

"Aw, not again," Gabriel said.

I had just finished transposing the number into the phone. The crazy casino had distracted me. "What is it, babe?"

"Another jam."

The traffic was veering into the right-hand lane, but still moving at a decent clip, like 45 or something. After a mile of this, I could see a couple of highway patrol cars parked across the interstate, blocking both lanes of traffic. A state trooper stood out in the middle, waving a flashlight thing and directing traffic to take the exit. There was still about an hour of daylight left, and somewhere off in the distance a thick wall of smoke blotted out the sun and filled the evening sky with this surreal haze.

"Wonder what's going on?" I asked.

"Who knows? Grassfire, maybe."

We followed the other cars and trucks down the exit ramp. Some turned right, some turned left.

"Right or left? Right or left?" Gabriel asked.

There seemed to be more cars turning left. Maybe they knew something we didn't. But then, we would be stuck behind them, and it was getting dark and we were already behind schedule. I just wanted to get the hell out of the car.

"Um, right! Right," I said, trying to pull up the GPS on my phone. It was lagging and my service had kicked over to 3G. "Freaking Verizon," I muttered.

We drove down a highway past empty fields fenced off by barbed wire. There were houses and barns and oilfield pump jacks every so often, but not much else. No gas stations or a sign of a town or much else, really. After driving into all this nothingness for a while, my phone completely lost service. The surrounding cars thinned out, and there was only a black SUV in front of us.

"Hey babe, I have no service and can't pull up the GPS. Wanna turn back around?"

"Nah, let's just keep going. We've come this far, yeah? We'll hit a main road eventually, get some service."

I sighed in response as he kept driving, let him know I didn't approve.

"We'll turn north soon, ok? All roads lead to Turner Falls."

I checked my phone every fifteen seconds, looking for a signal.

"C'mon Gabe, we're gonna get lost out here. Let's just go back, follow the other cars or see if they've opened up the interstate again."

"Look, this looks like a good road. We'll cut north here and drive aways and then cut back west toward the interstate. It's literally impossible to get lost out here. Just trying not to lose any more time."

But it wasn't so simple, and the nervous feeling in my stomach was validated when the road we drove on turned into gravel. The sun was long gone, and our headlights cut a tunnel through the night as barbed wire whizzed by, separating us from pastures that were elevated above the road on grassy rises. I feared the worst, thinking of every horror movie I'd ever seen that had started out this way: the headstrong man refusing to admit that he was lost and the increasingly pissed off and worried girl that was with him.

"*Babe*, please just turn around," I pleaded.

"Okay, okay. Still no signal, eh?"

I looked down at my phone. Finally, there was one bar of service. "Yes! Hang on."

"Oh, fuck. Fuck. Fuck. Fuck," Gabriel said, his voice growing louder.

What appeared in the rearview mirror was just as scary as any sort of Freddy or Jason or Leatherface from the big screen. My stomach dropped.

It was a police car with its red and blue lights spinning.

Gabriel pulled over and the police car shined a spotlight through our back window, flooding the car with light. Gabriel muttered obscenities and started digging for his wallet and insurance information before the cop could get to the window. His hands were shaking. We both had legal

Texas driver's licenses, but you never knew what kind of trouble you could get into when you got caught being brown.

"Wasn't even speeding or driving crazy or nothing," Gabriel said to himself.

His window was rolled down. Crickets and frogs and other nighttime noises filled the air. There was no sound of other vehicles. We were really alone out here. I couldn't even see any lights in the distance. Footsteps crunched on the gravel road toward us.

"Evening, y'all. Can I see some license and registration, please?" the policeman asked.

I could only see the bottom half of him through Gabriel's window, and not very well at that. He had his flashlight beaming into the car, blinding us. I thought of the time I went catching bullfrogs with my cousins one summer in East Texas, how the frogs would just stare dumbly into the spotlight they used to catch them, helpless and hypnotized by the great shining light. Waiting to be plucked up and butchered and not a damn thing they could do about it.

"Just a sec. Got it right here," Gabriel said, handing it over as he squinted into the light.

The officer wore a dark button-up shirt tucked into a pair of jeans. A belt with a holstered black gun wrapped around his waist. Even more strange than his wearing jeans as part of his uniform was the large belt buckle. It was a large skull, that one you see everywhere on trucks and stuff. Punisher, I think it's called. My anxiety about the situation ramped to about a thousand when I saw that. Why didn't he have a normal uniform? Was he like a special sheriff's deputy or something?

"Sir, do you mind telling me what I'm being pulled over for? I don't think I was speeding."

This was just how it was. You had to be all polite when

dealing with the cops, all "yes sir" and "no ma'am" and "thank you officer," make sure you dotted all your "i's" and crossed your "t's." I'd heard friends and classmates talk about how they would cop an attitude with the police, talk back and stuff, but I never had it in me to do anything like that.

"I'm getting to that," the cop said. "Just looking at your stuff here for a second. Gabriel Torres. You two's are a couple of Tejanos, eh? Texicans? What are y'all doing up here? Looking for jobs?"

"Just a little trip," Gabriel said.

"A trip, huh?"

"Yeah, we're going to Turner Falls," I said from the passenger seat, leaning over. I thought the more we said, the better. No need to hide anything. Didn't want him to think the worst.

"Well, how we doing over there, señorita?" the cop sneered. He leaned down a little as he said this, looking in at me. I could see his tacky black mustache that went past his mouth and down the sides of his chin like a horseshoe. A tattoo peeked out from the collar on his neck. He turned back to Gabriel. "So, does she love it when you call her señorita? Does she have a nice little taco?"

Gabriel squeezed the steering wheel tighter, saying nothing. Just stared straight ahead.

"I asked you a question, señor," the cop said and squatted down so he could stare in at us with his beady eyes. "Y'all best comply. I got my partner back at the car if y'all do any funny business. He's been dying to shoot out some windows with his new Mossberg. Be even more thrilled if it was a coupla Mexicans."

"Sir. We are just trying to get to our destination. We are complying, and you are being rude and disrespectful to both me and my girlfriend," Gabriel said.

I noticed something about the officer. He had no badge

or name tag. Things weren't sitting right with me. This wasn't going to end well. His hand had crept on to the gun in the holster.

"Excuse me," I said. "What's your badge number? Don't we have the right to ask you for that?"

"Badges? I don't have to show you no stinking badges," he said in a thick mocking accent and laughed. He turned to Gabriel. "Maybe I might have to give your girlfriend a little strip search. Make sure she isn't smuggling anything from across the border."

I looked down at my phone discreetly. I heard you could call 911 in these instances when you had safety concerns while pulled over. They could send another officer or escort you to the station or *something*. It was supposed to be one of your rights. I slid my phone to the side of my outer thigh and edged out the screen so I could see.

The fucking lock screen!

"So, the reason I pulled you two over on this fine summer night was you looked ... suspicious. That's right, *suspicious*. What are y'all even doing way out here?"

I entered the code.

"We got lost," said Gabriel.

The dialer was pulled up. The number entered from before.

BANG!

I jumped and looked up.

"Just what do you think you're doing over there?" the policeman said. He had smacked his hand on the roof of the car.

"Um, nothing," I replied

"Hand it over."

"No," I said.

My hands were shaking. I couldn't focus enough to delete the number and enter 911. I hit the green dial button. Maybe they could trace the cell tower to my cell number for whenever we went missing. Maybe the person on the other end of the phone would hear what was going on, testify at this fucker's trial for whatever sick shit he planned on doing to us.

"Hand. It. Over," the cop ordered, slapping his hand on the roof of the car again for emphasis.

"Look, sir. She doesn't have to. Why don't you just let us go? Okay?" Gabriel said.

The cop reached for his gun. We both ducked and Gabriel jerked the car into drive. There was the loud noise of the acceleration, the redlining, the tires peeling out in the gravel, the small stones spitting through the air and raining on the car like hail. It was all capped off by a gigantic explosion that filled the car and deafened me, screams coming out of me that I couldn't stop.

This was how I was going to die. I couldn't believe it.

And still there were more gunshots and breaking glass, and the grinding noise of the car skidding out of control. The headlights pointed straight for the ditch. The front end of the car dove low, which threw me against the seatbelt and Gabriel against the steering wheel.

I think we were lucky that the airbag didn't deploy. We ended up really needing those extra seconds.

We shook ourselves off from the collision, got our bearings. Gabriel opened his door and looked back down the road.

"Yuvi. Yuvi. Yuvi! Get out. C'mon, let's go. Let's go," he said, his voice rising to a panicked register I had never heard him use before.

I opened my car door and stepped out into the ditch, leaving the door ajar as the little "door open" alert chimed: ding, ding, ding.

"This way, babe. Over the fence," Gabriel said, scrambling up the ditch's incline toward barbed wire, reaching his hand out for me.

I looked back and I could see headlights coming for us, could hear the engine revving and tires peeling out on the gravel road. Fear coursed through me and led the way. Gabriel stomped on a strand of barbed wire and pulled another up with his hands. I ducked under, unable to do so cautiously. A metal barb cut through my back and tore my jeans and leg.

The black car slammed on its brakes and fishtailed toward us. Gabriel hopped the fence and tumbled to the ground. As I helped him up, I heard the policeman open his door and shout at us.

Gunshots echoed around us, and we ran. Oh, how we ran. The grass was tall and there was a half-moon floating in the sky. Off in the distance of the open field, I could see large circular shapes scattered about. Hay bales. We sprinted toward one that sat in the middle of the field, ducked behind it and lay on our stomachs in the grass.

For a moment, everything was quiet. There was only our panting breath and through that I could hear the night sounds once again, the crickets and frogs.

"Do you think he—," I started in a whisper, before Gabriel shushed me.

"Shh. I can see him. He's coming this way."

I hugged the ground and inched my face just past the bale of hay. I could see the figure of the policeman carrying his flashlight, sweeping the beam across the field. I didn't think he could see me peeking. Our hay bale was in the middle of several others and set back a ways. He was coming, though, and bound to find us.

My heart revved back up again. Somehow this was worse than all the fast-paced terror before, when everything happened so fast that my mind couldn't process it. I almost pissed myself right there in the grass.

"Yuvi. Duck down low and we can crawl to the next hay bale. Keep going until we hit the trees and can lose him."

Behind me there was another round bale of hay about 50 yards away. Going from our current safe place to the next would leave us exposed, and as I started crawling, it didn't seem like such a good idea to move so slowly with my back to the gunman. That flashlight would hit us before we knew it, and we would be stuck with no cover.

"Gabe, I think we should go for it," I rasped.

"Okay, okay. Go."

I shot to my feet and ran in a crouched position, going for the next bale and then the next, Gabriel hot on my heels.

I yelped as a beam of light crossed my path. It was too late. Gunfire erupted from behind me, and I could hear actual bullets whizzing past my head.

And in the chaos from there, we ran and ran. We ducked behind bales as we came to them, but only used them for brief cover, running and running, all along Gabriel telling me "go, go, go."

How many bullets did he have? Would he ever give up?

In a panic, I made a hard left. There were more hay bales stretched in that direction, and I had once heard that running in a straight line from a gunman was never a great idea. It made you too easy to hit.

With heels pounding in a sprint for a good distance, we slid behind yet another bale, putting some space between us and the gunman, his flashlight revealing his position.

He shut it off.

We stayed low.

He clicked it back on, swept the beam around. Closer. We could always consider that he could completely walk by us.

The light went off again, a pale darkness in the field. I thought I could still make him out, standing there. Waiting. Listening.

But there was something else out here. I heard a rustle

from somewhere to our left and a tall shape emerged from behind one of the hay bales. Long pale legs shimmered in the moonlight, bending at awkward angles. A thick body that tapered into a long neck and a skeletal head with glinting black eyes.

The thing made its way toward us, heavy footsteps thudding through the pasture. I curled into Gabriel and made myself as small as possible, his breaths heavy and ragged against my back, arms and body slippery with sweat as he clutched me.

The footsteps passed. We poked our heads out to see as the tall thing ran down an aisle of hay bales, its body growing *wider* with each step.

The flashlight came on again out in the field, but soon its beam went tumbling and it clattered off in the grass. There was a scream and a giant beating sound, and the sounds of a scuffle. The giant thing leaned over the cop and I could barely make out his arms and legs flailing and struggling against the creature as its long legs kicked. The silhouette of the body grew and contracted again and again, the beating of its giant wings.

I could hear his grunting and choking, one last scream that sounded like his mouth was full of

Soon, the cop moved no more.

There was a light in the distance, shining through the trees. A porch light and the frame of a house.

"You're all sweaty," I said to Gabriel as I helped him up.

"It's not all sweat."

"What?"

"It's uh ... nothing. I just think he . . . ah . . . got me somewhere back there."

I touched his waist and felt a damp warmth, pulled my hand back. My palm was soaked in blood.

"Oh, Gabriel."

He was weak in the legs, and I had to help him. His

body was all clammy, and he clutched his side. The weight of him was tugging me down, but I stood strong, and we made our way toward the house.

It was across a country road and down a short gravel driveway. No dogs barked as we approached the wooden porch. I didn't see any cars parked outside, and I hoped they were just out of view. No one answered as I banged on the door and rang the doorbell and yelled for help.

The door was unlocked.

"C'mon, Gabe. Let's see if they have a phone."

I found a light switch and saw that we were in the living room and there was a floral print couch and I helped him over to it to lie down. He looked bad, and that was putting it lightly. It was like he was a kid that had just come off the log flume ride at Six Flags, except instead of his clothes being soaked with stagnant water, it was sweat and blood.

I grabbed a dish towel from a kitchen counter that overlooked the living room, pressed it to his wound.

"Hold this," I said. "I'm gonna find a phone." Gabriel gave a small groan.

There was a phone hanging on the wall in the kitchen, right next to the fridge. An old-timey one with a cord and everything. There was a dial tone. I dialed 911.

I tried to remain calm as I talked to the dispatcher, but everything came out in a hysterical flood. How my boyfriend had been shot and was bleeding to death, how we had run from a man with a gun, how our car had been wrecked, and I didn't know where we were exactly and—oh, God . . . oh, God—could they please send someone quick?

"Remain calm, ma'am. We are going to dispatch emergency services to your location," the dispatcher said flatly. "Can you stay on the line?"

But I had a bad feeling.

"I've just gotta check on my boyfriend. Hang on."

"We'll be—"

His breath was shallow, and his eyes were closed. I kneeled beside him, crying and whispering to him. He said my name softly, but his eyes stayed shut. I helped put pressure on the blood-soaked dishtowel.

There was a knock at the door, hard and loud and urgent.

Was it the paramedics?

How could they get there so quickly?

What if it was the cop, somehow? He wouldn't knock though, right?

I went to the door and cracked it open.

"Ms. Yuvisela Moreno? You called?" a deep voice said.

I opened the door further.

It was a man. He didn't look like any kind of paramedic I'd ever seen. He wore a dark brown trench coat and was wider than he was tall, a fedora hanging over his stubbled face, and I swore for a moment there that his eyes were glowing red.

"Yes, I called 911. Are you the paramedics? Come quick, my boyfriend, he's back there!" I said frantically, looking behind him for any sort of ambulance. But there was only a big black Lincoln parked in the drive.

He held up a single finger, telling me to wait. "You called for a good time, did you not?"

A crushing feeling in the pit of my stomach, my mind unable to comprehend.

The number. My cell phone, right before we sped away from the cop. I had hit the dial button.

"Wha ... What is all this? Who are you?"

"I'm here to give you a good time," the man said. "Your boyfriend, too. Unless he's predisposed at the moment." He looked over my shoulder at Gabriel. "Looks like you two could use a good time."

"I don't want it. I don't need it. I need you to get help. I need you to—"

His meaty hand clamped down on my shoulder, held it tight. I felt frozen in place. "You need to hush. Here you go," he said and shoved a thick manila folder into my chest with so much force that I toppled backwards onto the floor.

Fuck that guy, whoever he is, I thought as he turned his back to me and descended the porch's front steps.

I scrambled to my feet. I had been away from Gabriel for too long.

Where were those goddamn paramedics?

His hand had fallen from the gunshot and lay relaxed on the ground, his whole body slumping in that direction actually, like he would slide off the couch at any minute. And he didn't respond as I screamed his name again and again, didn't respond when I shook him and pounded on his chest and pleaded for him to please wake up.

And God didn't respond as I begged and sobbed into Gabriel's still chest for him to take all of this away and to please bring Gabriel back, but I guess something else did.

So, yeah, I'm guessing you're wondering what was in the manila envelope. This whole "good time" thing the mysterious man had promised us. What could it be, right? Do I got you on the edge of your seat?

Well, it took a while for the chaos to die down and everything. I just carried that folder around with me for a day or two. To be honest, I was afraid of opening it up. The guy who had dropped it off and the circumstances with the broadcast and all we had been through. I just didn't want to have anything else to do with it, you see?

But when I finally opened it, I couldn't believe my eyes. Inside were stacks of documents and papers, official ones, with both of our names on them. There were certificates of naturalizations, passports, driver's licenses, letters from the

US Citizenship and Immigration Services. The crazy thing about all this was they had our photos on them, our actual photos. They looked real and everything too, and they *were* real. They ended up actually working.

"Yuvi, are you almost done? It's almost one o'clock and we've got a big day tomorrow. Gotta pick up the rental," a man's voice in the background says.

"Hold on, I'm almost done. I'm to the part where we got our papers," Yuvi tells him.

"Alright, alright."

"So, wait. Is that Gabriel?" I ask.

"Yes," she says with a laugh.

IT WAS THE STRANGEST THING. I was just sobbing into his chest. I thought he was dead. He was as good as dead. *Maybe* there was a pulse somewhere in there. I mean that makes the most sense. I don't think this was like a back-from-the-dead type situation.

So, I was just crying there with my face buried and my eyes were closed and I was waiting for the ambulance to arrive, but it never did. I was going to get up to call 911 again, and when I lifted my head up, we were no longer in the living room of that farmhouse.

We were in a freaking hotel room.

I looked down at Gabriel and his shirt was clean and dry and he was breathing, looking like he was just sleeping there. The manila folder was on a desk in the corner and I opened the door and it opened out into a parking lot in the middle of the day, a Motel 6 sign standing tall in the distance.

. . .

"So YEAH, is there anything else you need to know? It is really late over here. Different time zones and all."

"Where is over here?" I ask.

"Reykjavík," she responds. "Just got here this afternoon. Gonna rent a vehicle and get started on the Ring Road tomorrow. We've got so much to see."

Thackerville Times

A man was killed in the most unlikely of circumstances Wednesday evening. His death has even resulted in the answer to several unsolved mysteries that have plagued the area for years.

Randall Finkman was found deceased and disemboweled on a local rancher's property. The cause of death? An ostrich by the name of Oscar.

Property owner Ted Shamley has kept ostriches on his property ever since the fad in the early 90s.

"I used to have me a bunch of them," Shamley says. "You know, it was this big thing going on back then and everyone was getting them. But once all that died down, I liked keeping them around and have always made sure I've had a couple. They're good guard dogs, keep the coyotes away. Even got me a zebra from that exotic animal park up the way that got shut down. They were just *giving* it away. I feel like I'm out on a safari when I drive around my property. I've always heard stories they could kill a man. You know, they've got these really sharp claws and they'll rush up on you sometimes, but I never would've said they're *dangerous*. I would've felt awful about what happened and all, but he *was* trespassing, and you know there was that other stuff they found out later. I guess he had it coming. Sounds like Oscar was just doing his job, ha."

The "other stuff" that Mr. Shamley is referring to is the revelation of Randall Finkman's involvement in several missing persons cases. He was found to have a repurposed Crown Victoria, painted black with his own set of red and blue lights. It is believed that he was impersonating a police officer in the area, pulling over unsuspecting victims. There was a box of cellphones found in his trunk and several items of women's clothing.

At his property were driver's licenses belonging to two long-standing missing persons, Gina Bunch of Oklahoma and Sylvia Gardner of Texas. Evidence of human remains has been found on the property as well. Forensic and DNA investigations have been initiated.

Another vehicle was found at the scene, and it is believed that Randall Finkman had found a new set of victims, victims that possibly fled into the field where Mr. Finkman met his demise. Their names have not been released pending contact.

I got to where I was receiving fabricated incidents regularly, and I would have to thoroughly vet each of these before I would proceed with publishing their account. People would email me ridiculous stories that were obviously pranks or send me obscene photos. Some attempted prank calls.

Others were the writings of individuals that weren't intentionally trying to deceive; rather, they were obviously mentally ill. They claimed Buck Hensley was a part of the CIA, that he contacted them through their dental filling for some PSYOP program In one instance, I received an envelope with an extracted molar.

This sort of thing didn't do much for my own mental health.

Who's to say I was any different from these folks?

10

"COLD AS ICE"

I received a letter from an individual by the name of Daniel. He detailed a second-hand encounter with the rules, revealing something that had occurred in his childhood, decades ago This was a startling revelation as I had always considered the Buck Hensley broadcast to be a recent phenomenon.

THE AIR WAS heavy with cicadas and heat. The old man stooped on his haunches and stared at the faded etchings of the grave, traced them with his finger. He had a lit cigarette in his mouth, ash stretching to infinity. I worried it might fall to the grave. It seemed disrespectful to do that out here, but what did I know?

It had been a long drive, and any time Grandpa was outside on this trip he took it as an opportunity to have a cigarette, making up for the miles he had spent without the smoke swirling in his chest. He hadn't wanted to expose me to that secondhand smoke as I rode with him in my grandma's old Mercury Sable.

Mom had seen a commercial on TV and told him that

even if the windows were rolled down, I could still inhale the smoke and get cancer someday. It would be like a bullet shot into my lungs that wouldn't do damage until I was in my fifties, and by then the old man would be long gone. Wasn't it worth it to sacrifice a little for this hypothetical?

So, while we drove, it was Levi Garrett. He spit into a Styrofoam coffee cup stuffed with paper napkins that helped absorb the splash. I guess accidentally spitting on a grave would be a whole lot worse than ashing on one. Maybe that's why the meant by that saying, "ashes to ashes", after all.

"That's not it," he muttered to himself, rising from his crouching position.

We crisscrossed the rows of graves in a grid until we found it. The old man squatted once again and a ran his palm over face of the headstone like he could feel some sort of warmth there, a connection to his buried ancestors. After a heavy sigh, he nodded at me. I knew to swing my satchel across my chest and retrieve the materials, delivering them one by one.

He measured a piece of butcher paper from the roll with his eyeballs, sliced it with his pocketknife. The tearing sound it made reminded me of a dying man's cough. I worried we might wake the dead. He centered the paper over the gravestone, the etched names and dates, taped it up there. Next, he took the disk of black rubbing wax and smeared the paper vigorously. As he did so, it picked up impressions and imperfections in the stone, the engravings that had been made decades ago. The rubbing was mesmerizing, like the wax was a magical reverse eraser.

We had taken a winding road to get to the cemetery which lay in a patch of sun amidst the heavily wooded hills of the Ozarks. It was far from any sort of civilization. Near the cemetery's entrance, there was a tree with a thick and black-barked trunk. Underneath its gnarled branches were several lichen-covered tombs resembling stone benches. Any sign of who they belonged to had been rubbed off by time's steady hand.

"Check for ticks," Grandpa said as we crawled back into the car. He pinched one off of his forearm and smashed it between his thumbnail and fingertip. I caught a black one crawling up my leg and tried to imitate the same technique but failed. Instead, I flicked the live bug out the window where it would go on to crawl and suck another day, perhaps finding a feast on some mourner or more likely, a deer.

He was a quiet man—my grandpa—and this kept me from being closer to him than I ought to have, especially since I was his only grandson. So, when I discovered I'd have to spend an extended stretch of summer with him, I was less than thrilled. He lived three hours away, and I didn't want to be taken out of my usual summer routine of sleepovers, swimming pools, bicycles, fireworks, and movies with friends.

But I didn't have much say in the matter. My parents' relationship had grown rocky, and they were sending me away while they tried to sort things out in one last-ditch effort. They believed I had witnessed too many fights and I believed I had, too. I would return home to a house one person emptier, my dad staying in a studio apartment.

We made our way down the twisted roads of the mountain to stretches of straightaways and level ground where we found a town of sorts, just a church and gas station and a smattering of houses, really. We stopped at the filling station (his words, not mine) and he bought me a glass bottle of Coke and himself another pouch of Levi Garrett.

He laid a roadmap onto the hood of the car, pinning the corners with his leathery hands. There were circles of locations, of places we had been and places we were going. He rotated the map and squinted, got his bearings and I thought about asking him where we were headed next, but I didn't because none of the names meant anything to me. The only one that had stood out was Toad Suck, and I had already pointed it out after seeing a sign and asked if we would go there and we weren't.

There was more driving and more George Jones on the cassette deck and more silence.

"Why are we doing all this?" I asked in the way only an almost-eleven-year-old could get away with.

"Just always been a fan of genealogy, I suppose. See the places my people came from, I reckon. It's interesting."

"You gonna trace it all the way back to Europe? Rub some graves over there?"

"Maybe one day. I dunno. Maybe if your grandma was still alive. She'd want to see all that. Most of her ancestors are from the Georgia area and had been since before the white folks got here."

After stopping at a couple more nondescript cemeteries, we found ourselves at the end of the day. We headed back east, the blue evening and the twilight haze and the disappearing sun at our backs.

"Gonna find us a place to stop off for the night."

It would be our fifth overnight of the trip. I had lucked out once when we found a place with a swimming pool, but it was near the interstate. That perk seemed unlikely out here in the country, running through small towns on two-lane highways.

We pulled up to the Huckleberry Inn, a park-by-the-door motel with a couple strips of single-story rooms all in a row. It looked plenty vacant. I waited in the car while Grandpa went to the front office and paid for a room. He returned to the car with a keychain, and we pulled around to our room, unloaded our luggage.

I belly flopped onto the bed, the stiff comforter and lumpy mattress. I found the remote to the TV and flicked through some channels. I wanted to watch MTV or Nickelodeon or something, but I felt too self-conscious to watch something like that with my grandpa here. Instead, I left it on an episode of *Bonanza* while I took a comic book to the bathroom for a bit. After I finished, I wandered to where he was smoking outside.

He was just standing in the parking lot, staring out into the dark and taking drags.

It had become a ritual. No matter where we stopped on this trip, there was always a bucket of ice that we filled from the motel ice machines. It didn't matter if neither of us opened the individually wrapped plastic cups and helped us to a glass of tap water on the rocks. It didn't matter if we just had dinner and weren't thirsty. No matter the situation, we had to fill the little plastic tub full of ice and leave it on the plastic tray atop the dresser until morning came, until it was nothing but a flimsy bag of cold water.

I headed to where the ice and vending machines were, in a little alcove between the rooms and the motel office. The Pepsi machine gave off an ethereal glow. I pressed all the buttons and checked the change slot. Such habits could yield treasures like a free soda or fifty cents, but I came up empty that night.

The ice machine whirred and groaned as I tried to get it to dispense. I bumped it with my shoulder, looked up into the little dispenser hole, even snaked my hand up there to see if I could feel the cold. Nothing. I shrugged and went back to the room with an empty bucket.

Grandpa was lying on his back with his shoes off, twitching his toes through his socks. His eyes were half-closed. I set the empty ice bucket down.

"Get 'er filled up?" he asked.

"Nah. Machine was busted."

He sat up with a start. "What? So, there's no ice? Was there another machine?" He swung his legs off the bed and started lacing up his boots.

"I don't think so." I didn't see what the big deal was. I'd never seen him rise above his emotionally flat baseline and here he was getting worried about ice?

"C'mon, let's go see," he said.

We did a perimeter sweep of the property, just a boy and his grandpa and a plastic bucket. His pace quickened the further we went. You wouldn't say his behavior was frantic if you saw him but knowing him that was the word that came to mind. His version of frantic was anybody else's calm mood.

At the front office, we rang the service bell, rousing the owner from some backroom. The overhead lights glinted off of her glasses as she greeted us with sleepy eyes and a tired smile.

"Excuse me. Y'all's ice machine's broke. You got another somewhere?"

"No, I'm sorry. Supposed to have a repairman look at it next week. But I guess that don't help you now." There was a sympathetic smile. Fake.

"You got anything in the back?" Grandpa asked, looking over her shoulder.

"No, unfortunately," she said with a little frown that tried to cover up the fact that she couldn't care less whether we had ice tonight.

"There a convenience store around here?" Grandpa's mouth got smaller by a few millimeters.

"Up the road . . . but oh wait. What time is it? Nah, they're closed. I'm really sorry to inconvenience you folks like this."

Grandpa made a little clicking noise. "We're gonna head out. Any way we can get a refund?"

"On account of the ice machine? Geez, you fellas must

really like ice. I don't know if I can do that. Did y'all step foot in the room? Lie on the beds? It's not like there's a sign out front that says ice guaranteed."

"Look, we didn't even . . . whatever. Forget it. Keep it. C'mon Daniel," he said halfway out the door. I could only glance back at the front desk lady's perplexed face. Grandpa was already halfway across the parking lot, marching with purpose.

"Here ya go," I said, and handed her the plastic ice bucket.

"Look, you guys ever come back through. I promise we'll have it fixed. We've been trying to get the guy in here for weeks."

I only shrugged and jogged after Grandpa.

"Get your bag. We gotta get out of here. It's important."

He had already loaded his small suitcase in the trunk, and I went and grabbed mine. I had a nervous feeling in my stomach. For the life of me, I didn't know what was going on. I had never seen him the slightest bit rattled, but there he was. *Rattled.*

But I had forgotten my comic in the restroom. I went back to grab it and pondered taking a leak for the road.

"Goddammit Daniel, hurry up!" Grandpa yelled from the doorway. I had never heard him curse before and he had never yelled at me, either.

My body flushed with shame and anger, and I ducked my head and sat in the front seat of the Sable, comic book in hand. He peeled out of the parking lot, and we drove off in a haste. Whatever he thought was chasing us was still out there in the night.

I didn't talk, and he didn't talk. Still feeling like a scolded puppy from him yelling at me, an anger simmered underneath and took over. My wounded pride took precedence over the burning questions I had. Primarily, *just what in the hell was going on?*

There was close to an hour of driving, the forest around us frightening and imposing in the dark, like it was something that wasn't meant to be traversed at this hour. It triggered a primal fear. The fear was this: there were things out here that could kill you. Things that could drag you kicking and screaming out into the dark, never to be heard from again. Things that we had largely taken dominion over with guns and fire and electricity and extinction, but the fear remained.

We chanced upon a state rest stop. It was a mere pull-off parallel to the highway with a couple of 55-gallon drums and a picnic table or two. Grandpa pulled over.

"This'll do just fine," he said.

"What are we doing?" I asked.

"Pulling off for the night. You can sleep in the backseat. Could bundle up a towel for a pillow. I've got a blanket in the trunk."

"But *why?* What was wrong with the motel?"

"They didn't have any ice," he said, as if it were obvious. He yawned like a cartoon character, stretched his arms as far as he could. "Look lil' buddy. We better hit the hay while we can. Got a lot more miles to cover tomorrow. I'll be fine sleeping up front."

That was that. I sulked and curled down low in the backseat until sleep took hold.

I awoke to birdsong in the morning, shafts of sunlight shining through the trees. My jeans were balled upon the floor and for a moment I thought I had pissed myself, but it was just my briefs soaked with the sweat from sleeping in a vehicle on a humid summer night.

Grandpa wasn't in the front seat. I shimmied into my jeans and stepped outside. He was sitting on one of the picnic tables.

"Morning, sunshine," Grandpa said, acting like I had just emerged in the kitchen on a Sunday morning while he manned the waffle maker, ignoring the fact we were on the side of the road after fleeing into the night.

Still half asleep, I grumbled a response. The surroundings and circumstance disoriented me.

"Reckon we better head on down the road a bit and find us a bite to eat?" he asked.

"I guess," I said. "Look, why did we sleep on the side of the road? What was all of that about? With leaving the motel? My neck hurts from sleeping in the back."

He sighed. "It's a long story, son. I don't really wanna get into it right now. We'll just make sure that every hotel has an ice machine from here on out, okay? No more sleeping on the side of the roads. I'll tell you someday when you're older."

AND HE DID TELL me when I was older, but not until I was *much* older, not until that night we fled the motel was a distant memory, not until he had passed away.

I wasn't close to him when I was forced to take upon that venture, that quest across the southeastern United States where we scoured graveyards for proof of lives once lived, links in the chain. Yet that trip brought us closer together, and we would grow even closer still, him becoming a father figure. After the divorce dust had all settled, my mom would move us out to his town three hours away, where I would stay until I graduated high school.

I made it to my thirties before he got sick. As a smoker that hadn't quit until later in life, he had a pretty good run before something related to that got to him. In his case, it was lung cancer. They thought they had caught it early enough that they liked his chances if he did chemo. He was in his seventies and still seemed as full of life as ever, like he could get a decade or more if he beat it. However, he was reluctant to start the treatment.

"I'm only doing this because your mom wants me to fight it or whatever. I'd just take my chances if it was up to me. I feel about done. Like I'm ready to go see your grandma," he had told me.

I was married and out of state at this point, making trips home when I could because I was worried the end could be near and you never really know. The treatment for his cancer had been a series of forward steps and backwards slides, all amounting to little more than tires spinning in the mud. After he had finished the chemo, he had enough. No more trying this or that and just let him have his final months. He chose to take it easy and made comfort his top priority.

There was the last time I saw him, and then there was the *last* time I saw him. I don't count the viewing of his body at the funeral home or the visit I made when he was barely awake, moaning with his arrhythmic breaths and trembling hand. No, the time I count as the last is when he was at home on hospice and still lucid, dying but still living.

He shuffled around the house weakly on thin legs, wearing pajama pants and a stained white tee. It was strange to not see him in his usual uniform of trousers and a Dickies short-sleeve shirt, the uniform I had seen him in all my life.

We got to talking about his great grandkids and the missus and work and this and that. The conversation shifted to old times, fishing trips we had taken, how he hated golf, and finally it turned to that summer trip we took all those years ago.

"That reminds me," he said, rising from his chair and slipping down the hall.

He returned with a banker's box, setting it in my lap.

There were files and folded papers inside. I could see the butcher paper, the gravestone rubbings. The memory of that night at the motel stirred itself loose, bubbled up from somewhere deep down. I hadn't thought about it in years. I asked him about it, figured now was as good a time as any, really the only time left.

"There's a letter down there in the bottom," he said, nodding to the box of loose papers. "I wrote it to ya a few years ago. Always meant to send it, but it must've slipped my mind."

I shuffled through the folders and files and papers until I found an envelope with my name on it. It was sealed. I didn't open it. I gave Grandpa a nod and sat it back in the box.

"I'm in no hurry," I said, and he gave me a wan smile.

We talked a while longer until he drifted off and I eventually drifted out. The letter burned a hole in the box, begging me to open it. But I would not or could not open it. Not until after he had passed.

Sitting there in my home office one late evening, weeks after my grandfather had passed, I opened the envelope to reveal a handwritten letter inside.

I was glad I had waited.

DANIEL,

I GUESS I've gotta get this out somehow, and you're the only one that would really understand. You may remember that summer trip we took back when your folks were having problems, back before they split up. Remember that night we slept in the car because the motel ice machine was broken?

I remember that trip clearly. Most days I was still sad and angry over your grandmother being gone. I didn't do much of the things I used to. I didn't go to church or fish or go to breakfast on the weekends. I'd just work and come home and sit around that empty house. So it was good for you to come out on that trip with me. Got me out of a funk, I suppose.

I know I ain't the most outgoing sort of fella, never been one to show how I feel very much, but I was glad you were there.

Now what I'm about to tell you, I would've never taken you along if I didn't think it would be safe. It had been years—decades even— since these events took place. Your Grandma and I had traveled tons of times after and as long as I did what I was supposed to, I was fine.

It had been a few years since we had gotten back from the war and we had settled into our lives back home. College was never in the works for me, so my GI Bill was never used. I hadn't proposed to your grandmother yet, but we were in the courtship phase.

Shane Albright had served over there with me. He came to tell me about some work with the U.S. Forest Service. Said there were hiring preferences for veterans on account of it being a government job and all. So we both signed on and got jobs with the fire watch. They had us working near our hometown at first, but soon they shuffled us around, doing month-long stints at sites across state lines.

These out-of-town gigs paid a little more. We'd ride out together in Shane's Studebaker Champion, where we would arrive at the site and be stationed at separate towers, staring out across the rolling forests as we looked for fires. Then we were off for two weeks before we'd go back and do it again.

It was solitary work. I sometimes wonder if working that job made me quieter than I already was. I got in the habit of journaling, writing letters to the gal that would become your grandma, little love poems she kept in an envelope. They are buried under the earth with her.

Sometimes it would take us a two day drive out to these towers. We'd end up staying overnight somewhere along the way. Other times we'd get off on that Sunday and drive all the way through, taking shifts behind the wheel, collapsing back at home in piles of pure exhaustion with little memory of how we got there.

It was on one of these overnights when we heard it . . . the broadcast.

I was driving and the AM radio was going when suddenly a lady with the voice of an angel sang "Anchors Aweigh." Shane was half asleep in the passenger seat but started singing along to it. There was a burst of static and the sounds of explosions, the howl of klaxons and the shots of an ack-ack gun and someone whistling happily through it all.

Then there was a masculine voice, a cheerful *voice. He introduced himself as Buck Hensley and started rambling about the pilot of the Enola Gay and how he never lost a wink of sleep even after what he'd done: vaporized all those men, women, and children, and babies of Hiroshima. Said that maybe nuking a city worked better than a nightcap or a glass of warm milk as far as a sleep remedy. He said that he found the whole thing hilarious and pitiful from the outside looking in, especially knowing what he knew now.*

Now, at this point, Shane was sitting straight up in his seat. We were both enraptured by what we were hearing. The man on the radio then presented us with something he called "The Rules of the Road." The rule was this: if we were to stop at a motel or hotel at any point during our journey, then we were to request ice for our room from the innkeepers. He said there might even be an ice machine on the premises, that they would one day be all the rage at lodgings in the future. (And he was right, but that's beside the point. It would be clear that there was something uncanny about the guy on the radio well before his prediction came true.)

The consequences of not following this rule seemed vague. He said something about a visitor in the night that would give us cold feet. The man on the radio, Buck Hensley, he bid us a fond farewell and safe travels and just like that ... the radio went back to normal.

To cut to the chase, we were on the road once again, driving out to a job. We had stopped off at some roadside motel, not unlike the many you and I stayed at during our cemetery trip, just newer and less worse for wear.

It was late when we stopped. There wasn't a TV in the room.

Those were luxury items at that point, only a radio on the dresser. I remembered the warning.

"You really gonna do that?" Shane asked me.

"Sure. Why not?"

"The ice ain't free."

"I could use me a cold drink."

They gave me a small ice bucket at the motel office. It cost 5 cents.

"Well, if you've got it, might as well make the most of it," Shane said, and pulled a pint of rye whiskey from his bag.

He had a drink, and I had one as well. Betcha didn't know your ol' pops had it in him. That was then, though. I put aside all of that tomfoolery once your mom was born.

So that's how we all survived our first night at a motel after hearing that fateful rule. We rode off to our jobsite for another couple weeks of fire watching and isolation.

There was a late departure, and we found ourselves bone tired and miles from home. Even if we had pulled it together and drove in shifts, we wouldn't have gotten back home until noon.

Shane asked, "Why not take it easy and stop for a bite, maybe get a drink?"

There was a little town with a diner and a motel and a filling station. We had burgers and sodas and fries at the diner. It was getting late by the time we got into our room, and I wanted nothing more than to fall asleep. Shane had other ideas, though. He had eyed a pool hall off the main drag and wanted to go, begging me to come along with him. I shrugged and followed along.

We played some pool and drank some beers. As the night rolled on, Shane got cozy with a gal in a corner booth. I was on the sideline and getting bored. I made a signal to Shane that I'd be leaving. He pulled me aside.

"Look, pal. I play my cards right, we might find ourselves back at the room," he said with a wink. "Just wanted to give you a heads-up."

I just sighed and told him good luck and when I got to the room, I realized we only had a single bed. Being in the military, it was nothing for us to sleep in proximity like this. However, if he brought a girl back to the room, that might've made things complicated. I didn't really want to be in there, even if there were two beds.

It was decision time, and as welcoming as the bed looked to my drunk and tired body, I took one for the team. I made my way to the car and fell asleep in the backseat of the Studebaker.

The sleep was light and fitful. I tossed and turned in and out of a half-awake doze, my thoughts growing more agitated at my sleeping situation, when all of a sudden it hit me.

The ice.

We had forgotten the ice.

I shot up and opened the door. I didn't know what time it was. It was still dark out. The parking lot was silent.

I started for the motel room door. My hand was almost to the knob when the door creaked open and someone stepped out.

Was it the same gal from the bar? She looked different in the orange motel lights. Like her skin was paler. Her eyes were the bluest things I'd ever seen. Glowing almost. She smiled at me and her lips looked like they had a layer of frost on them.

"Care for a turn? Your buddy's tuckered out," she said.

That's when I noticed her blouse was unbuttoned. I could see her chest and the sides of her breasts, the heart beating under her translucent skin, her lungs inflating with each breath. Her skin was glass.

No, not glass.

Ice.

I staggered backwards into the parking lot, tripping over my own two feet and landing back hard on my hands and rear-end. I could hear the lady laughing, the laughter fading into the night. I got up to my feet, and she was gone.

I rushed into our motel room and flicked on the lights. That's where I found Shane, lying naked on the bed, eyes closed and face all contorted. He wasn't moving a muscle. His back was arched and rigid, while his neck was extended as far back as it could stretch, with the crown of his head touching the mattress. His heels were planted firmly at the other end, with toes curled.

"Shane, buddy. You okay?" I asked and instantly felt stupid.

Of course, there was no response. He didn't move to my touch and felt stiff, like rigor mortis had set in. But I wasn't an expert in such things, and it didn't seem to explain the fact that his body felt ice cold. I also couldn't ignore the fact that his back wasn't the only thing rigid. It almost looked like he had died mid-thrust, frozen in place. His now-permanent facial expression could've been one of pleasure or pain. The tips of various extremities looked black.

Frostbite.

I tossed a sheet over his lower half and went to the payphone to call the authorities.

THERE WAS no definitive cause of death, no mention of hypothermia. I wonder if he thawed or something like that by the time they got there. They wondered if a black widow spider had bitten him. It could cause muscle spasms like that, they said.

I told them I had seen a woman leave the room. There had been no signs of foul play. Maybe he had been poisoned? I didn't tell them that this was all because he had paid the price for not following a rule we had heard about on a mysterious broadcast. I didn't tell them that the woman's skin was ice, and you could see her heart in her chest, pumping the blue blood through her veins.

I'VE LIVED with this all these years. My life has been no different. The world keeps spinning and largely seems to play by the natural rules I've known all my life. The only thing is the simple inconvenience whenever I travel. Your grandma used to make fun of me about the ice machine habit, and I told her a version of this story with the crazier stuff taken out. I told her I do it as an homage to my ol' buddy Shane, gone too soon from this world, taken in a manner too strange to grieve.

You're the only one I've told the entire story to and here's why. I've had the feeling over the past few months that things haven't been right. I have a cough that's more than a smoker's cough, a cough I can't quite shake, a heaviness in my chest. Last week, the doctor took an x-ray and confirmed it: a mass in my lungs. He said it looked inoperable and offered chemo.

I know where I stand on that. I'm going to go out on my own terms. Not gonna wait until the cancer spreads everywhere, getting a little worse each day. I'm also not gonna poison myself with no chemo.

What I'm gonna do is go for a little drive. After a while, I'm gonna find me a motel room. I'm gonna sit back and watch a little TV, smoke my first cigarette in five years, and go to sleep. What I won't do is fill the ice bucket. I'll ignore the rule and I'll wait for her to come to me in the dark. It seems like a good way to go out, as good as any. One final kick of pleasure before I kick the bucket. A motel bed sure beats a hospital bed.

I hope you understand.

Love,

    Grandpa Doug

P.S.

Of course, I couldn't go through with it. I'm writing this postscript weeks down the road. Even now sick with the chemo, I still think about it, how it would be a great way to go out. Yet maybe I was scared, scared of the lady with the frigid lips and the icy skin, how it would feel to die that way.

But I don't think that's it. I think it's because of your grandma. After she died, I never had another woman. How could I see her in heaven with that as my final act? Even though I got ripped off and have missed her every day, she was enough for a lifetime.

I can wait just a little while longer.

So, we end up back where we started, me at a cemetery with Grandpa. Except this time, he's underground, and it's *his* headstone I'm thinking of rubbing, the one he shares with my grandmother. I don't go through with it though.

The act seems better suited to the older graves of faceless ancestors and he was anything but. He was my grandfather, a man I loved and knew. I'll carry him around in different ways, the quiet demeanor that I exhibit, the way I furrow my brow when lost in thought, the penchant for a good Western, and the bucket of ice I will fill at every overnight motel I find myself in.

"We've seen that you've clocked in late your past few shifts."

"I've had a lot going on."

"Well, we need employees we can rely on. Even before that, you haven't really been the most punctual, however showing up this late is unacceptable."

"Right. I understand."

"You've also been off on your counts quite a bit. Coming up short. Coming up over. You've never given us any trouble before, so we're trying to work with you. But you've also got to work with us, okay?"

"Yeah, for sure."

"Is everything okay?"

"Oh, yeah. Totally fine."

11
"LANDSLIDE"

Annie spoke with me over the telephone from an unknown location. She was in her thirties but had experienced the broadcast much earlier.

I DON'T RIDE in cars much if I can help it. I don't even have a driver's license. Everyone understands.

It's not quite a phobia—okay, well maybe it is—amaxophobia, they call it. A fear of riding in cars. But these days most therapists don't care to bother with terms of specific phobias and prefer to use the term post-traumatic stress disorder. PTSD. They say I have it and I have to agree with them, for my issues extend past the realm of being triggered by riding in cars or seeing vehicles.

I awake with nightmares. I get flashbacks. If I see broken glass on the road or in the street, whether it be from a windshield or broken beer bottle, my heart races, my palms sweat, and I have to do my breathing exercises to avoid a full-blown panic attack.

Sometimes, the breathing exercises aren't enough.

It all started back in the 90s. My family was going on

summer vacation, a trip that in my eleven-year-old opinion was going to be totally lame. I mean, even now it's still kinda lame, even if you remove the fact that I was a moody and sullen kid that didn't really like her stepdad and the trip he had planned.

His name was Tim, and he had a fascination with the Southwest. His home office was decorated with Navajo rugs and pictures of desert scenery and Native American pottery. He had even started rubbing off on my mom and now she allowed his interior decorating sense to infiltrate the living room. She even started sporting turquoise jewelry.

It bugged me more than it should have. I guess what really annoyed me about it all was how obvious it all seemed, how my mom was swaying under his influence, changing who she was right before my very eyes. Who was this guy that had come into our home and married my mom and started changing everything? I'm not trying to say I was *right* in feeling that way. Whenever I look back on those days, at how ungrateful I was, I cringe with guilt.

It's these sorts of things you figure out once you're an adult, looking back at it all through a mature and experienced perspective. It's not like Tim was this awful guy. He *seemed* like a good guy to my mom. He never yelled at or scolded me. The most he did was sigh at my petty shows of rebellion, the disrespect I gave my mom, maybe tell me she was trying her best and loved me and if I could just be a little more agreeable, he would appreciate it.

So, we made an uneasy truce. I never gave him any lip or mouthed off to him because I would rather not interact with him, rather just ignore him completely and act like he wasn't there. If we ever had some sort of confrontation, that would only make his existence in my life more real.

If the addition of Tim had caused an inner turmoil within me that my pre-teen self couldn't quite understand or articulate, my mother's pregnancy really sent me into a tailspin. I sort of blocked these months out, which is strange because I wish I could block out so much more.

I know I spent a lot of time in the principal's office for disruptions in class and some fights here and there. There were parent-teacher meetings because I quit turning in my homework. Lots of time was spent holed up in my room, drawing and listening to the radio.

However, when Jackson arrived, and I saw that sleeping, peaceful bundle, I softened up a little. He was half my brother after all; we shared the same mom. Still, I wouldn't hold him. I circled him from afar like a curious dog, afraid to get too close.

When he smiled at me for the first time, my barrier cracked even more. I was able to reinforce it, however, when he started crying through the night. He suffered from colic and was quite fussy through stretches of his infancy. His incessant crying would set me on edge, nails on a chalkboard.

I was nearing my twelfth birthday and Jackson was almost two when my mom and stepdad got the bright idea to take a prolonged family trip. Tim wanted to see the Grand Canyon and various other sites of the great Southwest, including some place called Monument Valley. My mom and I had never been. Jackson wouldn't remember.

It wasn't enough to just fly to Phoenix and drive over to see the "biggest damn hole in the world." No, according to Tim, we needed to take a lengthy road trip in order to get the full experience. He said we needed to cross through various climates and sceneries in order to appreciate the distance traveled, long drives of nothingness.

"You just won't get a feel for the sheer amount of space out there otherwise," he had said.

Driving all the way from New York was too long, though, even for him. So, he compromised, and we flew to

Denver, where we rented a station wagon and headed south.

It was boring for an eleven-year-old. If you saw one giant mountain, you had seen them all. Thus, I stared at my Gameboy Color or my sketchpad as we careened through the Rockies until car sickness forced me to lean my head against the passenger window and stare. I listened to my Discman and nodded off to pass the time. Jackson sucked on his binky, sang songs to himself, and napped. I played with a little tiger puppet to entertain him. He was a good little traveler so far.

The mountains receded, yet still loomed largely in the background over a flattening landscape. We stopped for the night at a hotel somewhere in the lower left corner of Colorado. I was thankful to be out of the car and even more thankful that the hotel had an indoor pool.

My mom let me go down to the pool by myself while they got Jackson to bed with his complicated nighttime routine. There was nobody else at the pool, so I spent my time doing cannonballs and dashing from the hot tub and the pool to see if I could withstand the disparities in temperature. I had even snuck an orange Slice from the vending machine with some of my own money. My mom didn't really let me have soda, so this was a kind of special and forbidden treat for me.

The glass windows of the pool room were fogged up and the tile floor was damp and there were wet towels scattered about the place and the scent of chlorine was heavy in the air. I reclined on a plastic lounger and sipped the sweet, refreshing drink, pretended like I was a rich lady at a fancy summer resort. I felt calm and content, oblivious to any of my outside worries. Looking back, I can now see that this was the last time I would experience a moment so pure and peaceful.

The next morning, we visited the ruins of some American Indian cliff dwellings. Later, we headed west and descended into the desert. The land was red with a cartoon blue sky and lunar scenery. You looked out the window and half expected to see a coyote zoom by with a big red ACME rocket strapped to its back. Trees choked out a meager existence, never able to aspire to the great heights of their cousins from the lusher environments. It was boring after ten minutes.

Tim was ranting and raving and stopping to take pictures every five minutes.

"Isn't this neat, guys?" he would ask.

Every time he pulled over to take a pic, he would dart back into the car and apologize to Mom for making us stop.

"It's fine," she would say and smile, but after the eighth photography stop I could see her rolling her eyes in the rearview mirror whenever he slowed down to pull over.

Then Jackson started crying.

And crying.

And crying.

He had been so good this whole trip, too.

"Can you give Jackson his pacifier?" my mom asked.

"He keeps spitting it out and throwing it, though," I responded.

"Well, see what he wants. Can you smell his diaper?"

"Eew!"

"*C'mon*, Annie."

"Fine," I groaned and stuck my nose near his stomach and kicking legs. "He's good." Jackson's face was scrunched up, his eyes shut and his skin turning red.

"Can you sing him a song? Distract him for us."

I tried once again to put the pacifier back in Jackson's mouth, but his gaping, screaming piehole wouldn't close around it. It was all bared teeth and curled lips. He didn't respond to my renditions of "Twinkle, Twinkle, Little Star" or "Mary Had a Little Lamb" or "Kissed by a Rose" either.

"Mom, he won't shut up," I protested.

"He's just tired. Fighting sleep."

"Can we pull over? This is stupid, and he's *so* loud."

"Just give him a little bit."

Around us, barbed wire fence and sand and little scrubby bushes whizzed past. There were no signs of life to be seen. We passed a lumbering semi-truck.

"I don't know why we had to drive all this way with a freaking toddler," I said.

"Annie Elaine," my mother snapped.

"What? It's true. It's not like *you* would've wanted to come out here. You hate outdoorsy stuff and rocks and the desert. You like beaches and cities and taking it easy, but *noooo*. Tim had to see the Grand Canyon. Tim *had* to drive. Tim *had* to—"

"Enough!" my mom shouted. Normally this would've been enough to shatter the car into silence, but Jackson continued his wailing.

Tim gritted his teeth. My mom put her hand on his shoulder and whispered something in his ear, then patted him on the back.

All the while, Jackson cried.

"Next gas station or rest stop we see, we're stopping. Okay? Is that alright with *you*, Annie?" He said the last part in a snide tone that he had never used before. I had crossed some sort of line with him. It made me uncomfortable.

"Fine," I muttered.

I turned on my Gameboy and fished in my backpack for my headphones. Anything to drown out everything, anything to distract me. The tinny music of Super Mario Land 2 filled my ears, the sound effects of Mario jumping and collecting coins. I had already beaten the game before, but I liked it and was playing through it again to find secret levels.

I got to the end of a level I had beaten many times

before and there was this pipe I had never seen before. I don't know how familiar you are with the Mario games, but he goes down these pipes and they are basically portals to different rooms and locations. Most of the time these pipes are green. Yet this pipe was a shiny black, the color of an eggplant and with purple borders like neon lights. The colors extended way past the capabilities of my Gameboy; I had never seen it pull off something like this. The color *pulsed* out of the screen.

Mario descended the pipe. That familiar sound effect chimed in my ears, but then a throbbing hum filled my earphones. I became dead to the world around me: didn't hear Jackson crying anymore, didn't sense the car's motion. The next location loaded, and the pipe emerged from the top of the screen, jutting from a bizarre and alien ceiling of mucus, tentacles, and thorns that dripped orange liquid. Mario slid out of the pipe and fell off-screen. As he fell, Mario appeared slick and slimy, like the pipe he was just in had been full of some sort of alien goo.

Mario dropped to an empty street, buildings lining the background. They reminded me of New York's brownstone apartment buildings in all of their glory, but rendered in 8-bit style. I made Mario walk down the unassuming street. There were trees planted along the sidewalk and little animated leaves fell from their branches. I walked past cars and fire hydrants and the other minutiae of an empty city street until my character could walk no longer. At the last brownstone, a door creaked open at the top of the stoop.

I went inside.

There were stairs I followed until I reached a landing and an open doorway. It all looked familiar, somehow an 8-bit rendition of our apartment in Brooklyn, but somehow not, like the way locations are in dreams.

Inside the doorway was our living room, a couch and TV. There were two characters, a man and a woman. The male character wore Tim's eyeglasses and had his dark hair, while the woman had my mom's wide hips, the floral print shirt she liked to wear. Both were cute and cartoony, smiling with arms around each other. And Mario was no longer under my control. From somewhere off-screen, a little girl ran into the frame, blonde hair and pigtails, *my* blonde hair.

They shooed her away and she sat in a chair in the corner. A baby boy crawled on the floor toward them while they laughed and picked him up. Mario frowned, his eyes forlorn. The screen turned black. There was a tinny exploding noise.

We had entered another scene in the video game. There was no Mario present, just a parking lot with a vehicle in the middle and these red desert rock formations and cactuses off in the distance. The video game versions of my mom and Tim materialized, my mom carrying baby Jackson. They all hopped into the car and drove off in a cloud of exhaust.

The little blonde girl, the avatar that had been fashioned in my image, suddenly appeared chasing the car for a while, big cartoony tears erupting from her face as she wailed and sucked exhaust and crumpled into a crying pile. All around her everything started fading to black until there was nothing but her at the center of the screen in front of a black background.

Meanwhile, in the real world, Jackson was asleep. My parents continued driving, oblivious that I was in the backseat playing on a supernatural Gameboy that was reading my wildest fears. I continued watching, the console slick in my sweaty palms.

The blackness slowly receded. My character was now in a motel room. An old-timey radio player sat on a nightstand. It squirmed to life. My 8-bit doppelganger stood up and stared at it with her black, unblinking eyes. The noise from the radio played into my earphones, and this cheerful old guy spoke.

Howdy folks, Buck Hensley here with a friendly reminder that your conscious self and soul is all just an illusion, and that the universe is just a bunch of individual parts of the same whole with everything trying to differentiate itself from the faceless, egoless black mass. Won't you join me in turning back to the solidarity?

You won't? Doesn't sound too appealing, does it? I get that. Well, at the very least can you join me in offering a salute? Us here at "The Rules of the Road" have a fondness for travelers and drifters. And who better exemplifies that spirit of the open road than the lonely truck driver, miles underneath his rubber and many more miles to burn?

Won't you join me in offering a salute to those long-haul heroes of the highway, the hardworking mother truckers who miss their husbands or wives and kids and girlfriends? Don't you know these assassins of the asphalt have been on the road for so, so long? They're awful tired. The least we can do is give them the proper salute. And just how might we do that, you might ask? Well, I'll tell ya...

If at any point during your journey, you make eye contact with one of these proud denizens of the diesel, these sailors of the street, then you must hold up your arm, cock it at the elbow and pump your fist vigorously. In turn, this buccaneer of the boulevard will acknowledge you with a loud (but friendly) blast of his or her horn. Sounds fun, doesn't it? What better way to let our little trucker friends know we're thinking of them. Think of it as a "thank you for your service" for these tramps of the turnpike (and baby these tramps were born to run.)

Now I know what you're gonna say. You're gonna say, "Bucky, I don't like to look over at the other drivers when I pass them. Every time I glance over, they look at me, and I fear they're gonna suck my soul out through my eyeballs. Don't you know the eyes are the window to the soul? So how am I gonna know to look over at a vehicle when I pass?" And to that I say, "Fair enough, but in this instance, you want to make eye contact with the driver. If they don't see you, then you're off the hook!"

What happens if you don't follow this rule? Well, you may find that something will rain down from the sky, creating an unfortunate situation for your party. That's all I can say on that. I don't know what will rain down. It varies depending on just when and where you are.

Welp. Looks like it's getting a little late for me. Stay safe. Stay sane. Stay lively. Stay lonely. I'm Buck Hensley and these are "The Rules of the Road ..."

THERE WAS a tapping on my shoulder. I jumped. "Annie," my mom said quietly, neck craned over her headrest. "We're about to make a pit stop. Do you need to go to the bathroom?"

"Um, what?" I asked, pulling the headphones out of my ears, glancing down. The Gameboy was off, a blank screen.

"Shh, Jackson's finally asleep. We're about to stop."

"Oh, okay."

At the gas station, my mom asked if I wanted anything, and I told her Cheez-Its and I went in to use the restroom while Tim pumped gas. The images from the Gameboy played in my mind and I had this paranoid feeling as I made my way through the aisles of snacks, the tops of strangers passing by over the shelves. I almost wanted to ask my mom to come to the restroom with me, that's how nervous I felt.

My mom had been right behind me while I was in the restroom, but when I got out, she was nowhere to be found. I felt panic rising.

She's just out at the car already, I thought.

The car wasn't by the gas pump. I looked around frantically, my heart in my throat.

It's just like the video game. They've left you. They've forgotten you.

A little mewling sound caught in my throat, and I hollered out, "Mom!" and ran to the gas pumps. Strangers gave me odd looks. "Mom!" Tears ran down my face.

A silver horse trailer rolled past the canopied station of gas pumps and there they were, parked by the air pump machines.

I stomped over.

"Puttin' a little air in the tires," Tim said happily. "What's wrong?"

"Nothing," I growled and made my way to the backseat where I shook and clenched my fists and took deep breaths.

Miles down the road and humming along the interstate, Jackson stirred awake, and my mom asked me to get his milk. I unbuckled my seatbelt and fished his sippy cup out of the little ice chest that sat in the back of the station wagon. I've always wondered how lucky I was to have done so or if the end results would've been the same, regardless.

They say it was my lack of a seatbelt that saved my life, that had I kept it on I would have surely been dead.

I plopped back in my seat and handed Jackson his sippy cup. He was thirsty. He sucked the milk and made little contented sounds and stared at me with his bright blue eyes, a curlicue of hair plastered to his forehead, his cheeks pumping. I smiled at him, and he gave me back a toothy and frothy-milked grin.

I turned to shut the ice chest and out the back window I saw it coming, a flash of white on the horizon, a bright glare signaling its arrival. A semi-truck coming up fast while Tim milled about in the left lane.

The radio, I thought. *I gotta salute the truck driver. Make him honk. But what if it's a trick?* I thought about the images on the video game, what it was saying about me and my situation, how I thought they had left me back at the gas station. What did the radio say, that something would rain down on our party? We were in the desert. They could use a little rain out here, right? Maybe it would mess up a day of Tim's travels?

I looked out the window and up at the cab of the semi. The driver looked down at me, aviator sunglasses and a big bushy beard. He lifted the glasses and gave me a little nod. I held my right hand up, forearm cocked, made a fist ready to pump, and ... extended my middle finger.

The trucker only laughed and returned the favor and sped along on his way.

"Jesus. Slow down, buddy," Tim said from the front seat.

"Maybe get out of the passing lane?" my mom offered.

"Yeah, yeah. He just came out of nowhere," Tim said, changing lanes.

I'm sure you've seen those semis that haul the new cars around, like to the dealerships or whatever? There will be six or eight cars all stacked up in a double-decker trailer. Growing up in New York, we didn't drive far places very often, but I had memories of seeing them several times on trips upstate. Anyways, we were coming up behind one and Tim was just hanging out in the right lane and I can remember looking up at all those cars stacked on top of each other, some at angles. It was all one car, two car, red car, blue car, and those cars looked awfully precarious as they sat up there, shimmying and shaking from bumps in the road.

THERE ARE a few images burned into my brain, still photographs I can't shake no matter how I try. The first is a dark blue sedan on the upper level of that car hauler, standing upright as if its back tires were feet, its headlights and front windshield pointed straight to the sky. That vehicular monolith towers over us, eclipsing the sun and casting an impossible shadow over our car.

The next image is that same blue car, suspended in midair. The once perpendicular car is now parallel to the ground, albeit upside down. There's nothing we can do. We're frozen too. On our inevitable path.

Sound accompanies the final image. It's the collision of the blue car with the front of ours. It's the sound of dumpsters being dropped, only ten times louder. And it's intermingled with my mom's scream and the breaking of glass. The windshield is buckling, the ceiling is crumpling, glass is spraying.

That's the last thing I remember.

THE IMPACT THREW me clear of the vehicle when it rolled. The first responders found my unconscious body on the side of the road, bleeding from superficial cuts and scrapes. If only my mother hadn't asked me to get Jackson's sippy cup. If only I had had my seatbelt on, that life saving device would've saved my life in a much different way. It would've kept me in that vehicle where I would've died with the rest of my family, saved me from the pain that followed.

My grandmother flew from New York to Utah to pick me up at the hospital. They kept an IV in my arm and saline running to replace the tears that I continually cried. It didn't feel like there would ever be enough.

Annie's story gutted me. How could someone endure this? I couldn't even begin to imagine. 'You were just a kid,' I told her.

I did this.

I was just a kid.

I was just a kid, but I did this.

How could a kid ever bear that weight? The guilt? I spent years underneath the weight of it all and many times since I've wished that I had gone with them. The event is always there, always a part of me and its shadow hangs over everything I do.

I've told therapists, counselors, and psychiatrists over the years the things I heard on my Gameboy, how the accident was my fault. Nobody believes me. They tell me things like how my young mind couldn't accept the terrible tragedy that occurred, that it fabricated this other reality to cope with the trauma. They tell me that survivor guilt is a real thing and that if I had this fiction where I was truly at fault, then I could continue to feel bad about what had happened, continue living in my pain, the pain that was comfortable and familiar.

I'm told that letting go doesn't mean I completely forget, that just because I no longer hurt doesn't mean I stop caring.

When I found your website and the stories, I felt validation. Honestly, I felt better with that confirmation than I ever had in years of therapy. This changed everything for me. I felt at peace.

I now know what I have to do.

It was a month before I heard from Annie again, and this time it was through a mailed package. It contained a typed letter and a sealed envelope. A note advised me to not open the envelope until I had finished the letter. I did so.

I GUESS I should get into the gist of what my life was like after the car accident. My biological dad had long been out of the picture, and I had never even really known him, so I went to live with my grandma in Manhattan, my mom's mom. I had always liked her, and she liked me, and before the accident she often let me hide out at her place whenever the new family dynamics overwhelmed me.

But I was different now. How could I not be? Grandma tried her best with this new me, and I pushed her to the absolute edge. I fell in with a rough crowd at school, a quiet tagalong looking for a place to belong. Their antics distracted me from the pain: smoking cigarettes, petty shoplifting, graffitiing, hanging out late at night at the park and worrying my grandma, the thrill of getting away with it.

She threatened me with boarding school a few times, but never followed through. Having lost her daughter and grandson, she was hurting too. Her wine filled days allowed her to tune me out half the time. Little more than an afterthought to her pain, the rest of my childhood was unsupervised. Fortunately, I made it through with no run-ins with the law.

My grandma said she would pay my way to college.

NYU or Columbia? Get real. Not with my grades. I went to a community college in Ithaca where I promptly failed out after the first semester.

I spent years drifting from job to job, doing anything to feel nothing. There were strings of bad relationships and many casual encounters. I started self-medicating. It was nothing illegal, mind you, nothing you couldn't buy from a liquor store or get from a pharmacy (even though my name was rarely on the prescription). Years went by in a haze and at my lowest point I found myself on a week-long stay at a substance abuse treatment center in Ithaca, court ordered.

At this point, my grandma had cut me off, and money was getting tight. I found myself spiraling downward, flailing about to grasp for any sort of stability I could find. So after years of fucking up and fucking around, I got a steady gig at this strip club called Kuma Charmers.

It was meant to be a part-time thing, but I made more from a few nights a week than I had at any other job I ever had. Dancing enthralled me. During those periods performing on stage, I didn't think about anything else. I had quit the pills and got to where I was hardly even drinking anymore.

I met Daryl on the job. He was handsome and gave out some really nice tips. Living in a rural town nearby, he spent a lot in the oilfield and made good money and spent lots of time on the job out in Pennsylvania. This was his justification for why he'd stop off at the club.

"Don't got time to meet a girl at church," he'd say. "'Sides, they're all boring, anyways."

It got to where we would talk between my stage time, and he was charming and made me laugh. He started in with the talk of how he could take me away from all of this and was pretty persistent, and soon we started dating.

He was good enough and I think I felt something like love at the time. I really didn't analyze how I felt, I just went with it. When he asked if I loved him, I said yes. When he asked me to move in with him, I said yes. When he asked me to marry him, I said yes.

I guess there were the signs that I ignored, the proverbial writing on the wall. He drank too much, and when he was out of town, he called at all hours of the night to see if I would answer. God forbid if I didn't answer him quickly enough. He would get furious if I slept through his call and accuse me of cheating on him. I would then be tasked with talking him down and reassuring him. He would apologize profusely for his paranoia, tell me how he had been through infidelity before and how it had wrecked him. Then, he would return home with flowers and some lavish gift and everything would be ok for a while.

He offered to let me travel with him, said that during the day I could hang out in the hotel or go shopping or hiking. I had to explain my phobia of driving long distances. He was supportive and understanding, listened closely when I told him what I had been through. It was this side of him that kept me around, I guess, even though I never told him the part about the Gameboy and the broadcast. At this point, I must've convinced myself what the therapists had always told me.

I had quit my job at the club. He didn't like me being there, and I really didn't need the money anymore. There were enough encounters with the occasional creepy customer that quitting sort of felt like a relief. However, my human interaction was now cut off. I pissed away the hours of the day by drawing, taking walks, and vegging out on bad TV. I started looking into going back to school, starting another job.

I missed my coworkers, so one day when Daryl was gone, I stopped by the club to hang out a bit and catch up. It was so good to see my friends and acquaintances again, to walk into that club to a chorus of "howdy stranger" and "long time no see." However, the hours got away from me. I was having such a good time that I didn't even see the seventeen missed calls or the thirty-three text messages that had occurred within a two-hour period. The alcohol I imbibed didn't help and the night ended with me catching a ride with a friend to my house, where I promptly passed out.

I awoke hung over, oblivious to any worries, until I picked up my phone. The phone was filled with missed calls and texts, all from Daryl. There was a dropping sensation in my stomach, followed by fear and anxiety. I started to scroll through the messages, but I didn't get far.

I looked up, and he was there, standing in the doorway. There was a wild look in his eye, his jaw clenched.

He was on me before I could say a word, his hands on my throat, my cell phone knocked from my hands. I would have whiplash for days from him shaking me and a bruise on my hip from where I hit the floor. My ribs would creak every time I took a deep breath, and I was sure they were broken.

The whole time he asked me, "Why? Why? Why?" and didn't give me the chance to speak as he tossed me around the room, smacking me until he got a shocked look on his face. He backed away with his hands raised until he hit the wall by the door and slid to the ground, sobbing.

I was on my hands and knees, catching my breath, my body aching and my face throbbing. He was right by the doorway. I couldn't leave unless I went out a window. He crawled toward me, begging and pleading and saying my name. I was just numb as he bowed before me, his face buried into the carpet, hands wrapped tightly around my legs. He cried and cried about how big of a piece of shit he was. I couldn't squirm away.

My mind and body had shut down. I saw no exit from the situation I was in. I was afraid of him. He looked me straight in the eye and said, "Please. Give me a second chance. If you don't, I'll kill myself. I wanna kill myself right now for what I just did, but please let me make it right."

His pupils were dilated, and he was twitchy. There were sores on his neck and arms.

Was he on something? This wasn't the Daryl I had known. Maybe he needed help.

I only shrugged and said, "Whatever."

"I swear you won't regret this," he said.

I already did.

GIVING Daryl a second chance got me out of that temporary situation. It didn't matter that he took time off work to tend to my injuries. Didn't matter that he offered to pay for any schooling I wanted. I was still skeptical.

There was a small part of me that believed he could change, but I didn't really care and didn't want to be around for it. Fear and numbness kept me there. I knew he owned guns, guns he kept in his truck and in a gun safe he wouldn't give me the code to. If suicide was a response to not being with me, then why not take me out too? If he couldn't have me, then no one else could.

He left for his job for two weeks, begged me to come, but I resisted. This was as good a time as any to leave, but fear won out. There was a persistent worry that he was watching me, that he was having someone else spy on me. I kept seeing this black car on our street I had never seen before. I got it in my head that this was some sort of test, a test he wanted me to fail.

I holed up in the house for the whole two weeks. I did a lot of self-reflection, deep dives into where everything went wrong. That's when I found your website. That's when I contacted you.

. . .

"I ALWAYS FIGURED you were faking about how bad your phobia actually was," Daryl said to me from the driver's seat.

We were driving west toward Pennsylvania. I had agreed to go with him for his next stretch of work. The car ride still made me nervous, but there was no longer a paralyzing fear. I knew this was something I had to do.

"Excuse me?" I asked.

"The whole fear of cars and long drives and stuff. You just wanted an excuse to stay home and fuck around."

I often wonder if this trip could've had a different outcome, if I would've changed my mind had he been the perfect gentleman for the duration. But there was an edge in his voice.

There was an edge.

Traffic was thick as we drove, and I had made sure to look down anytime we passed a semi-truck. Ahead of us, two semis were in both lanes, puttering along at similar speeds. Daryl whipped his truck in between cars and muscled his way up to the truck in the left lane, rode the semi's ass. Slowly, we made headway.

I rolled down my window, watched the cab of the slow lane semi creep into view. I waved my arms, got the driver's attention.

We locked eyes . . .

THAT WAS the end of her letter. I stared over at the sealed envelope. The one that said, "OPEN LAST." Inside was a news article.

Cayuta Man Killed In Overpass Construction Accident on I-99

A CAYUTA MAN was killed by a piece of falling concrete from an overpass outside Lawrenceville Sunday evening. Repairs have been ongoing for the past several months.

"I was about a hundred yards from the truck, and I thought I saw something drop from the overpass. Suddenly, the truck swerved, and I thought 'Oh, boy,'" an eyewitness reported.

Daryl Phillis, 46, was en route to his jobsite in Pennsylvania when a chunk of concrete the size of a basketball fell from the overpass and entered the windshield, striking him in the head. He was killed instantly. His fiancée, Annie Rushing, was in the passenger seat. Annie was able to safely steer the car to the shoulder. After being evaluated at the scene, she was released with no injuries.

NYSDOT has started an investigation into the overpass and the construction project. The southbound interstate in that area has been converted to a single lane and special supports have been installed to ensure no further debris can fall onto motorists.

THE MONTHS PASS. I still get occasional news articles in the mail from her. The stories are largely the same. A motorist traveling east or west or south or north is fatally injured in an accident. The deceased are always men. The differences are in the details. There are different locations, different people, different ages, different objects falling from the sky.

Accompanying these letters are separate, older articles detailing old crimes and allegations against the deceased, charges acquitted or dismissed. There are court documents of restraining orders against the deceased, names listed on the sex offender's registry.

There was the 53-year-old man from Nebraska who perished on I-40 when a spare tire fell out of some good ol' boy's truck and went airborne and squashed his torso and face like a ketchup packet in a parking lot.

There was the guy who had beaten the rap of his ex-wife dying in a mysterious trailer house fire, the same ex-wife who had filed a restraining order a month previously. Well, this guy was driving under the High Five interchange in Dallas when a piece of rebar fell from the top of the highest ramp. It plummeted a hundred feet down and through the roof of his car where it pierced him like a shish kebab. This eight-foot piece of metal entered his skull, excited out the bottom of his jaw and into his lap, impaling him to the seat and floor. They had to use the jaws of life to extricate his body from the vehicle.

There were decapitations and crushed skulls, and in one bizarre instance, a man buried alive in his convertible by several tons of wet cement.

In many of these articles, she was there. As a passenger, as an eyewitness, as an acquaintance or significant other of the deceased. Sometimes I saw her in the background of photos of the wreckage: attractive, yet plain and anonymous, thanks to the newsprint.

She could be anyone you passed on the street.

I can imagine her walking away from the wreckage in slow-motion, untouched and unfazed. She's off to find another target, to be at the right place and right time once again. I want to know so much more. I have so many questions to ask. There's never a return address, though. And from the looks of it, she doesn't stay in one place for long

"Who are these people you keep talking to on the phone? These text messages and emails you get? Something's off."

"Babe, I'm not cheating on you."

"I'm not saying that at all."

"Really? Cause it kind of sounds like you are."

"You ever trace these numbers that call you, these emails? You ever notice they don't respond after a certain period of time?"

"What are you saying?"

"I'm worried about you."

"My work is important."

"Your work? Oh, come on. You're reading about terrible tragedies and case studies in the newspapers and you're making up these elaborate fictions after the fact. I never hear the voices of your so-called subjects on the other line. We can't listen to my white noise machine anymore because you say it sounds too much like static. And what the hell happened to your tooth?"

"Oh, I get it. I get it. You don't believe me."

"Please. Get help. I can't do this anymore."

12
"LEFT OF THE DIAL"

John Pratt had been a touring musician for many years. The road had been his home and livelihood as he and his band had crisscrossed the country, playing shows most days out of the year. You could hear the weariness in his voice. Whether this was from his high mileage lifestyle or an encounter with "The Rules of the Road," I didn't know. I'd let him tell me.

ONCE UPON A TIME, we were on the cusp. Fame. Money. Recognition. *Greatness*. Or that's what we all believed. I suppose there was a time when we still bought all the lies that rock-and-roll had sold countless young fools before us, that hard work and perseverance paid off, that dreams come true. That final year we were on a cusp alright: the cusp of complete failure and self-implosion.

With a name like Spit Weasel, I suppose it was an uphill battle from the start. At first, it was just a name that we had thrown together because we needed a name for the flier. Then, we had used it for booking our next batch of shows because we were lazy, and it was the path of least resistance. We had always planned to change it to something cooler down the road. We had never expected it to stick. By the time we had ordered the first batch of T-shirts—a skinny rodent rocking a Gibson Flying V underneath the name Spit Weasel—it was all she wrote.

"At least we didn't go with Shit Weasel like we'd first talked about," Bret said one afternoon while we were bemoaning our unfortunate moniker.

"Always looking on the bright side," I said.

"History's full of dumb band names that hit it big. What the hell's a 'Foo Fighter'? How about The Lovin' Spoonful? That's a band that's *literally* named after jizz. Didn't stop them from hitting it big. It's like a badge of honor past a certain point. When the fans love us despite our name, then that's when we'll know we've truly arrived," Bret said.

"Loving Spoonful is jizz?" I asked.

"Totally. I mean, think about it. How much do you have, when y'know ... you shoot your load? Not much more than a teaspoon, right?"

"Shit, man. I guess. Ain't ever really measured it."

"The average volume of ejaculate in an adult male is roughly five milliliters. So that equates to your big ol' lovin' spoonful."

You had to be careful when Bret started going off on one of these rants. He loved the sound of his own voice, and he could go on forever. However, he wasn't the only one that loved the sound of his voice. Being as he was our lead singer and all, I guess that was a good thing.

Bret continued his routine and talked about Steely Dan and The Buzzcocks and The Flaming Lips and Chuck Berry's "My Ding-a-Ling," while we all zoned out like the spouse who had learned to tune out their significant other by nodding along. Except at this point none of us were nodding, we were just staring blankly out the windows of the van. Unless we were on stage or doing an interview somewhere, we had no interest in putting up a front. Even then, it was getting harder and harder.

Speaking of spouses and divorce and things that end, I don't think there's a marriage counselor on earth that could keep a band together once that particular acrimony sets in. A marriage on the rocks has nothing on a band that is destined to break up. It's like a fuse that's been lit. There's nothing to do but sit back and watch the demolition.

That final year we were tired, oh, so tired. The road had taken its toll. After years of believing that we were finally gonna grab that brass ring, we had the sudden realization that the ring had been all greased up, that it had never really been within reach at all, a carnival game rigged against us. It was a game none of us wanted to play anymore, at least not together. A low simmering resentment had set in amongst the group and secret unspoken alliances had been made. Sides had been chosen.

I JUST NOW REALIZED I never properly introduced the lineup of Spit Weasel. Bret Hilton (previously mentioned) was our front man extraordinaire. He was the guy at the center of all the promo photos, the guy the music journalists flocked to and who answered most of the interview questions. The guy described in Pitchfork as the "tousled haired lead singer of Spit Weasel … with an animalistic fury that was hard to ignore, his voice only matched in raw power by his piercing blue eyes."

Next, there was Keith Hayes, the drummer, whom I'm pretty sure we only kept around because his name was Keith, and we thought it would be good luck to have a drummer in a rock band named Keith. Name notwithstanding, he wasn't the best or most imaginative drummer, but I guess we didn't really need him to be with the kind of music we played. That same Pitchfork article described Keith this way: "with his frantic drumming, flesh-colored beard, and receding blonde bushy hair giving him a clownish appearance, Keith is the quirky heart and soul of the band. He is just as likely to keep the rhythm as he is to do a flying leap off of his trap set or bang the cymbals with his forehead."

You had Ted Lang, the bassist. Silent and stoic and steady as a rock. The magazines and blogs frequently described him as "looming." At 6 5" or 6 6" or however tall he actually was, I guess you could say that he loomed. I don't know if it was because he was so big or what, but I can't rightly say that I ever saw the man ever get drunk. This wasn't for lack of trying, either. It was like the alcohol didn't have an effect on him.

Finally, there was me, your humble narrator, John Pratt. I was the one Pitchfork described as "putting on an intentional nondescript presence" and having "a silence that belies his role as the verbose songwriter and lyricist of the band." It's not that I was really that quiet. I just let Bret and Keith have the spotlight while I smirked in the background or offered a witty aside or two. It was too hard to compete when those two were going at it. And Ted, he didn't have to move a muscle to get noticed, a towering statue. So I guess that left me all nondescript with my heart on someone else's sleeve, my words coming out of Bret's mouth.

Spit Weasel was formed in the 90s. Keith and Ted had been in a band that played the sporadic weekend here and there. I was in another band as lead singer and guitarist and had gotten to know them at some gigs, gotten their numbers. Bret, he played covers at open mic nights and Ted had sort of been familiar with him. I had started jamming with Ted and Keith on some weekends, just trying each other out. We seemed to have a good chemistry and had an affinity for the same sort of sound. One day, Ted brought Bret along to watch us.

I don't remember the specifics, but Ted and Keith and I all agreed that we wanted to make a go at this whole touring musician thing. I was a little shaky on my singing, and I wanted to showcase my guitar playing, which I was quite proud of. Being center stage with all that attention was a role I wasn't suited for. If we had a true lead singer, someone with presence, then we could really take off. Somehow, Bret was there at the ready, waiting in the wings.

We started out with no idea of what the hell we were doing. It was clear from the get-go that once we decided we were going to be a band, our first step was that we should practice and play and do it a *lot*. A routine was established, with us practicing at least four times a week. We did this in the basement of Keith and Ted's rental, descending into that cinder block dungeon for hours on end before emerging again. We would piss in a little sewer drain that sat at the corner room and we would fill a hubcap ashtray with butts and a 55-gallon barrel with crushed beer cans until it spilled over, the air an oppressive fog of sweat and cigarette smoke and humidity.

I had already had a nice cache of songs that we pulled from. We got to where we could play them frontwards and backwards, drunk or sober. There was never any desire from any of the other guys to write songs. They all contributed in their own way to the development of the tunes, but I was the guy behind all the lyrics, the general shape of the song.

As for college and jobs, none of us had a lot going on. We were all a mix of part-timers and drop-outs. Nobody had any serious girlfriends, and we all kept a couple of temporary low-skilled jobs with fluid hours. In other words, we had plenty of time to devote to the band.

We started up playing some shows at local open mics and bars and eventually got a weekly gig at one of the chill dive bars that leaned toward the punk side of things. At this place called The Observatory, we made acquaintances with a regular.

His name was Tyler Overholser, and he was a financial adviser by day, music fanatic by night. The long story short of this cat was that he was older than us, like late thirties. After a divorce, he had undergone something of a midlife crisis. He had always been a music fan and even had some aspirations in his youth of doing the very thing that we were doing. As is often the case, life had gotten in the way, and he had finished college and entered the workforce and did all the other things that you were supposed to do, like marriage and kids. All of this left him unfulfilled, however.

"I guess you could say I was . . . unsatisfied. My dreams were unfulfilled, and I graduated unskilled," he said with a wink and a grin. He was prone to talking in the aphorisms of his favorite bands, chiefly The Replacements.

Tyler hung out at the local rock clubs, scoping out bands. He felt as if he was far too old to get into the game as a musician, but his current aspiration was to manage a band, to help them go the distance. He was just waiting for that certain group.

"Out of every band I've seen here—and believe me, it's a lot—you by far embody the rock 'n roll spirit more than any other act I've seen. I think your group is something special," he told us after seeing us play several times.

His offer was that he wanted to become our tour manager and booking agent. Said he knew people and had connections with a recording studio, told us he could show us the ropes of the biz. He was even willing to front some of his own money.

"The only thing I ask though," he said, "is you let me come with you. I wanna be a part of the magic. I want a front-row seat."

We were skeptical. It seemed too good to be true. We

hedged our bets and told him we were going to find our own way for the time being.

"You've got my number if you change your mind. You know where to find me. But I want you to know that gone are the days of the A&R guys hanging out at these clubs and approaching you with a record deal. I know how to put in the work."

The next few months we buckled down hard and played more local shows, expanded our radius. We all moved into Ted and Keith's rental so that we could save more money for the band fund. It was a brotherhood.

From all of our penny-pinching we had saved up enough to buy a van, a used Ford Econoline. Our goal was to start touring, going further from our home base. The only thing is, we didn't know where to start.

We called on Tyler. He was ecstatic to be working with us. We were glad for the opportunity, figured we had nothing to lose and could back out at any time. It's not like he was having us sign any big contract; it was a handshake type of deal. He was earnestly looking for a group to live vicariously through, experience the things that he had missed out on, maybe get some credit for any success we might stumble upon. And that's one thing he stressed about success, that it was something that luck played a big part in, right place at the right time and all that.

First on our agenda was to record an album. We certainly had the songs, more than an album's worth of them. Tyler booked us some time at a local recording studio, got an engineer and an old producer guy to help us record the thing. We tracked our album live with minimal overdubs, just the way we liked it. They even got a dude to come in and lay down some keys, B3 and piano and the like for a few songs. It really fleshed out our sound.

The cost was never brought up. It had to have come

completely from Tyler's own pocket. It was his deal, and he was having a blast, beaming from the recording booth.

Summer came, and it was time to go on our first real, bonafide tour. This would be in support of the release of our debut album, *Half-Empty*.

We played pool halls and dives and nightclubs and biker bars and casinos and bingo parlors and restaurants. On more than one occasion, we played the early evening slot at a busted-ass strip club in the middle of nowhere, rocking out while a lone dancer with a c-section scar twirled on the pole and cowboys and ranchers drank from bottles, uninterested.

Wherever we went, people weren't actively coming out to see us. We hadn't been a band long enough for that. It was all just happenstance. They happened to be in the bar that night. They happened to be stopping in for a bite to eat. They happened to be there to see the headliner. Whatever the circumstance, we hoped they would catch us, actually listen to us and fall in love. We were trying to grow a fanbase one fan at a time, win 'em over any way we could.

The most memorable show from those early days was this Vietnamese karaoke lounge in Vegas. Yeah, our first big Vegas show, and it was in a strip mall. I don't know how Tyler booked the place, but it was packed with old Vietnamese men and some younger kids. They ate it up: the kids played air guitar, the men nodded. We sold ten CDs that night, cleaned up in tips, and scored a bag of banh mi sandwiches.

Tyler, he went for broke booking that first tour. It was something like thirty dates all across the U.S. Money was tight and we slept in the van a lot, drove through the night to the next gig, showered at truck stops or KOA campgrounds. Sometimes, Tyler would have enough of this type of rough living, and he'd spring for a Motel 6 or something. He'd get his own room, and we'd get ours. Other times, venue owners or newfound fans would offer us up a couch or a living room floor.

Starting out, we were wide-eyed and innocent. We didn't want to fuck up too badly, and even though we were playing for sparse crowds and empty rooms, we didn't get too drunk and rowdy at our shows. That's not to say we didn't bring the energy, though. At least that's what the people who actually paid attention to us said.

"Man, you guys really bring it," they would say. "Helluva workout up there!"

It was a world of wonder. I couldn't believe that we were actually doing it, living the dream. Sure, we were scraping by, but every night I was doing what I loved. I knew after that first tour that I would do nothing else. Anything else would just be pretending. I didn't want to end up like Tyler, full of regret and lurking around clubs, pushing forty and driving across the country with a van full of twenty-year-olds, trying to get a contact high from the rock and roll glory we all sought.

After the tour, we took some time off back home to regroup and recharge. It was back to finding some temporary employment and figuring out what our next step would be.

In those days, the internet was becoming more mainstream, and more and more people were turning to online websites and blogs and message boards for music recommendations. Music fans were using MySpace to preview songs. They were downloading stuff off Napster. We would show up at shows and people would already know our songs.

We did a second pressing of our debut album, made it an actual official release with actual cover art and everything. Tyler sent copies off to every online music website and blogger that he could, anybody that had a passing interest in rock and that would give us a review, all those local rags. It was a total DIY promotional thing. What we really needed was a publicist, but for now this would suffice.

We started filling up the local joints every time we played, even had a couple sellouts. Local girls took notice of us and actually gave us the time of day (although Bret had never had a problem with that, even before the band). Yet when we were out on the road, our fanbase was mostly male. The biggest fans were always 30 to 40-year-old white dudes in jeans and band T-shirts and tennis shoes, dudes that reminded us of Tyler. We drew some punks and scenesters, and as we went along, the crowds slowly grew and diversified.

By the time we were ready for our second tour, we had grown cocky. We fancied ourselves as veteran traveling musicians now. More and more Tyler felt like a thorn in our side, a mother hen trying to corral us from gig to gig. We were young and dumb and didn't want to be told what to do. We didn't want to outright fire him, though. Without the backing of an actual label, he performed so many of the duties that allowed us to function: manager, booking agent, bus driver, merch guy, publicist. Yet, an unspoken contempt grew in us. He had wanted to experience something like the train wreck of The Replacements in their heyday. Well, we'd try to give it to him, just not to the self-destructive degree of those alt-rock icons. We were still going to actually *try*.

By the time it was all said and done, he had front row tickets to the shit show. I think he got his money's worth.

Alcohol was our drug of choice. We lived to get liquored up before a show and during, just like our heroes did. Although there was always enough weed to go around, we didn't really dabble in anything harder. We were aware enough of rock 'n roll's history to know that rarely ended well.

The exception to all of this was Keith. If you had some pills, he'd take 'em. A handful of some weird brownies passed around at a show? Good as gone. Shrooms? Sure. I saw him snorting lines of unknown powders on numerous occasions. The way he would toss back the booze was like he was trying to burn the candle down at both ends, like he was trying to get a head start induction into the 27 club. The only good thing is that I never saw him break out a needle or tie off a vein.

There was the time that we got pulled over by the cops outside Gary, Indiana. Busted taillight or something like that. Tyler white knuckled it in the driver's seat, while we lounged in the back, laughing at our situation with reckless abandon. He was scared shitless that we were gonna get busted with the weed that was stashed in the guitar case, that the cop would take notice of the powder in Keith's mustache. When the cop did his back-and-forth between the van and his patrol car, he screamed at us to take it seriously, that this was a big deal and that he would roll over on each one of us, if it came to that. Still, that didn't stop Keith from firing up a big-ass joint right as the cop drove away and left us with only a warning.

"I think you could use a hit of this," Keith said to Tyler. "That vein in your forehead's looking mighty big."

Tyler only gritted his teeth and drove on. He knew the price of admission.

Our shows had become more drunken, raucous affairs. All of us (except for Ted and his magical constitution) had puked on the stage at least once, a sort of initiation. We got banned from certain clubs for our behavior, with the most deserving a ban for the egregious offense of grand theft bobcat.

Grand Theft Bobcat. Now there's a band name for you. Might've been preferable to Spit Weasel and incidentally it became the name of our third album. What happened was, we were headlining a show at The Drifter's Lounge in Lincoln, Nebraska, a cool little venue with a chill atmosphere. What was notable was a stuffed bobcat that sat on this ledge overlooking center stage. We had a pretty good turnout for a weeknight and a good score on merch sales. Only thing is that the owner was a dick. The sound guy was a dick. Even the bartender was a dick.

We were packing up our gear, and we noticed Tyler arguing with the owner over getting paid. Something over the percentage of the cover charge versus a flat rate. Everything was loaded and Bret and Ted and I were standing out by the van, when all of a sudden Keith burst out the back door with the stuffed bobcat under his arm, Tyler right behind him.

"Get in! Get in!" Keith yelled, and we did.

I was closest to the driver's seat, and I hopped in, while everyone else piled in behind me, including Tyler. Not much choice. We were running with or without him.

"Goddammit, Keith!" Tyler screamed as we hauled ass out of there.

The bobcat came to be known as Steve, and he became our de facto mascot. We'd place him on an amp wherever we'd play, put cigarettes in his mouth and hats on his head.

The infractions continued to pile up. There were wrecked hotel rooms, Keith passing out in a Waffle House bathroom, bad acid trips and ruined clothes, Sharpie dicks drawn on Tyler's passed out face. There was the time Tyler got locked out of the hotel room while we drank and smoked and partied and didn't miss him until we found him the next morning sleeping in the van.

There was a cruelty in how we singled out Tyler like a bunch of high school bullies, the resentment bubbling over and he the focus of our ire. We were too stupid to figure out how to get going in the business, and he had been a godsend. However, we also unfairly blamed him for any of our failures. Not getting as far in the business? Tyler's fault.

Bad show? Tyler's fault. CDs not shipping on time? Tyler's fault. A motel with bed bugs? Tyler.

We'd call him out from the stage and throw crushed empty beer cans at him. He'd laugh it up and pretend to be a good sport, but I could see we were wearing on his last nerve.

"You know we love you," we'd say, and we'd get good and drunk, and all would be forgiven for the time being.

Tyler finally came through for us. He had booked us a showcase at SXSW, the music festival in Austin. SXSW was a big deal even back then, but not near the level of overexposure it is today. You could still get a label deal if you played at the right place at the right time and rock and roll was still alive here.

The showcase was our next success. We were signed to a mid-tier indie label, Grindstone Records, which gave us access to more resources for promotion and touring. But this meant Grindstone relieved Tyler of the many roles he fulfilled. There could still be a place for Tyler, other jobs we could have him do. We had a long debate on what to do with him, but ultimately he answered the question for us at our celebration party.

"Well, guys, it's been great."

"Yeah, man. We really appreciate it. You've been a blessing," Bret said. "You know, we've been talking and we would—"

Tyler interrupted. "Don't say it. I want to get this out before I hear what you say and change my mind. This needs to be totally my decision. It's time to pass the baton. I don't think I can handle much more of the road. My liver's *begging* for mercy. I just can't handle the antics."

"Is this about the girls I brought to the room that one time?" Keith asked.

"The hookers? The ones you picked up at the truck stop when you were buzzed as hell? The one that gave me the clap and those weird bumps? I mean, nah, it's not about them. Well, that is part of it. And all the other shit you pulled."

"Oh. Sorry."

"Look, I wanted to enjoy this rock and roll lifestyle for a bit, catch up on what I missed. You fellas helped me with that. Gave me more than I could handle."

"Well, thanks again," Bret said.

"Yep, and I hope to one day see the children by the millions sing for Bret Milton to come around. I hope to read about your band in some *national* page and you guys remember to mention my name," Tyler smiled.

"I see what you did there," I said, noting his super obvious references to that Replacements tune. Corny bastard. Lord knows how lucky we were to have never ridden in a plane with him, to hear him refer to the stewardesses as "waitresses in the sky" ad nauseam.

"Hey," Tyler said, his eyes twinkling with tears. "If I don't see you guys in a long while ... I know where I can find you: left of the dial."

I DIDN'T MEAN to get into this whole VH1 *Behind the Music* type of deal, but I think it's important to see how we started out and how we got to where we were and how stagnant it really all became. That cusp I mentioned earlier? We spent years there. It came in a series of little advancements, but ultimately no matter how far we got we weren't that much better off from where we started out.

Despite the success of being signed to the indie label and getting a two-record deal, we were no closer to hitting the big time. Despite getting reviews in more esteemed publications, despite the stronger promotional arm behind the bigger label, we were still struggling. We still scraped by in poverty, barely making enough for our cost of living. Forget health insurance or putting anything back in savings.

We opened for some really big bands in some really cool venues. We played some big festivals; played on a European tour, we even played a spot on Conan. It still didn't amount to much in the way of fame and fortune, just some cool stories we might tell our kids one day.

Maybe we just weren't as good as we had all thought. Or maybe they just weren't buying what we were selling. The type of music we played, the "drunken earnest heartland rock with the yearning guitar solos and melancholic lyrics", I guess most people didn't want to hear that. They wanted something a little more fun.

Whatever our resentments were about our lack of success, one thing was certain: there was a certain draw to Bret by all parties involved. From the audience, from the label, from the press. The interviews of the music mags all heavily focused on him. There were a couple of dreamboat photo sessions the label paid for featuring him with his pearl snap shirt unbuttoned all the way, his jeans down low. I got the sense that they were trying to make a star out of Bret, that a rebranding was coming down the pike. Bret Milton and The Weasels.

Unless Bret wanted to take a night off, he didn't play a single show without having some new chick end up in his hotel room. I know that's not saying much in a rock band, but Lord knows how often the rest of us struck out.

Speaking of all that, I tried my hand at various long-term relationships during this time period, but none of them could withstand the distance and lifestyle. These painful endings continued to fuel the subject of my songs. Bret and Keith, they couldn't give less of a fuck about maintaining any sort of long-term relationship. The closest Bret came was a singer or two from other bands with which we toured, and he cheated on them constantly.

As far as Keith cared, pussy was just another drug, and an inferior one at that, something best experienced while under the influence of more drugs.

The exception to all these romantic failings was Ted. Good ol' reliable Ted. He was anchored in life to whatever he decided, and in his case, it was life in the band and a good woman named Heather. She had understood the lifestyle and remained by his side through it all, had even served as our merch girl on several tours once we had signed to Grindstone. When she wasn't around, Ted was constantly calling her or sending her postcards, buying souvenir keychains with her name on it from truck stops.

The years passed on the road, each one a blur indistinguishable from the next. The struggle continued: the poverty, the hard miles, the nights of playing to a crowd of fifteen in Dubuque, Iowa. Yet still, when I was on that stage with that guitar in my hand, that was the only time I truly felt normal. For that moment in time, all was right with the world. I wouldn't trade it for anything. I couldn't go back.

I remember some late-night beers on the roof of a club that we had played at. It was nice out and the owner said we could stay the night up there if we wanted. There were hammocks and beach chairs. Bret and I sat at the edge of the building, smoking and drinking, our feet dangling over the lamplit street below. It had been another night with a less than stellar turnout.

"I've been thinking," Bret said.

"Always a risky endeavor."

"Nah, I'm serious. I'm so tired of this. All this hard work is getting us nowhere. I think maybe it's time we hung it up."

The suggestion hit like a sucker punch. "What? Are you fucking with me right now?"

"We've had a pretty good run, but this shit's getting tiresome. It may be time to regroup. Take a little break, y'know? We're not getting any younger. How many years you got left in the tank? How many bands you know that hit it big with a bunch of old-ass bastards?"

A sudden desperation overtook me, and I couldn't stop myself. I grabbed him by the front of the shirt, pulled him back from the edge of the building, his beer bottle falling and shattering on the street. Pressing my face up to his, I said, "I'm never fucking giving up and *you're* not either."

His eyes got wide.

"This is it for me, Bret. I'm not doing anything else," I said.

He pressed his hands against me, more in reassurance than resistance. "Okay, okay, man. I was just feeling you out. I'm just a little tired, that's all."

I let go of him. "Sorry, man. I'm tired, too. I get how you're feeling. We're almost there though . . . almost there."

AND EVEN AFTER THIS CONFRONTATION, after that current tour, we ended up back at our home base with the longest break we had taken in a long time. We only played the occasional regional show here and there with months long gaps in between.

Ted and I, we both fell into jobs for the time being, Ted as a bartender and me working at a music store and giving guitar lessons on the side. Keith, who had looked real sickly toward the end of that final tour, entered a treatment facility and disappeared for a while.

It seemed the brotherly bonds we had formed on the road were growing weaker.

Bret became scarce. He would answer our calls and would hang out some, but he was distant, and we didn't see him much. We'd soon find out why.

Bret had signed on to record a solo album with Vitality

Records, an imprint of Warner Bros. So, in other words, a major label, more or less. The big time.

That almost ended it all right there. There was a big confrontation, a band meeting. Even Keith was there, newly sober for the time being. The rest of the band simmered in suppressed rage and jealousy. Bret spoke his piece. We spoke ours. He explained that this could be a big step for the band, that after he recorded and toured this solo piece, we could get back together and make a new album. All we could do was hope that he was trustworthy.

The rest of us took the dreaded hiatus, the death knell of so many bands before us. We sunk down into the drudgeries of our new lives.

Keith took up a job painting houses, and his newfound sobriety slowly slipped away. "They told me it could take several tries," he told me at the bar one time.

Ted seemed happy bartending and playing in the occasional cover band. He and Heather got married. I'd talk with him and jam sometimes, ask if he'd heard any updates from Bret.

As for me, I fell in love with a brunette bartender that worked with Ted. Her name was Evie, and her eyes were green. She looked like a dream and had an array of tattoos that began at her elbow and went upwards, the black ink intricate on her pale skin. She was cool as hell. Dug music, too. The good kind.

For once, it seemed like I was going to finally make a relationship work. It helped that I wasn't on the road all the time. We moved in together, a small yellow cottage with white trim and a muddy yard. I felt happy, a measure of peace that I hadn't known in some time, the big dream slipping away from me to be replaced by something else.

That "something else" turned up soon enough. In that whirlwind of romance and moving in together and getting after it whenever we could, Evie missed a few days of her birth control, and before we knew it, she was pregnant. After our son, Benjamin, was born I started thinking, maybe I should just give it up.

Maybe this was it.

Evie was my cheerleader, though. She came through in ways that made me feel luckier than ever. She encouraged me to give the thing one more big try, what with everything falling into place with Bret's solo record more successful than anything we had ever done. Why not give the band-thing one more try with his new popularity behind the tour?

"If you don't try one this more time, you'll always be wondering, 'What if?'" she told me.

While at work, when I wasn't pining to return home and hold my son, I daydreamed about being back in the band. I longed to be in the studio again, getting back out on the road, at different clubs on different nights, and with friends in every town. The strict routine of my day-to-day life was getting boring. I could yawn just thinking about it. I guess that's why they called it a hiatus, which I once read was the Latin word for yawn.

We titled our fourth and final album *Sometime After Never*, a not-so-sly nod to when I thought we would finally achieve real success. I had a plethora of songs to choose from for this album, songs I had written during the break. I chose the best of the best and we recorded what was probably my favorite of all of our albums.

After signing a deal with Vitality Records as a band, I felt like a real professional musician for the first time. We had budgets and managers and green rooms and everything. The only thing they skimped out on was the mode of transportation. I had hoped for a tour bus with a driver. Instead, we got an Econoline van with a trailer. At least it was a van that had a model from the current year, much less the same decade.

It was here that the cracks in the foundation widened,

and the facade crumbled. After the initial buzz of our first few shows back together, it was clear we had drifted apart.

I found myself more and more annoyed by Bret. He was such a phony now. He always had that potential, even back in the early days. But Bret didn't become the current Bret we now knew until after the solo record, his ego and worst traits amplified like a guitar hooked up to a Marshall Stack. He acted like he was doing us all a favor by schlepping it with us.

Keith had long since fallen off the wagon after his rehab stint and he was drinking as much as ever, mostly the hard stuff. He was losing weight, barely eating, but he still seemed as wild and lively as ever. Bret didn't seem to get under his skin that much, though. As long as the party kept going, he was fine with whatever. Keith took umbrage with Bret's obsession with image, however, and he was the only one of us that would mock Bret's newfound vanity with impunity, even go so far as doing it on stage. Keith would unbutton his shirt all the way and leave his alcohol swollen gut hanging out in the breeze, prance around with his black jeans down to his pubic hair.

Ted was ever the stoic one. The only sign of his annoyance was how he talked less often, which I didn't think was possible. I even caught him rolling his eyes a few times when Bret was talking. For Ted, this was like announcing his inner thoughts on a billboard. He would never give that much away.

We noticed that on this tour that the crowds started getting prettier and younger and more dominated by the fairer sex. The cruel irony of the situation was that I could no longer play in that sandbox; Evie and Benjamin awaited me at home. If only this development had happened a lot sooner, back when we were all younger. Oh well. What I had with them was more stable and more fulfilling. I had plans on buying a ring once this tour was over, finally making it official with Evie.

We were driving to Boise after a gig in Missoula when I heard it. Bret was driving, and I was riding shotgun. We didn't have a driver for this leg of the tour, and it was only the four of us in the van, just like old times.

Per the long-established bylaws of the band, the van's driver had dibs on the stereo. Bret had something playing quietly. Whatever it was sounded eerily familiar.

"Hey, what's this?" I asked. "Sounds familiar."

"Oh, nothing. Just that solo album," Bret responded.

"Solo album?"

"Well . . . mine."

That's a little vain, I thought. Guess I should expect nothing less from ol' Bret.

"I'm just picking it apart. Seeing how I can grow as an artist, what I can do better the next go-round." He must've sensed my thoughts.

Had I heard that song before? I had never even listened to the solo album in its entirety, perhaps out of jealousy.

It didn't sit right. I turned the stereo up and started the song over, noting some lyrics. That line that went, *I'm coming undone, I don't want to be the one*. And then there were those chord changes: the D-minor to B-flat, the F to the C. I pulled my phone out and looked at the notebook app where I would often write lyrics and ideas down.

There it was. The lyrics I had written over a year ago were almost verbatim to what was coming out of the stereo. I had even written the chords. I had never gotten around to completing it and practicing it with the band. There it had sat, long since forgotten, stolen somewhere along the way. Had he ripped it directly from my phone? He wouldn't have had to necessarily. I could've been playing it on my acoustic in the motel room, and all he had to do was covertly record me with his phone.

How many of my other song sketches had he snagged this way?

"You motherfucker," I said, looking over at him, reaching to turn off the music.

"I wouldn't touch that dial, Johnny-boy," a voice from the stereo speakers said, clear as day and loud as hell. *"Not unless you wanna miss out on the feel-good hit of the summer by our favorite rock and roll rascals, Spit Weasel."*

"Wait, what's going on? Someone playing our songs on the radio?" Ted asked from the backseat. "Turn it up."

"I haven't touched anything," Bret said.

The voice on the radio continued.

"Yessiree, we've got the latest from those fellas coming up right here in a jiff, right after the latest edition of 'The Rules of the Road.' Here's a taste to wet your whistle."

Just then, there was Bret singing the chorus of a song from our latest album, with us playing behind him. It cut off and went back to the disc jockey.

Buck Hensley here with a special musical edition of "The Rules of the Road." That was Spit Weasel with a cut off their latest album, Sometime After Never, and we'll hear more from them in a minute. But first we've gotta get to our usual business.

You ever hear of a Chinese fire drill? I don't know if it's kosher to use that term nowadays. Heck, is it even kosher to use the word kosher? Guess they started calling 'em Chinese fire drills on account of having some sort of issue with the Chinese, fear of the other and all that, as more of those folks found themselves over here. Maybe it was an inferiority complex?

Whatever the case may be, seems to me like yet another entry in a long line of entries of humans

and whatnot fearing the dreaded "other." Now, I reckon you'd do well to be afraid of the other, but you're wasting your time if you think it's somebody in the same species, much less an organism made from the same molecular elements.

I mean, we all breathe oxygen, we all put our pants on one leg at a time. It's not like we use super special sonic vibrations to stun our prey. It's not like we then turn this vibration up to eleven and sever their covalent bonds until their internal organs liquefy and leak out into a delicious human slurry that we then slurp up with our funnel-shaped proboscis. Them's the kind of other I'm worried about.

But I digress, I know you fellas are eager to hear your song on actual cosmic radio. On to tonight's Rule. If at any point during your journey you come across a train on a railroad crossing that you have to wait on, then you and your party must perform that unfairly named ritual known as the Chinese fire drill. Why don't we call it the label executive fire drill or the focus group fire drill? Everyone in your party must exit the vehicle, run around the perimeter of said vehicle, and return to their seats. All while the vehicle is in park, of course!

What are the consequences of refusing to follow this rule? Well, I'll tell you. If you don't perform this harmless little prank, then you will lose what you love most. Isn't that something? Kind of unfair, don'tcha think? Small price to pay to avoid this, though.

Welp. That's all I got for tonight. I'll be signing off to the sweet soulful sounds of Spit Weasel. Y'all stay safe out there. Stay rockin'. Stay rollin'. Stay

lonely. I'm Buck Hensley and these are "The Rules of the Road."

HIS VOICE FADED into static and the familiar opening riff of "Bullet Train" rang out over the car speakers. As the song progressed into the verse, it seemed different somehow. Heavier and more layered, slower and slower and slower. The song cascaded over me in slow-motion waves like I was super stoned. I could barely move my head to look over at Bret, everything passing so slowly, the weight of the song crushing me, crushing us all.

When the final notes rang out, we realized we were now parked off on the shoulder of the interstate with no idea of how we had gotten there.

"What in the fuck?" Bret said to the quiet van.

Keith rose with a start from the very back. "What's going on? Van trouble?"

"Are you serious right now? You slept through all that?" I asked.

"Slept through what? Just had this dream that they were playing us on the radio."

THERE WERE two weeks left on the tour. As soon as it was over, I was done. Done with the band, done with Bret. I avoided him whenever I could and only spoke the bare minimum to him. Quitting would have affected my pay, so all I could do was lie low. There were no big confrontations after being interrupted by the strange radio broadcast, and I didn't bring it up again. I was thinking of getting a lawyer involved over the stolen song as soon as I got back home to see what my options were. I wanted to take him by surprise.

We never figured out what was up with the radio broadcast. We had some theories, from a shared hallucination brought on by white line fever, to a prank from the label, to Keith spiking us with LSD somehow. Keith was adamant that he didn't spike us, said there was no way he'd waste good drugs that way.

The tour petered out in a series of headlining shows, each one with less of a draw than the previous. Somewhere in that final string is where it happened, the inevitable.

Leaving a club in Lawrence, Kansas, there was a railroad crossing. We were on the outskirts of a dying industrial section that had made some attempts at revitalization. A closed restaurant to our right and a liquor store to our left, the club we had played at in our rear view. There was the telltale sound of a train's horn, the red-eyed sentries chiming and lowering their candy cane arms and me stopping the van. I looked back at everybody, put the vehicle in park.

"Y'all remember the rule?"

"C'mon, John. It's late dude," Bret said.

"I think we should do it," Ted said. "That was some trippy shit. What could it hurt?"

"What rule was this?" Keith asked.

"We're supposed to do a Chinese fire drill or some bad shit will happen," I said. "We received this supernatural radio signal."

"John, do you know how crazy that sounds? Do you actually believe it? I'm not sure what we heard," Bret protested.

The train was barreling down now, it's light boring through the night a couple blocks away. We were running out of time.

"What have we got to lose? I'm getting out," I said and opened the door.

Ted stepped out of the passenger side. I could see the back door open and Keith ducking out and sliding toward the back of the van. Bret stayed inside.

"Goddammit Bret. Are you really gonna fuck us over? Get out of the fucking van," I said, reaching toward him.

We were running out of time. How long could the train be?

"Keep your fucking hands offa me. I'm not doing this paranoid shit." Bret slapped my hands. It was hard to get to him in the back of the van.

"You're not gonna ruin this too," I said through gritted teeth.

Just then, an enormous hand grasped my shoulder, pushing me aside. It was Ted. He plucked Bret out of the van with ease, tossed him over his shoulder.

"Ted, Goddammit!" Bret yelled, kicking his feet.

"Look, he's laughing," I said. I could see the strained smile on Bret's red face as his struggling waned.

"Let's hurry. Train's almost passed," Ted said as we scurried around the vehicle. I rounded the back and jumped into my open door. I could see the end of the train coming a few blocks down like a dark line being erased. Ted tossed Bret into the van and plopped down back in his seat.

I looked around. "Wait. Where's Keith?" He was nowhere in the vehicle, nowhere nearby.

Nowhere at all.

I looked toward the other side of the street at the liquor store. His bald head shined under the lights as he stood at the counter, checking out. I rolled down my window and started screaming at him. He gave me a little wave and held up a brown paper bag, shuffled toward us.

It was too late. The train was long gone by the time he got to the van, horn blaring off in the distance as it chugged off and away to destinations unknown.

The DJ's words rang out in my ears like feedback from a stage monitor: *If you don't perform this prank, then you will lose what you love most.* The days and nights were filed with dread, sludgy stoner-rock power chords building and building until ... what, exactly?

I texted Evie constantly. Waiting for the day when she wouldn't respond, waiting for the phone call that would come to tell me of Benjamin's sudden death from choking or SIDS or smoke inhalation from a house fire.

But nothing ever came. The fear slowly faded and the belief that the world was bound by laws and science returned. I slowly focused on the reality of my current situation, that the band I was involved with was likely to be dissolved as soon as the current tour ended. At least I was leaving. I didn't see it surviving after my departure. Keith would be too unreliable for Bret's ventures and Ted would likely hang it all up to spend more time with his wife, Heather. He had been talking about starting a family.

A final show in Chicago that wasn't advertised as one—but one that sold out all the same—and all of my fear, all of my unhappiness, all of my doubt evaporated. Up there on the stage and the music flowing through me, I was the happiest I'd been in a long time. For that moment in time, music was the cure for what ailed me. My only true salvation. Hail, hail rock and roll.

FORGET GOING BACK to Richmond with the rest of the guys. I was going to take the next flight out of O'Hare. Ted would make sure my amp got back safely, and I took my Tele and Martin with me. I didn't even have a farewell drink with them, couldn't stand to be around any longer than I had to.

My flight was scheduled to leave around noon. I got a room at an airport motel, smoked a cigarette in the parking lot, and told Evie I was coming home early. I could hear her smile through the phone, could practically see it.

"I'm done, baby. I'm done," I said to her, my voice cracking.

THE FAMILIAR DARKNESS of a motel room and the intimate hum of those window air conditioner units that you've known all these years. You're waking up to the feeling that someone has slid into the room with you, that it's maybe the ghosts of all those who've slept here before. But you feel it watching you from the shadows, and maybe you can hear them breathe. Your eyes are blurry and out of focus and you chalk it up to still being half asleep or maybe even still dreaming. As your eyes adjust you see that, no, this is happening. There is a silhouette, a figure at the foot of the bed. You can't move and you can't scream, and you've heard the stories about sleep paralysis and maybe it's just that, maybe all you have to do is wait for it to pass. Pray that your heart doesn't beat against your chest until it stops, that your breath keeps going in and out.

And somehow the lamp is flickering beside you on the nightstand, and you catch sight of the thing at the foot of the bed, the thing that is crawling onto the covers. With its vinyl black eyes and the bloody tongue wrapped in guitar strings and one rigid arm dragging behind it, it pulls itself closer and closer. The rigid arm spinning around mechanically, the shirt sleeve sliding down its wrist and it's not a wrist at all. It is an arm, just not a human one but the arm of a turntable, an arm that ends in a needle, a needle way longer than any record player ever would need, two feet long of gleaming metal. When the needle enters your ear, there's pain, but you can't react and this must be what it's like to wake up frozen in anesthesia on the operating table, aware of everything.

When the darkness returns and you can move again, you

see a shaft of light shining through the curtains and realize it's morning and you call back home and find out that everyone is okay. You splash water on your face and you're so thankful that it was all just a dream.

Except as time passes you find out that it was anything but.

THEY CALL IT MUSICAL ANHEDONIA. At least, that's the closest approximation of it I could find through my internet research. It's the lack of pleasure derived from listening to music. We've all seemed to know these people throughout our lives, these weirdos who don't care much for music or have never been moved by a song. Well, I'm one of them now.

What I have seems to be more of a unique case of it, though. It's not that I just no longer enjoy music as is the common case of musical anhedonia, it's that it all sounds like an atonal wash of sound. I can't even pretend to like it; it's painful. There's no difference between listening to "Born to Run" or "Let it Be" or "Stairway" and the dulcet tones of a jackhammer on sheet metal. The first time I picked up a guitar since that visit in the hotel room, I tried to play a G chord and it was like pulling out a splinter. I got nauseous with each strum, sick with worry that something was drastically wrong.

Sometimes I think it would've been better to have lost all of my hearing instead. At least I would have all those songs in my head. I could revisit those glorious places in memory, hear the guitar solos on crunchy low wattage tube amps, the chord changes and drums, the triumphant howls. Hell, I could probably even still write and compose music as a deaf guy like Beethoven composing his 9th Symphony.

The more severe symptoms have faded with time and music is just background noise to me now.

It all sounds like tinnitus, painfully annoying at worst, easily ignored at best. I haven't picked up my guitar in years, and I sold most of my record collection years ago, keeping any leftovers for Evie and Benjamin. I got a job in a factory. The beeps of my forklift backing up instill in me the same joy as the songs I hear Evie singing in the shower.

Of course, there were the others. What was to become of them and the things they loved most? It was different for all of us. Some were worse off than others.

Ted's wife Heather was dragged from her bed late one night. Her screams echoed through the neighborhood and her fingers clawed tracks through the yard. They found her body in a ditch with a broken neck and numerous bite marks. Ted was at work when this happened, came home to an empty bed and a wide-open back door. Her bloody fingernails lay on the threshold from when she had clung on for one final second before she was dragged away. Ted was never a suspect, working at the bar and all. They weren't even sure that what got her was human.

When I heard about what happened to Keith, I couldn't help but chuckle in the face of it all. I'm glad one of us got out unscathed. And when it was all said and done, what else did we expect Keith to love the most? What was it he lost? Well, he got completely sober and joined the seminary. Now, he gets high on Jesus and preaching, and he's on the straight and narrow. He has no use for the rest of us heathens now, and Ted and I have no interest in hearing about how everything that happened to us was part of God's plan. We haven't spoken in years.

That leaves Bret. What was Bret's one true love? It wasn't his talent or his career or his status that he had lost; it was what he loved most. One late spring night, Bret went missing. A girl he had been dating said he had gone out for a long walk along The James. He was apt to do this, liked to get high and stare out at the water and think of songs. He never came home. They scoured the river and never found his body. There were no reported sightings of him. He had simply disappeared off the face of the earth.

The label scraped up enough new studio demos, B-sides, cut tracks, and other stuff Bret had lying around to release a posthumous album. It got an 8.7 on Pitchfork and made numerous "Best Of" lists at the end of the year. I didn't listen to the album to see if any more of my old songs were on there. I wouldn't have been able to tell the difference.

Sometimes I think maybe he wasn't going to the river to brood, but rather to stare at his reflection in the water like good ol' Narcissus, the guy from Greek mythology. Maybe there's a wildflower growing along The James with Bret's name on it, coming back year after year accompanied by its one true love: the reflection of itself on the river's surface.

There's a void in me that will never be filled, something that once gave me so much joy that I can't find a replacement for. When I look at my wife and child, I realize I'm lesser than the person I could have been. I'm just not as happy.

Yeah, I hate to keep harping on myself and boo-fucking-hoo on me when there are people that have actually died, but my experience is all I've really got. There's a more disturbing implication to what has happened to me, something that I'm ultimately thankful for, but that I'm not sure I can ever forgive myself for.

If I look into my heart of hearts, I know that the rules were right. My family was spared because there was something out there that I simply loved more. What kind of guy leaves his woman and kid behind alone at home while he goes off and chases his little rock and roll fantasy? The kind of guy that has other priorities.

I remember something a roadie once said during one of

our bigger tours. He was grizzled and had the appearance of a man who had been ridden hard and put up wet. As we smoked and drank at one of the many aftershow parties, he said this with experience in his voice: "Women come and women go and divorces happen and friends die and kids grow up. But in the end, the one thing that is always there, is the music."

Except in my case.

Perhaps I was cracking up. Perhaps I needed to take a break. Perhaps I was at risk of being swallowed up by "The Rules of the Road." Perhaps it had already happened.

"If the radio signal was coming from a stationary point in a specific location and was continually broadcasting, then the radio direction finder might lead you there."

"So it won't work on a signal that's broadcasting through time and space, potentially another dimension?"

"Do what now?"

"Like this signal I'm looking for has been broadcast in different regions and time periods. We're talking all across the country."

"Then, no, I'm afraid it won't help you. You might have better luck paging Elvis or giving E.T. a ring."

13

"LOSING MY RELIGION"

Timothy Harper had never shared his story with anyone else before. It was a written account compiled from journal entries and writings from his adolescence. The truth he had seen and the truth that was later reported were two different things. He would come to accept the rational explanation while keeping his own truth buried for years.

That is, until he found my website.

I remember the backseat: David and I next to each other amidst piles of luggage, the suitcases and duffels and backpacks forming a shelf behind our headrests where we stashed junk food and bottles of Mountain Dew. Between us on the seat was David's bright yellow Panasonic Shockwave, the portable CD player that was guaranteed not to skip no matter how rough the terrain was. It was built like a tank. You could flick the thing, like thump it really good, and the song would still play without missing a beat.

David's dad had acquired this marvel of technology by some sort of Marlboro cigarettes rewards system. You could trade in box tops for points and exchange the points for all sorts of merchandise, like ten points per pack and 150 points for a carton or something like that. This was back when cigarette companies could actually bribe you to smoke with promotions. They hadn't planned on the craftiness of David's dad, though. Dude didn't even smoke but went ham on those things. Cashed in on all his co-workers that smoked like chimneys, bought 'em from people for quarters, picked up litter.

We each shared the earbud headphones that snaked from the player into a fork into our separate ears. David with the right and me with the left. I think we were listening to blink-182 or some other pop-punk band that played catchy music with power chords and irreverent lyrics about sex and alcohol.

We were headed toward some sort of youth conference put on by the Baptists. I guess that listening to vulgar music with cuss words on a CD player sponsored by Big Tobacco while we rode in the back of a church van seemed a little contradictory, but we rationalized it in the way only good Christians could.

I was a God-fearing kid at that point in my life, an everything-fearing kid, actually. Teachers, my parents, bullies, girls—if it had some sort of power over me, I was afraid of it. It's not that I walked through those years as a fearful ball of nerves like some sort of quivering chihuahua; I put on a pretty good front. I believed it was important to have a good poker face and keep a low profile. That's how you kept them from noticing you, from seeing the weakness. But on the inside, I was a giant wuss.

Fifteen hadn't been a good year for me. I'm sure it's that way for a lotta folks out there. I mean, what could you possibly have going for you? An awkward body and hormones raging and stupid, impulsive thinking and not knowing who or what you are, and you have these emotional storms and you're hungry all the time and you don't even have a driver's license yet and you still have to do homework.

Maybe it would've been different if I was one of the cool kids, a time of great discovery and new experiences. But I wasn't. I was unathletic as hell and unmotivated to boot, a slacker just trying to get through each school day with good enough grades to make my parents happy and without getting my ass kicked. The high school was big enough to be intimidating to a kid like me but small enough that I couldn't float through anonymously.

On top of all of this teenage angst and anxiety, I was nursing a devastating and embarrassing lovesickness. To my fifteen-year-old self, it was a turmoil the likes of which I had never known. I carried the pain of this unrequited love longer than I should have. I couldn't get rid of it, no matter how hard I tried.

Her name was Emily Bruenig, and she was beautiful and smart and funny. I was in love with her. Her eyes were shimmering almonds and her lower lip was as plump as an overstuffed sofa cushion. My daily thoughts settled heavily upon her and her gleaming white smile, the auburn hair cascading down onto her shoulders. I even had dreams of her, dreams where her disembodied voice called me down a long hallway and I followed her and never could quite catch up.

Back in eighth grade, I had my chance. Several times, circumstance would have it we'd be sitting by each other in the bleachers for some school function or another and I would be cutting up and getting her laughing so hard that her mouth would be agape with her teeth shining white. She would lightly touch my arm in an "oh stop" sort of way and my insides would fill with something like warm, bubbly soda.

Toward the end of our eighth-grade year, I got her phone number. I had a string of successful phone calls with her, conversations that stretched long into the night. I would imagine her in her bedroom and how she looked as she sprawled out on her bed, the phone receiver next to her face. There was an intimacy in all of this that threatened to swallow me up. Her voice and breath in my ear, traveling those few miles across town through the landline. And though I desperately wanted to take her out to the movies or something, I could've died happy right there in those moments.

Of course, I never asked her out. The anxiety kept me from doing so. It wasn't fear of rejection that kept me from asking her. Sure, there would be a finality in hearing her say no, but I feel like I could handle *that.* Anything would've beat the zone I currently occupied, the purgatory of "what if she says yes" versus "what if she says no." I certainly didn't have her now and that hurt. What kept me from asking her was something more primal. It was abject fear and anxiety. I'd freeze up. My words caught in my throat many times, unable to come out. I was a kid pacing back and forth anxiously in front of a roller coaster before deciding that he's too much of a chicken to take a seat in the cart.

As the first couple weeks of summer passed, I sensed a shift in my phone conversations with Emily. She seemed distracted. There were long pauses. I think she was getting bored with me and I became self-conscious. I definitely couldn't ask her out *now*. She probably liked me less now than she ever did, could barely feign enthusiasm on the phone with me. How could she possibly get excited about going to the movies with me?

"Welp. Guess I'll see you around this summer," I remember saying in our final phone conversation, the awkwardness between us a chasm I just couldn't cross.

"Oh, yeah. Sure. See ya around, Timothy," she said, her voice suddenly bright once again. Even though the new positive tone in her voice was out of niceness or perhaps a joy that she was finally getting off the phone with me, I hung on for dear life on the way she had said my name. It replayed on a loop in my mind.

See ya around, Timothy.

Timothy.

   Timothy.

She wants you to call this summer.

Don't push your luck. Give her a little space.

She's bored and at home alone and wants to hang out and do something.

Call her. Ask her. Call her.

   I never did.

WE WERE in a caravan with a couple of other church vans and a small shuttle bus. All in all, there were about twenty-four kids and about six chaperones composed of the youth minister, parents, and whatever other volunteers they could muster from the church.

Our destination was Fort Worth, Texas. The Baptists had rented hotel rooms and had purchased tickets for Six Flags in Arlington. David's the one who had invited me to this whole ordeal. It was his church, after all. We were responsible for paying fifty bucks and whatever extra meals we might need. The church covered the rest. I guess they figured that roping in a few nonbelievers or getting a few converts by way of a flashy youth convention and a day at Six Flags was worth the expense.

Why I was going on this whole trip was not out of obligation or anything like that. I wasn't even Baptist (I was Methodist). It wasn't even for the Six Flags trip (I didn't like roller coasters). It was one reason and one reason only: Emily. She was attending with some of her friends.

It was going to be about eight hours of driving from our sleepy Kansas town. Fine by me. With the CD player at my side and our stash of junk food, let me ride in the back of this van all day (although the constraints of my filled bladder had me rethinking the Mountain Dew). That stretch of road down I-35 wasn't the most scenic, just flat land and nondescript prairies. It wasn't even impressive in its flatness. It had enough tree cover and shifts in topography to keep it from being an expanse of limitless horizon, but not enough rolling hills to be interesting. Billboards and semis and fast-food restaurants and piles of red dirt and interstate rolled past.

The van David and I found ourselves in was heavy on dudes. A feisty old guy named Jerry was the driver. He cursed the traffic in a nice Christian way, darns and hecks and all that. The other seats were staggered with some obnoxious younger boys I didn't really know and a couple of letter-jacket-wearing kids from our class, jocks with crispy gelled hair who mostly ignored me and David.

I didn't know whether to be relieved or disappointed that Emily wasn't in our vehicle. How could I start up a conversation? What would I say to her? Could I only sit back in jealousy as the Dustins and Harrisons with the bleached tips stole her attention? I needed to psych myself up. Maybe I could find myself in her vehicle for the ride back, break the ice at some point during the trip.

I would be lying if I said I hadn't obsessed over all of this and had some designs on how I could imagine this trip playing out. Once we had entered high school, I kept tabs on Emily's relationship status. She dated an upperclassman for a while, Josh Livingston. He was a basketball phenom that was the leading scorer on the team as a Junior. But they had broken up, and she was single now. And maybe somewhere in the back of my mind I had a chance. We would hang out on this trip and have fun and I would make her laugh and then, toward the end of the trip somewhere, I would finally ask her out. I would do it this time for sure.

I even prayed over it, asking God to please grant me the strength to ask her out, bargained with him and told him I would be perfect from now on. Or at least I would try to be.

The caravan convened at a hotel in downtown Ft. Worth, and the kids piled out of their respective vehicles, milled about the parking lot. I could see Emily from afar, amidst a group of girls from our grade: Liz Crenshaw, Stacy Deviney, and Jill Freeman. I tried my best to not obsess over her and instead focus on the present moment. Any sort of desperation at this point would be off-putting. I knew I had to play it cool. As we awaited our room assignments, I watched from afar.

David and I got matched up with a weird younger kid named Billy that had a bowl cut and constantly talked about Pokémon. We had a chaperone named Jay, a deacon of the church, according to David. He was sort of a country cowboy type of dude, sported jeans and boots and a mustache.

"What the hell's a deacon?" I asked David.

"Don't really know. They hand out the offering plate and sit in the back of the church."

This would be the room set up for the rest of the trip. Not just the two nights here in Arlington, but also our final night at a different hotel on our way back home. I got the sense that Jay would've been better suited with some different kids, someone he could talk football or hunting with. He wouldn't find that with us: a couple of scrawny nerds and video game aficionados. And I definitely couldn't see him striking up a conversation about Pokémon with Billy. At least we'd all be pretty quiet and easy to ignore.

The conference was called "Extreme Devotion: Becoming Radical Followers in Christ" and it was being held in this big-ass arena with steep stadium-style seating. It was this whole extreme sports theme. They gave us program booklets with motocross guys plastered on the cover and there were large screens playing footage of skateboarders, skydivers, hang gliders, and bikers. Up on the main stage was a half-pipe and some rails and ramps. To the right of that was a full band set-up. A haze of artificial fog wafted up to our seats in the nosebleed section.

The main speaker was a spiky-haired lad who wore jeans and tennis shoes, played it like he was a hip guy who wasn't far removed from our current ages and could totally relate to the trials and tribulations of teenagers. Since we were all teens, the talk focused heavily on the things that teens liked to do: sex, drugs, rock and roll. They told us all about how all of those things were bad news and went against how God wanted us to live. They used specific verses from the scripture to back themselves up.

Our body was a temple that drugs and alcohol would only defile. Wasn't it enough that there was addiction and overdoses and drunk driving accidents? In attempting to banish us from these sins, God was only trying to protect us from terrible outcomes. Or were these simply the punishments he doled out for disobeying him?

As for rock and roll, it only glorified all of which we should abstain from. It was a gateway that led to corrupt thoughts and desires. We were told to be selective about what we let into our minds. Nobody said it was the devil's music during this conference, but when read between the lines, it was heavily implied.

"Christian rock is definitely okay, though! All in the name of our heavenly Father," the hip preacher guy said before the band played a few songs, complete with a guitar solo that the lead singer said was heaven sent.

At some point, the talk had moved on to sex. The speaker had a lot to say on that subject. Being as we were an arena full of teenagers and the hormones were dripping off the rafters, he probably felt like he had to address the elephant in the room. It was the usual talk about the preciousness of virginity and the importance of abstinence. Marriage and sex were a sacred covenant between a man and woman, the act of them becoming one flesh.

I couldn't help but think of Emily during all this sex talk. Was she still a virgin? I sure as hell was. I had never even kissed anyone at this point in my life. What if we could lose our virginity together? Maybe not wait until we were actually married, but had been together a long time, long enough to be in love and love each other? Wasn't that what was important in the eyes of God? Love?

I looked back to where she was sitting a row behind me. She was with Stacy and Jill. Nearby were Todd Higgins and Ricky Frizzell, a pair of popular upperclassmen. Todd tapped Emily's shoulder, leaned in close, and told her something. She laughed and said something back. An irrational jealousy surged through me, an urgency that my time was running out.

The hip minister of the thing had now moved on to homosexuality, told us how God had designed men to be with women because he had made Adam and Eve, not Adam and Steve. That was just one of the many zingers he had to share regarding gay people. I had heard about the Baptist obsessions with gays from David, said that it was a topic of many a fiery sermon and the pastor frequently said America was on the brink, in part because of the gays.

There was a break in the action. Lunch at a BBQ place and a quick detour through a shopping mall where David and I bought *Surfer Rosa* by the Pixies. Coming out of the store, we ran into Emily and Stacy.

"Careful. They say that's a gateway drug," Emily said, gesturing at the Sam Goody bag in my hand.

"Oh, this is definitely Christian music," I said, holding up the CD. It featured a topless lady on the front. I don't know why I showed her. I think maybe I wanted to impress her? In the album's background, a crucifix hung on a wall. "See, there's a cross."

Emily was unfazed. Kinda raised her eyebrow and made a clicking sound with her mouth. "Are those titties Christian?"

"Hey," David interjected. "Boobs are proof that God loves us and wants us to be happy. I think Ben Franklin said that."

"Oh my *God*," said Stacy.

"Tsk, tsk. Lord's name in vain," Emily chided.

At this point—with none of us even realizing it—we were walking and talking with them, strolling through the mall like we were all friends. Our break was running out, and we were supposed to be making our way back to the conference. Across the mezzanine, we could see more members of our youth group making their way to the mall's exit.

"Hey, look! It's Adam and Steve!" a voice boomed from behind us. It was Dustin Phillips, an annoying sophomore prick. He was talking about me and David.

"Just ignore him," Emily told me. "Probably pissed off that there's no Abercrombie in this mall."

And then we were exiting the mall and entering the arena and filing down the aisle into our seats. I was sitting by Emily. My luck was actually playing out, and I was filled with both surprise and a belief that this was all destined to be. Sometimes good things did happen to mediocre people. You just had to wait.

We talked and whispered through the remainder of the conference. I cracked jokes and made her laugh. We were sitting close enough in the cramped seats I could smell her perfume or body spray or whatever. I never found out what it was called, but sometimes while walking in public I'll catch a whiff of it and I can feel my heart sink way down deep into my guts and I get tears in my eyes.

The next morning, I sat in the backseat of the church van alone. I had snuck down to get some time to myself and get a listen to my new CD. We had done an impromptu devotional service in a small conference room at the hotel and everyone else was packing up and clearing out the rooms.

Our next destination was Six Flags Over Texas in Arlington. We would spend the day there and then start the drive back, staying overnight at a hotel along the way before arriving back in Kansas on President's Day.

I was familiar with the song "Where Is My Mind" by The Pixies and that had been my motivation to purchase the album. The rest was unfamiliar territory for me, and it sounded kind of weird and quirky. There were songs sung in weird barking vocals and lyrics in Spanish. A song started playing that sounded instantly familiar; in fact, I was certain I had heard it that very weekend.

It was a song called "Sanctuary," a staple that was played by acoustic guitar-wielding youth ministers in churches all across the region in those days. It's a classic sing-along tune with a simple melody, but here playing on my headphones was something more sinister and disturbing. A full choir of voices was singing, and I could hear the crackling of flames and distressed cries of pain and sobs and screams elsewhere in the background. All the while, the choir sang on and on, undeterred.

My world shrank to that backseat, and I ignored the luggage and bags being tossed behind me, the filing in of the occupants of the vehicle. There was a jaunty run of high-pitched notes played on an organ, and then a voice spoke, addressing me. A voice that I can only assume has spoken to so many others.

How we doing out there today, folks? Oh, what a glorious morning it is, ladies and gents. I'm feeling mighty blessed on this fine day. Does it get any better than waking up to find that they're not shoveling dirt in your face? That you've still got air in your lungs and tears in your eyes and aches in your joints. I tell you it's a blessing to simply be alive despite all the bullcrap we have to put up with to simply walk around on this earth. At least that's how I feel today. Ask me again tomorrow or the day after, or one of the many days beyond infinite. I'm sure I'll change my mind.

Whoops! Got a little off track there and forgot to introduce myself. Buck Hensley's the name. I'm the voice behind a little program known as "The Rules of the Road." You may have heard of it. If not, well, stick around. A lot of folks have heard of it and it's come to my attention that a lot of people ain't too happy with "The Rules." They're saying that "The Rules" are too hard to follow. They're saying that the rules are simply not fair. Many are saying that the rules are just downright evil.

And to that I say, "horse pucky!" Oh, sure some folks have died or gotten maimed along the way, but that's not my fault. Everything happens for a reason. It's all part of God's plan. I mean, I guess. Speaking of God and rules, he sure has had some doozies. Some of those rules and consequences make "The Rules of the Road" look like something you'd find at a daycare.

I mean, let's run through a few of 'em, shall we? Don't look back at the destruction of this city or I'll turn you into sodium chloride. Your husband will think of you every time he seasons his popcorn. Don't cut your hair or I'll take away your strength.

Sorry, I kinda screwed up on the design of the whole male genitalia thing so you're gonna have to cut a bit of meat from your baby's peepee or I won't let him into heaven. Don't eat this delicious apple that I put here just to tempt you, or I will take away your paradise.

Not trying to deflect or nothing like that. I'm just saying I ain't the only one that has a history of this sort of thing. And I think that I'm a little more fair than the other guy, if I do say so myself.

With all that said, I've got an easy rule for y'all to follow. No, seriously. Trust me. No fakeouts and no tricks. Scout's honor. Cross my heart and hope to die, and believe me, I've been hoping and wishing and thinking and praying for that.

If at any point during your journey you come across a cemetery, then you must hold your breath when you pass. I am talking about the entire duration that you or your vehicle is parallel with the final resting place of so many dearly departed souls. The dead get jealous of our living breath, so you must hold it until you are well past them.

What happens if you fail to follow this rule? Then the dead will catch sight of that juicy breath of yours and break a couple little rules of their own. Hopefully, you don't find out which ones.

I reckon that's all I got for you today. A simple little rule for a simple little boy. Hope that teenage romance works out for ya. They so seldom do. Stay safe out there. Stay lively. Stay holy. I'm Buck Hensley and these are "The Rules of the Road."

> I came out of my trance with David tapping me.
> "How is it?" he asked, nodding at the CD player.
> "What? Oh. Dude, listen to this creepy-ass skit."

I handed the headphones over to him and I cued up the track. He smirked a little while it played. I could hear music through his headphones, the vocals and music of the Pixies.

"That's not it. Lemme see. It was right *here*," I said to myself.

Try as I might—skipping through all the tracks, fast forwarding—I never found it again.

There are certain things I'll always remember about my day at Six Flags. They were all centered on Emily. In hindsight, I wish I hadn't been so dead set on those moments spent with her; other things were worth remembering. Yet, they have slipped away into the blur of things forgotten.

It's not like I had her completely to myself that day. It wasn't the equivalent of a date or anything like that. David was with me, and her friends were there, and the older guys Todd and Ricky drifted in and out of the picture. But there were moments I shared with her and her alone.

I remember riding up in the front cart with Emily on the Texas Giant, a massive wooden roller coaster, her saying, "I may grab you if I get too freaked out," and me hoping it would happen (it didn't). I remember her thighs pressed up against me in the cart, the wind whipping her hair into glorious tangles and the air on her teeth as she screamed and laughed as we plummeted down that first hill. There were the freckles on the bridge of her nose and the spoon gliding in and out of her mouth. We shivered and ate Dippin' Dots on a bench under naked trees and a winter sky while we waited for the others to get off one of those upside-down coasters.

Soon we were making our way to the exits, toward the waiting church vans. I could feel an encroaching dread as Emily's group got separated from mine and David's, and I could see her from afar, talking and flirting with Todd. Was he going to steal my chance? Time was of the essence.

But luck or fate or God intervened once again, and somehow, I ended up with her sitting beside me in the church van. We rode off into the night, the lights of the urban sprawl all around. Crisis averted for now. I knew I couldn't blow another chance. I would do it this time, no excuses. I would finally ask her out. My mind raced at what could only be inevitable.

I will be your boyfriend. This summer I'll get my license and I'll be the boyfriend you never knew you could have. We can talk long into the night and I'll rub your back and we'll go on adventures in my new car, see things none of us have ever seen. I'll always listen to you and be there for you and I will worship the ground you walk on because you deserve nothing less.

I just needed to wait until closer to the end of the trip in case she said no, so I wouldn't have to endure any awkwardness for the remainder.

She won't say no.

We were herking and jerking through stop lights and traffic. The flowing ride of the interstate was not yet in sight. On my right and under orange streetlights is where I saw it, behind a brick retaining wall. The headstones and markers were visible above the waist-high wall, and I could see a sign that read: Parker Memorial Gardens. I stopped breathing, held the last inhale I had taken right there in my chest. If only I had seen it up ahead, I could've gotten a big breath in advance, could've told Emily what I was doing.

Emily, who was saying, "Did you hear me, Timothy? What's your dream car?"

I could only raise my eyebrows and shrug at her, look out the window and watch as the cemetery creeped past.

"Something wrong? Are you getting car sick? I swear to God if you puke in here, I'll be right behind you. It will be like that one movie."

I shook my head no, gestured at the graveyard, puffed out my cheeks.

"Oh, I know this," she said. "You're doing that thing! Holding your breath for good luck. My sister and I used to do that." She glanced back at the graveyard and our position in relation to it. The van was stopped. The interior stained red as rows of brake lights blared in front of us. "Hope you're an Olympic caliber type of dude or else I don't think you're gonna make it."

I wiped my brow, tapped my wrist like a watch. My lungs were burning a little. Could I go until I passed out?

Emily got a mischievous look on her face, a look I sometimes replay in my mind on certain dark nights. Her fingers were wagging at me. She pounced. I tried to croak out a *no*. The brake lights blinked out. The van creeped forward while I staved off the attacks on my armpits. I writhed and twisted in my seat, squirming away from her. She only laughed. It was the stomach that did me in. Flinching and exhaling, I forgot all about my task at hand and joined in with her laughter.

"Dammit. Do you realize what you've done?" I asked.

"No?"

I thought about it for a moment. I really had no idea what was going to happen. There was no reason to believe the rule was a real thing, that it would hold me to its consequences.

"Me neither, " I said.

Still, later we would ride in a comfortable silence and Emily would nod off in the seat next to me, her head eventually finding its way to rest on my shoulder. The weight of it there, the warmth of her face. It was enough to give me a raging hard on. I would weep for a time so simple and losing an innocence such as that, a world where a girl's head on your shoulder was some sort of steamy foreplay. I could mourn for this loss of innocence if there weren't so many tears that have been shed since then.

It was a Holiday Inn Express with all of the usual trappings: green carpet lining the halls, keycard entry, mass-produced Thomas Kincades hanging on the wall, an indoor pool.

Down the hall from the pool, there was a continental breakfast area with tables and chairs. I was down there with David and Emily, Liz, Stacy, and Jill. We were playing Uno until lights out. Ricky and Todd and some older girls were in the indoor pool. I could hear their loud voices and laughter echoing off the tiled walls.

After this game, I was going to ask Emily. I was too nervous to ask in front of all of her friends. My voice would come out all shaky and embarrassing. I would distract her and pull her aside where it was just me and her and say, "do you wanna go to the movies sometime?" When I put it that way, yeah, it seemed ridiculously simple. It was just my stupid teenage brain that had inflated it to a monumental task.

In came Todd from the pool, shirtless and with a towel wrapped around his waist. He was all cut up and six packed and muscled arms. He plopped right by Emily, his hair dripping.

"Ew, Todd. You're gonna get me wet," Emily said, and then he raised his eyebrows and everyone at the table laughed except me. "Shut up. Not like that!" She said and hit his arm.

I got a burning, jealous feeling in my stomach.

Soon our room chaperone Jay had appeared and was telling us, "Fifteen minutes, guys." We wrapped up whatever game we were playing, and I couldn't help but notice Emily wasn't into it as before. She was too distracted as Todd kept teasing her. It was the way she smiled at him, the change in her body language and the subtle shift in the way she sat in her chair. Before I knew what was happening exactly, Emily and Todd were sneaking off ahead of us down the hall and into the stairwell, to destinations unknown.

"Bummer, dude. Older guys are always gonna have a leg up. You ok?" David said. It was just us. Everyone else had gone up to their rooms on the third floor.

My mouth had gone dry. I said nothing because what was there to say? Besides, my voice might crack into a sort of cry, as I could already feel my eyes water.

"I'll be up in a sec," I choked out. I burst into the lobby restroom and stared at my pathetic face and red eyes before splashing them with cold tap water.

Coming back into the lobby, I encountered a strange sight. The bare back of an elderly man, pale and liver spotted. He wasn't even wearing *pants*. Just boxers and dress socks pulled past his calves. He stood at the front desk counter and my eyes were glued to him in bewilderment while I crossed the lobby. His head remained fixated and staring forward, tufts and strands of gray hair combed over a bald peak.

I kept my eyes fixed on him as I passed. He had a blank expression, facial muscles slack and corners of his mouth drooping. Deep-set, sad eyes stared into nothing. Above his collar bone was some sort of surgical repair, thick white cord woven through the skin like a baseball stitch. He pounded on the service bell with a flattened palm, the chiming of which I heard over and over as I made my way down the hall into the stairwell.

The bizarre scene got my mind off Emily for the time being, but the respite was short-lived. The First Baptist Church had the entire reign of the 3rd floor. As I entered the third floor, a head darted in and out of a darkened room.

"What up, Timmy?" Todd said as he looked down the hall both ways and realized it was just me. "I'm just making sure the coast is clear. If anyone asks, you never saw me here. Emily, too."

"Emily's back there?" I asked, trying to look past him in the darkened room he was leaning out of. His body blocked my view. The door that was partially closed with a sign that read HOUSEKEEPING.

"Nope," he responded and gave me a wink, and shut the door.

Our room was located in the middle of the hall, the stairwells on either side and a bank of elevators in the middle. I slumped back there and stumbled over Billy sleeping on the floor. A solitary lamp was on and deacon Jay stared up at the ceiling. David was already nodding off in the bed we would share. I brushed my teeth and put some gym shorts on and crawled into the bed.

Sleep wouldn't come. Dark thoughts filled my mind. What was going on in that utility closet with Emily and Todd? Didn't she know the type of guy he was? I knew about Todd and guys like him. He had been an invite to this youth thing. It wasn't like he was a strict practitioner of Christianity and chastity and abstinence. He had the reputation of being a player. If anything, he was going to use her for one thing and one thing only, another notch in his belt. Is that what she really wanted?

Oh, Emily. I would never want you for just that. We will be each other's firsts and it will be special and something we'll never forget. I'll put candles on the windowsill. We'll drive out to an empty pasture with blankets and sleeping bags and make love underneath the stars.

I could hear Jay snoring in the opposite bed. David was motionless beside me. My heartbeat wouldn't slow down, and neither would my thoughts. This feeling was not going to go away unless I got out of bed and walked down the hall and found out for myself if the worst was actually happening. I tried to rationalize it. What if Todd was taking things further than Emily was comfortable with? What if she didn't want to go all the way? I could be her savior from all the guilt and shame that would surely follow.

I tried to ignore the images that played in my mind. My stomach filled with dread at what I would find in the closet. Surely there would be lots of clean sheets and pillows for them to be comfortable on. Towels to clean up with after. A dirty laundry bag to put the evidence in.

The housekeeping room was just up ahead, past the ice and vending machines. The hallway was empty, and I couldn't hear a thing. No talking or laughter from the rooms. Everyone was exhausted from a full day at Six Flags no doubt. I could hear the hum of the ice machine and a fresh batch clattering in the machine startled me.

Then I heard several deep gasps, something wet. I froze where I stood, a stone sinking in the pit of my stomach. It wasn't too late to turn back. I didn't have to see this. I could just turn around and go back to bed, forget I had ever even seen Todd, forget that Emily was with him. What would've changed if I did? Maybe I wouldn't be here. I could have drifted off to sleep and never woken up.

But I never made it to the utility closet. The sounds weren't coming from there, but from the adjacent room. I struggled to process the scene laid out before me. There was a hissing noise coming from a gaping mouth, a pool of dark blood on linoleum, wet, clammy skin. A busted can of Dr. Pepper fizzed and bubbled out on the floor in front of the Coke machine. Ricky Frizzel lay with his body twisted at an odd angle, wedged against the wall. A weak hand clung to a mess of gore spurting at his throat. His tongue protruded down below his chin, hanging not from his mouth but from the shredded flesh of his neck.

I could see the bare back of the old man that was hunched over him, the man from the front desk. The fingers of Ricky's other hand were in his mouth, his jaw working. His lips and neck and shirt had the look of a man at a sloppy joe eating competition. Ricky's glassy eyes stared up at me and he strained to call out, but only a wet gag escaped.

My trembling legs carried me back to my room, to a door I couldn't open. I had forgotten my damn keycard. Fearful of making too much noise, I tapped lightly on the door and waited, scanning the hallway for anyone following me.

There was no answer.

A little louder.

The hallway remained empty.

I gave a continuous knock until the door jerked open, Jay squinting into the light at me.

"What in the world, Timothy?"

I pushed past him and into the dark room, slamming the door.

"Ricky . . . it's . . . he's ..." the words were caught in my throat. I had never been so utterly speechless, like the speech center of my brain had been knocked out by pure fear.

"What are you doing out of the room?"

"He needs help," I managed.

Jay flicked on a lamp, grabbed me by the arms, and sat me on the bed. "Okay, just calm down and tell me what's going on."

I took some deep breaths. "Ricky's bleeding. I think a dead guy bit his throat out. A dead guy from a funeral home." The words came out fast, all mushed together.

Jay rubbed his eyes, winced, and tried to process the insanity I had just given him. "Look, Timothy. Do you think you might have had a nightmare? You ever been a sleepwalker?"

Something about his incredulity and exasperated tone took me back to reality. "I know what I saw. I'm telling you that Ricky's seriously injured. We need to call someone and help him out."

"Look, where was he?"

"Down by the Coke machine."

"Okay. I'll take a look. Will be careful and even take this," he said, rummaging through his duffel bag. "Brought my concealed carry just in case. Gotta love Dallas," he said, tucking a holster into his waistband. "When I get back you *have* to get some sleep."

He slid out the door. I thought of watching him from the doorway but figured it best to just hunker down in the room and await the gunshots. Or—hopefully—wait for him to come into the room shaking his head, telling me those crazy upperclassmen had pulled quite the prank, that I was only the fifth one they had scared that evening. But five minutes passed, and I got nervous.

David was still asleep. Hadn't even moved a muscle since I had come in. I poked him awake.

"Sup, dude?" he asked with his eyes closed.

"David. Man, something bad's happened. You're never gonna believe it, but I think Ricky's dead."

David sprung up. "What?"

"I'm as serious as a heart attack, dude. Somebody killed him. Jay's investigating it right now. I thought maybe . . . I wasn't so sure what I saw. Maybe a hallucination."

"What do you mean, killed him?" He sure was awake now.

"Cut his throat. Chewed his throat. I dunno. But I found him, and I think the guy who did it was still there. He didn't see me."

"Where's Jay now?" David asked.

"I don't know. He should be back now."

"Dude. You're fucking with me." David rose to go to the door, but my desperate look and how hard I pushed him forced him to reconsider.

"Do. Not. Go."

"Alright, alright," he said, holding his hands. "If you're

that serious, you need to call the front desk. They've got security at these places or people they can call."

"Duh," I said, amazed at my ignorance.

I picked up the phone. There was no dial tone. I hung up and tried again, traced the cord back to the wall. It was plugged in. "There's no service. Like it's been cut or something."

"What? Let me see." David investigated the phone and concluded the very thing I had just told him.

"I told you so."

"Well, shit, what do you want to do? Just wait it out? Sure, we could be safe in our room," David said.

I thought about it all for a while. There wasn't any harm in waiting a little while longer. I got to thinking about it all, what it was I had seen. This was all because of that rule I had failed to follow. Had to be. What was it that the Buck guy had said? That the dead would get jealous and break a few rules of their own?

I had seen a zombie movie or two. Whoever they bit and killed ended up just like them, joined their ranks. Maybe that's what we were dealing with. The old guy at the counter was clearly the undead, a zombie or something. Or maybe he was a vampire. Whatever he was, he was coming, and there was a chance he was making more of them.

"I think he got the front desk lady," I said.

"Who?" David asked.

"Dead guy that killed Ricky."

"*Dead* guy?"

"You know what that means. Means that she could help him cut the phones. Means that she could make a master keycard."

"Dude, what are you talking about?"

"Imagine them silently going room to room, finding people asleep in their beds. They don't even need to break in."

"I'm seriously thinking about going back to bed."

"Their army gets bigger and bigger with each room they clear," I said, thinking aloud.

"Man, I don't . . . hey, did you know Billy was gone?" David asked.

I looked down at where I had stumbled over him on my way to bed earlier, the gap between the two queen beds. There was just an empty pallet. The bathroom was empty, too.

"He was right here. I tripped over his ankles on my way to bed," I said, lifting the comforter and pillows from the floor that formed the pallet.

Just then there was a knock at the door, slow and steady. David started for the door as if nothing had happened, as if there wasn't a potential hotel siege going on.

"David, man. Check the peephole," I said from my vantage point between the queen beds.

"It's just Billy," he said, with his face pressed against the door.

David cracked the door open. I could see the black dome of Billy's bowl cut, his glasses, the Gameboy tucked in his hand. "Hey, buddy. What are you doing out so late?" David turned back to me. "Must've snuck out to get a Pokémon session in. Or hey, maybe he was meeting up with —woah, easy dude."

Billy had wrapped himself around David's midsection and started pushing off with his feet on the floor, the wall, the door. That's when I saw that the back of Billy's shirt was soaked, the strips of skin hanging underneath his shirt tail. David was being pushed back, tripped and screamed, Billy now upon him as they fell between the narrow gap formed by the beds and the dresser and TV.

It was like trying to separate a pair of fighting dogs, thrashing and clashing jaws and limbs. I didn't know where to put my hands, where to grab without getting bit.

David had a handful of chili bowl hair, and was screaming, "Get him off me! Get him off me! He's fucking biting!"

"I'm trying! I'm trying!"

My bare toes stubbed on Billy's skull as I kicked, to no avail. Even grabbing him by the ankles and yanking back as hard as I could, it only seemed to make him clamp down harder and give David a rug burn as they slid across the carpet.

There was blood. So much blood. David's yelling had devolved into a high-pitched wail, and I knew I had to think of something fast. Leaning out in the hall and screaming bloody murder for help may have been the most logical decision, in a world without rabid zombie ten-year-olds, and maybe even still. But I could only focus on getting Billy off of David.

There wasn't an extra gun in Jay's duffel. He hadn't been that paranoid. I started thinking of blunt instruments. The phone was heavy plastic that only glanced off Billy's head. What did it was the porcelain tank lid off the back of the toilet. It broke in two after the second strike and it was enough to daze him, knocking him back far enough for David to scoot to safety.

Billy lay on his back, blood and shiny pieces of tissue covering his face and mouth. He snarled and slobbered and looked ready to strike again. I couldn't hesitate. There was no turning back from what I had started. So, like Moses coming off Mount Sinai, I raised my porcelain tablet high and drove it down again and again into that snarling mouth, those glazed over eyes. Teeth scattered on the carpet, and he still wouldn't quit snapping. Finally, after a clear separation between jaw and cranium, a gaping hole between the two, Billy's second death was achieved.

David was a wreck and fading fast. When I saw the damage, a cry caught in my throat. My bare feet squished through the blood-soaked carpet as I rushed to his side.

That's when I saw he got the same glassy look in his eyes that Ricky had, his breathing shallow. All I could do was look frantically around and mumble obscenities, tell him to hold on that I was getting help, and wad up a bedsheet to place on his wrecked stomach.

God may have been pulling the strings on all of this, but that didn't stop me from pleading for his help in my brain. I had no plan from here. I could stay barricaded in my room until David perished, test the hypothesis that we were actually dealing with zombies here, zombies that could spread. That seemed like a sitting duck option, though. And I didn't really want to smash my best friend's head in, even an undead version. Better to just leave him shut in here, sneak out, and run to the nearest convenience store to call for help.

As always, my thoughts returned to Emily. I needed to make sure she was safe. Warn her and anyone else of what was going on, drag her with me. Hadn't I seen Emily coming in and out of a room at the opposite end of the hall when we first got here? Down by the stairwell?

I looked back at David one more time. "Hang on, man. I'm going to get some help," I said—for myself more than anything. I took a deep breath and stepped out into the hall.

It was a dumb idea. I should have at least poked my head out, gathered the lay of the land. But if I had, the sight I beheld would have kept me from ever working up the nerve to even leave my room.

To my left was a congregation of people at the end of the hall. They shuffled amongst each other like bodies trying to make their way through a crowd in a subway car. Some walked into walls like glitching video game characters, continuing their paces as if they could just slide on through solid matter eventually. I could see familiar faces and haircuts, kids and chaperones that had attended the conference. Ricky Frizzell with his torn open neck and missing fingers,

Liz Crenshaw with her blonde hair all disheveled and a wad of someone else's clutched in her hand. Bodies littered the floor.

Emily was nowhere to be seen, thank God. I made sure I scanned every face before ducking my head and going the opposite direction. Nobody seemed to regard me in any particular manner, and maybe it was because the leader was preoccupied. The last thing I saw was the old dead man in the boxers and the front desk lady opening another room. Several paces later, a scream followed.

I hadn't seen Jay either, which left me with a little hope. Maybe he was holed up somewhere with the gun that would save the rest of us. A little of that hope was dashed as further down the hall I saw his brown leather gun case, unzipped and strewn on the ground. Empty.

I went to where I had been going all along, picking up speed, wary of anything lurking around corners, past the bank of elevators where there was a ding, where Jerry the van driver pawed at his stainless-steel reflection and smeared a bloody handprint on the door.

In the dark utility room, the fluorescent lights flickered on, and I was greeted with the envious scene of Emily and Todd lying on a bag of laundry as if it were a beanbag chair. They were wrapped in each other's arms, and if there were ever a time I was glad to not see her naked, it was right now. Both were fully clothed, her in the crook of his arm with her head on his chest, eyes closed and long lashes resting on her cheeks. I remember that even in my panic and adrenaline-stricken state, my brain still found enough reserve to think, *God, she's gorgeous when she's sleeping.* And even after everything that had already happened, my heart sank a little over the implication of finding the two of them like this.

"Psst," I said, crouching beside them.

Todd stirred awake, his eyes squinting under the bright

light. "Timbo! Oh, shit dude. Is it late? You're a lifesaver. Em, Em," he said, shaking her awake.

"No, guys, it's serious," I said, waving my arms. "Bad shit is happening. People are dying. There's a gas leak and they want us to evacuate the building." I realized that explaining it that way would be easier to process.

They both sat up with a start.

"What do you mean, dying? Are Jill and Liz okay? Stacy?" Emily asked.

"You don't think anyone knows we didn't end up back in our rooms, do you?" Todd said.

"Guys . . . it's bad. We've got to go."

The door swung open, and a determined Jay moved swiftly across the room, gnashing his teeth. His head looked all wrong, a flap of his forehead hanging over his eye to reveal a patch of smooth pinkish skull, one of his arms shredded and dangling. He was gunning straight for Emily, who was closest to the door.

Todd leapt to action, cut him off with a shove and a right cross to the face. This only served as a mild distraction for undead Jay, only allowed enough time for Emily to scramble to her feet and me to pull her to the corner of the room.

"Timothy, what's going on?" she said in a hushed cry.

Todd and Jay were locked arm in arm, pushing against each other toward a goal that neither one of them really could understand.

"The hell's wrong with you, man?" Todd said through gritted teeth, bending Jay's fingers at ninety-degree angles. Jay only clacked his teeth in response.

I'd like to say that I was brave, a hero that could spring into the thick of it and save the day. But the truth of it is that I was hesitant. I hoped Todd would subdue Jay on his own, that I wouldn't be called to action. Todd was hollering with a chunk of his forearm bitten open and Emily was screaming at me to "do something! Do something!" before I did anything.

There was a fire extinguisher on a shelf beside us. I grabbed it and blasted a foamy white cloud into Jay's slobbering face. This was enough for Todd to break free, enough for Jay to be dazed and blinded and vulnerable. I swung the end of the extinguisher at his head, ineffective.

"Here," Todd said, swiping the blunt object from my hands.

He then kicked the shit out of Jay's legs, some sort of karate kung fu leg sweep. Jay hit the ground hard. He never even saw the rest coming. Emily covered her eyes. Foam and blood splattered the room, Todd caught up in the adrenaline and violence of the moment. He panted and looked at the crushed skull, the teeth and blood pooled sinuses and matted hair, all deformed into a crumpled Halloween mask with shards of gristle jutting from it.

"The fuck, Timbo? What the hell is going on?" Todd said as he caught his breath.

"I'm telling you, man. You ever see those zombie movies? It's like that. People are going crazy and biting each other. There's more like Jay. We'll be outnumbered soon. David already got bit pretty good. We gotta get outta here, hit the stairwell. Call for help."

"You sure we can't help the others?"

"Maybe hit a fire alarm on the way out. Alert them," I said.

"Emily, you coming?"

She nodded, tears running down her face. She was quivering. I don't think I'd ever seen her cry before. I wanted to comfort her. I found an alternative, something reassuring.

"Wait. Help me roll him over," I said, pointing at Jay. Tucked in the waistband of his pants it was there, the cold metal, the gun.

"You ever use one of those?" Todd asked.

"Not really," I shrugged.

"Give it to me." It was a simple revolver. He checked the cylinder and nodded, looking at both of us with a serious expression. "You guys ready? I'll take front. Emily, best you get in the middle."

Being as we were near the end of the hall, the stairwell wasn't far away. We could make a mad dash for it as soon as we exited the room. I guided Emily behind Todd as he crouched in a defensive posture and started for the door, emulating every cop or SWAT team we'd ever seen on TV. I took the fire extinguisher, figured it was better than nothing.

There was a stampede. Rows and rows of staring faces, just a couple yards away. There was weeping and gnashing of teeth. The hallway funneled them toward us. All those familiar faces, those people we knew, now dead-eyed and changed. The dead man in the boxers and dress socks stood toward the back, leading his charge by pointing a bony finger, his mouth agape and emitting some silent instruction the horde somehow understood.

I had to hand it to Todd. He could've easily veered to the right toward the stairwell, and they would've been on us in an instant. But no. He saw the mass a couple yards away from us and engaged them head on, spreading his arms wide as if he was going to cure them with a big ol' hug. When they did not heed this display, he drew the revolver, looked back at us.

"Go on. Go on!" he said, and there was a deafening gunshot.

There was no time to argue with him. The mass of people was right there, shoving Todd into us as he fired again and again. I pushed Emily toward the stairwell and grabbed the red fire alarm next to the door. But really, at this point, I don't know how much it would help. For the moment, it only added to the chaos.

I tried to yell back at Todd, to tell him he could make it,

but he was in the throes of the deadly mob, his body disappearing under limbs and hands, feet trampling him. His painful scream followed us into the stairwell.

Determined fear carried us down to the first landing. Emily winced and halted, a little cry like a wounded animal escaping her throat. There were more of them coming *up* the stairs. They crowded the stairwell like sardines, mouths flapping like fish out of water.

"The roof! The roof!" I shouted and now I was in front. I slammed my shoulder into the 3rd floor doorway. It rattled under immense pressure. Emily passed me and went up. I followed while the door banged open behind me.

We burst out onto the roof. The cold air was jarring, the dark sky overhead. There was the smell of tar and our feet crunched on gravel. Behind us, they came.

They were all there. I had made out Jill and Stacy and Liz in the crowd. Dustin Phillips. Ricky Frizzell. I even saw David in their midst, loops of intestine dangling. I guess he had figured out how to open the door. Todd and the dead guy in the suit walked side by side.

Shredded legs carried them closer on twisted ankles. Some crawled on hands and knees. Spittle flew as teeth clamped down over and over.

When we made it to the edge, we walked the perimeter of the roof. They would be upon us soon.

"Looks like as good a place as any," I said, looking at the tarped-over swimming pool below.

"I can't Timothy," Emily said. "I can't."

"Yes, you can. It'll be like jumping on a trampoline. It's only 3 stories. I'll hold your hand."

Our fingers intertwined, and I squeezed her hand.

She squeezed mine back.

I said a quick prayer.

"But I never heard about any zombie attack in the news," you might say.

You're right. Nobody did. If you look back some years though, you may read about the tragic story of the youth group who stayed the night at a Holiday Inn Express on their way back to Kansas, the youth group that perished in a freak carbon monoxide accident. Most of them had perished in their beds. Others were in critical condition and recovered with intensive treatment and therapies. Those survivors reported having the most awful dreams about the deceased. The dreams were the same.

Included among the perished was a funeral home director. He had been en route to transport a body for embalming. The director had died in his room on the second floor. The strange thing was that he had brought the body into the room with him. Despite the grim jokes that arose from this weird situation, nobody could explain why he would do such a thing. Maybe the carbon monoxide had put him in a delirious state?

Maybe it was oxygen deprivation that led two of the youth members to the roof. Did you hear about them? The ones that thought they could jump into the pool, the pool that was empty, and the tarp that gave away? The one that almost died and the one that did?

You may have heard the story from the bible about Jonah. You know the dude that got swallowed by the whale? Before that whale swallowed Jonah, he was fleeing God's call. He took refuge on a ship and God sent down a storm to root him out. The tumultuous storm threatened everyone aboard that ship. It wasn't until the sailors honored Jonah's request of being thrown overboard that the storm ceased, and the waters calmed.

Much like Jonah, I could've stopped the storm that we went through. By sacrificing myself to the dead, I could've ended that massacre that night. I didn't have it in me. Todd certainly did. I think about how he didn't flinch when it was time to step up, when he knew what he had to do.

I haven't had a lover since. Not out of a broken heart, but out of penance. I wasn't good enough to date her, wasn't good enough to save her. I often think about how differently things could've gone for her if I had only been a different person.

MY MOM SAYS, my dad says, "why don't you get out there and find yourself a nice girl?"

My coworkers say, "so and so has a sister that's single," and "I've got the perfect person for you to meet."

My dad says, "Look, it's ok to go out and *see* someone from time to time. It doesn't have to be anything serious."

But no, I say. I've already met the love of my life and she's dead and it should've been me. There's no one else that can replace her. We held hands on the way down. I cradled her limp body in my arms and kissed her bloody head and told her what I had always wanted to. And even if I was just a stupid kid that didn't know what those words really meant, had never actually felt the true versions, even though I never would feel those feelings again, I said them all the same.

I still say them to the yearbook photos I keep in my nightstand drawer, on the nights when the Jameson doesn't do what it's supposed to.

I DON'T PRAY ANYMORE. Just don't have it in me after the most important prayer of my life went unanswered. I guess

He in all His infinite Holiness couldn't have found it in Himself to save a young girl with her whole life ahead of her. I guess it was more important that He teach me a lesson about love and loss.

I'm no longer scared of Hell, either. Looking back, I never liked how they tried to scare us into believing with threats of fiery furnaces and lakes of fire. Yet, I've found some things don't work as well without a little fear. It gives us that extra motivation. Sure, the promise of paradise and eternal reward is a pretty good motivator, but the threat of hell really greases the wheels.

And I have seen hell on earth, brought about by a deity on the airwaves. A god that stuck by his word, a god that didn't pull any of this vague nonsense about it all being a part of some mysterious plan. Maybe that's a god worth worshipping?

I'd had enough; it was time to quit screwing around.

14

"THUNDER ROAD"

I followed the rules to a T. I answered the call of every unknown number, tucked a sock into every lone shoe on the side of the road, and I made sure I had plenty of cash on hand. I even held my breath past every graveyard.

I never saw any speed limit signs reading 67 MPH, and I never found any souvenir keychains with my name on them. My given name is uncommon, so no shocker there. Nevertheless, I still kept my eyes peeled.

Not one Geo Metro appeared before me in any Wal-Mart parking lots, and believe me, I looked.

I was far from the southeastern United States, so my diet was free of boiled peanuts.

I brought along ear plugs for any religious or titillating billboards I passed, and I was never more thankful that my car's sound system had never been very loud.

The perplexed faces of convenience store clerks still made me cringe with embarrassment when I gave them a thumbs up and told them, "I'm looking for that sassy sweetness." None of them knew what to do, and many had laughed.

No bridges collapsed.

No feminine beings composed of garbage suffocated me in my sleep.

I didn't see any two-headed pit bulls.

Carla never called.

Life went on. The miles in my odometer ticked away, and the scenery blurred past. Other than whatever havoc sitting behind the wheel for hours at a time was doing to my health and body, the road left me unscathed.

Surely I failed at following the rules on more than one occasion. There had to be loads of missed opportunities I passed by without knowing, panhandlers and cemeteries I drove by without acknowledging. I was only human and could only see so much.

That wasn't the point, though. So far, the rules seemed to only affect those that had heard the corresponding and specific broadcast. If you hadn't heard the broadcast, you were in the clear: no harm in not following any rule that you may have read about in these accounts that I've shared with you. I had heard the broadcast about the single shoe on the side of the road, so it was imperative that I follow that one, but any other was purely optional.

My point in following all these rules, in spending so much time out on the road, was this:

I was trying to get *his* attention.

Yeah, Buck Hensley, the down-home demonic DJ, the phantom broadcaster, the plague of the airwaves, the ruler of the radio. That folksy *fucker*.

Somehow, I thought he might be watching me, noticing me doing all these rituals and rules. It may have been naïve or self-important for me to think so, but I persisted. He was bound to turn up, eventually.

It was the least I could do to force some sort of confrontation with him. No longer was it enough for me to sit back and collect the stories of those who had encountered "The Rules." I was going to have to get more information from him and see what he actually wanted. Ask him if he could stop.

But then again, what was so special about me to warrant Mr. Buck Hensley contacting me himself? Who did I think I was?

I PREFER the vast expanses of the West and always have. All that endless space stretching out before me, the drastically changing scenery from state to state. Besides, I was more familiar with it and mostly grew up here, so that's where I focused my journey.

Since Buck Hensley mostly contacted people at night, that's when I did the majority of my traveling. I'd start in the late afternoon and early evening and go until I just couldn't anymore. Sometimes I'd pull off at a roadside motel (always remembering the ice). Other times I'd just sleep in the back of my car, knees and legs cramped and bent, awakening with a soreness in my back.

Many a night was spent all by my lonesome, my headlights shining over never-ending white lines, the radio playing. He never came.

My money was running out and so was my patience. Was this all a goddamn joke to him? How could he enter someone's life and just disappear, never to be heard from again? He was the one that had chosen me. I never asked for this and now I was doomed to look for shoes every time I traveled. God forbid I should miss one.

I had many questions for him. Like, what the fuck, Buck? What did any of these people who'd had an encounter with "The Rules of the Road" do to deserve such punishment? How could it end so badly for most, yet others came out unscathed or even blessed? Was he behind these atrocities? Was he the man behind the curtain, pulling the levers and pushing the buttons?

• • •

Now you might ask: was I concerned for my own safety? What did I expect to happen if he were to finally send me a broadcast? I must admit that when I found myself as the only car on the highway in some rural and forgotten place, my headlights cutting through dark desert or tunneling through the blackness of empty plains, I would become downright scared and shut my radio off. Those were the times that I had to pull over and find some place to hole up the rest of the night, the times when I was glad that my quest was coming up short.

My journey might have even made me riskier and more foolish. I looked for the strange and the bizarre. I roamed the forgotten corners of the United States, on desolate roads and empty highways, miles away from civilization or emergency services, cell phone signal unresponsive. If there was a weird roadside attraction, I stopped and had a look. Strange museum or store? You better believe I was going to make a visit.

It was at an abandoned gas station outside of Amarillo when I found my first clue. I had stopped at a roadside attraction of spray painted and rusted Cadillacs buried halfway in a field when I drove along an access road for a while and saw the abandoned station. It was covered in graffiti and I decided to stop and check it out.

Broken glass and debris crunched under my feet as I explored the hollowed-out shell of the former pitstop. Spray painted obscenities and names and indecipherable tags covered every inch and there it was in big letters:

ROTR

Stay Lonely

Energized by this find, I vowed to continue and to keep exploring things off of the beaten path.

This risky behavior is probably what led me to the decision to pick up the hitchhiker.

I was near Clines Corners, New Mexico, taking 285 north in the middle of the night, trying to make Santa Fe at a reasonable hour. There was a winter storm advisory in the region, and snow flurries were falling. Soon, they were swirling all around me, sticking to the road.

The further north I drove, the more I could tell that the storm had hit here much earlier. I instinctively slowed my speed and tightly gripped my steering wheel. I wasn't sure if I was hallucinating the car losing its friction on the road every time I tried to speed up, but it *seemed* like it was, so I bore straight ahead, slow and steady.

Headlights seldom passed me going the other direction, and no one was behind me. I was truly all alone out here and it was strange because it was only about ten o'clock at night. Maybe all the locals and truckers were wise enough to avoid driving in the winter storm. I had probably miscalculated how severe the storm was going to be. I was probably fucked.

I crested a hill and saw him out of the corner of my eye, the silhouette of a figure standing on the edge of the road, a bag or some type of luggage at his feet. It took me a second to register that it was a person out here in the middle of nowhere, standing on the shoulder. How in the hell did he get out here?

It had to be a sign. I slowed and veered off onto the shoulder and turned around. As I came back slowly in the opposite direction, I could make him out more. He was wearing winter clothes, gloves, and the hood of his jacket pulled down low. I couldn't make out his face.

As I approached, he turned toward my car and stared. He couldn't see me through the windows, but I could feel him looking right at me. I got a little nervous. I knew this is what I had come for, but I had to fight off the urge to speed away and leave him standing there. Pulling off to the opposite shoulder, I rolled down my window.

The wind was a bitter cold, and the snow whirled around as I leaned my head out and yelled.

"Need a lift?"

He nodded, his hooded head bobbing as he ducked down, grabbed his bag, and darted across the road. He came around to the passenger side of my car and I leaned over and opened the door for him.

"You can throw your bag in the back," I said, and he did and then slid into the passenger seat. "Where ya headed?" I asked.

"Santa Fe." His voice was a hoarse whisper. I could make out more of his face in the dimming interior lights. He was a white dude of average build with a beard. He still kept his hood up.

"Headed there myself," I said. "I can take you all the way."

"Hm."

That was all he offered, and we drove in silence for a while, him only shrugging as I asked some basic questions like, "you from around here?" or "what were you doing out here by yourself?"

I felt uncomfortable with the silent passenger next to me, always watching him out of the corner of my eye. Every horror movie trope about this exact situation played out in my mind, and I took deep breaths and resigned myself to the fact that I was probably going to end up dead in a ditch somewhere. I imagined a knife shoved into my neck, the barrel of a gun pressed against my temple, a mouthful of razor-sharp teeth gnashing at my face. My skin trembled in anticipation as we drove, and I felt on the verge of a panic attack.

Maybe this was it. I don't know why I had expected anything different. Being on the road for so long, going down any rabbit holes I could find, I was bound to come upon some trouble.

But I had come this far. Why let fear overtake me now? I gambled.

"You travel a lot?" I asked.

No answer.

"Ever listen to the radio? Wanna listen to something? I've heard about this strange broadcast that plays late at night. I've actually heard it myself."

He shifted in his seat.

I threw out some names to gauge his reaction.

"You ever hear of Buck Hensley? Does that name ring a bell?"

Silence.

"What's with you, man? You know it's not polite to ignore someone doing you a favor. You were likely to freeze to death out there."

He sighed. "I've . . . I've been on the road a long time," he responded in that hoarse and cracked voice.

"James? Jimbo?" I asked. I don't know why I said that, but I thought of James, the individual who had called me about his experience with The Rules and how he had been doomed to travel forever.

"Who?" he asked.

"Never mind. You just reminded me of a guy I know. Liked to travel and hitchhike. What about Carla? You know her?"

I didn't see it coming, but a flash went across my eyes, and I swerved a little and I heard the loud SMACK! My cheek stung and flushed. He had slapped me across the face, hard.

"That is a dead fucking name," he said.

Now it was my turn to not respond. I put on a stoic poker face, not reacting to my stinging face and the shock I was in.

"Who told you to say that? Who sent you? Was it Frank?"

"I don't know Frank," I said. "I think this is just a misunderstanding, okay?"

"You can let me off up here."

We were coming up on the outskirts of town. I could see the lights of a residential area off in the distance. The snow had stopped. I eased over to the shoulder, and he opened the door angrily and left it open while getting his bag out of the back. He leaned into the car before he shut it, pulled his hood back off his head.

The interior lights lit up his face. He was just an average-looking guy. Nothing remarkable about him at all.

He smiled at me and said in a clear and smooth voice that was no longer hoarse, "Stay safe out there. Stay lively. Stay lonely." There was a glimmer in his eye.

He slammed the door and hoisted the bag over his shoulder. I jumped out of the car and ran around the side to catch him, but he was far away from me, having jumped a barbed wire fence and moving fast. Before I knew it, he was gone, disappeared into the desert night.

I WAS on the last of my funds and taking a meandering route back home. The road had taken its toll, and I'd had enough. I fantasized about the familiarity of my humble abode, down the hallway to my bedroom, and collapsing into my bed into a forever sleep. I didn't even listen to the radio.

My brain could take in no more scenery, and I slipped into an uncomfortable numbness somewhere in the panhandle of Texas. I felt like I was coming out of my skin, and I just had to go, go, *go*. If I were to get pulled over, my speeding ticket would be outrageous.

The car shook. The headlights flickered and the instrument panel dimmed. The steering wheel vibrated, and static blasted from the car speakers.

It was him.

HOWDY FOLKS, Buck Hensley here. We interrupt our regularly scheduled programming of "The Rules of the Road" to talk about some things I've had on my mind lately. Seems that some of y'all out there ain't too happy with the way things have been going lately. You say you're tired and frustrated and you want answers.

Well, I get that. I want answers too! My math homework is due in the morning, and I still have fifty problems to finish and I can't for the life of me come up with the solutions to these brain stumpers. So, if you could slide me an answer sheet real sneaky like, I'd be much obliged. I promise I won't let the teacher know.

Anyways, where was I? So you're wanting answers and you're wanting them from little ol' me. Who am I anyways? Why do you think I would have what you're seeking? I've seen you out there, out on the road and all. Oh yes, I have. Betcha thought I'd forgotten all about you. Betcha were thinking about giving up.

Well, don't give up buttercup! Ol' Bucky's here for you. And I've got answers, loads and loads of answers. The problem is that these answers are for me to know and for you to never, ever find out. I know, I know. I'm stingy that way. Mama always told me I never liked to share, and Carla did, too.

She'd ask, "Whatcha thinkin about, buster? Care to share with the rest of the class?" and I'd say "Nah, I'm good." Then I'd get to sulking and poutin' and being all quiet, smoking my cigarette and staring out the window, thinking about the things we could never change and the lives that would never be, the goddamn pointless absurdity of it all, and how she could be so chipper and happy in the face of everything, none the wiser.

Ha! Blissful ignorance. They oughta sell that in bottles. I'd buy some for a dollar. Might even give Buck's Sassy Sasparilla a run for its money.

Do you know what it cost me to obtain these answers? More than you could ever know. You could've left well enough alone. Gone about your own business and not tried to stir things up, but ya didn't. So here I am. What exactly is it you want, ol' buddy?

I WAS DUMBFOUNDED. I couldn't speak. Did he want me to respond? Could he hear me here in the car? Of course, he could. He was Buck Motherfuckin' Hensley.

"WHY?" I asked.
He laughed long and hard at that.

WHY NOT? There is no answer to this "why" question, amigo. There may have been at one time, but I can't seem to recall at this moment. I told you, I ain't giving you no answers. So if all you've got is a bunch of questions, you best be getting along little doggy.

. . .

I DON'T KNOW where the spark of bravery came from, but I suddenly felt angry. He couldn't just blow me off like this. I shouted, there in my empty car, screaming to the blank radio speakers to something that I wasn't even sure was actually there.

"People are dying, Buck. How can you sit back and be responsible for it? How can it be so bad for some people and just fine for others? Who are you? *What* are you? Can you just stop with the broadcast? Leave us alone? We've got enough shit to deal with here without you coming along and fucking things up further."

How do you know I'm responsible for these so-called atrocities? Maybe I'm just a warning signal. Did ya ever think about that? That these terrible things always existed and I'm trying to provide a way out? Sure, it can end badly for some folk, but maybe it was always going to. Just because I'm the messenger, doesn't mean I'm the one to punch the card.

Hell, I'm doing my best buddy. I may be omnipotent, but I'm only human after all.

With that said, that's gotten me thinking about a "Rule of the Road" that I better warn you about. You're gonna wanna turn your ears on for this one. Make sure you got your calculators handy, too. This one is almost as hard as my math homework. By the way, you got that answer sheet yet? But I digress . . . on to tonight's rule!

If at any point in your journey, you find yourself in a thunderstorm, use the old trick you learned in Cub Scouts to try and find how far away the light-

ning is. You know, you see the flash of white and then count one Mississippi, two Mississippi until you hear that thunder. Once you hear that thunder, count the number of seconds you have and divide by five. That number you get is how many miles away the storm is.

Now listen closely, because this is where the Rule comes into play. Once you see that the lightning is less than a mile away, then get out of your car. Get out of your car and run. Run toward that lightning. Embrace the lightning. You will not get struck. You trust me, don'tcha? When has Ol' Buck ever steered you wrong?

Hold on a second, I know what you're gonna say. You're gonna say, "Buck! You want me to run out in the middle of a bleeping lightning storm. Do you think I'm crazy? Everybody knows the safest place to be in a lightning storm is in your car. Why I like to sit in my car during any type of storm. Bottle of wine. A couple good books. That's what I call a nice little night. I'm not about to get out of my car during this storm and miss my leisure time."

And to that I say, "Fair enough." But if you don't get out of your car, then you and your car will be completely obliterated. If you don't get out of your car, you won't get to see what's at the end of the rainbow—pardon me—the end of the lightning bolt! Believe me, you wouldn't want to miss that!

Welp. I guess that's all I've got for tonight. Don't beat yourself up too bad over not finding out more information. Sorry I couldn't have been more helpful. I hope you stop and smell the roses from time to time and don't bother your little head with these questions you won't find the answers to. You stay safe out there. Stay alert. Stay lively. Stay lonely.

I'm Buck Hensley and these are "The Rules of the Road."

I POUNDED my fist into the steering wheel in anger. Over and over again. The staccato beeps of the honk echoed across the frozen plains, my furious cries of frustration following after.

It was miles down the road when I saw the flashes of lightning on the dark horizon, photo flashbulbs that briefly illuminated the dark wall of clouds that hung in the night sky. I started counting.

One Mississippi.

Two Mississippi.

Fuck this.

No. You know it's real.

Five Mississippi.

Six Mississippi.

I am not about to run around in a thunderstorm and get struck by lightning.

Then turn around and drive the other way. If it doesn't get within a mile of you, then you're fine. That's five seconds until you hear the sound.

Nine Mississippi.

Ten Mississippi.

I heard the low rumble of thunder. Rain pelted my car. Two miles away. I pulled over and made a U-turn, pointed away from the storm. I stayed parked on the shoulder.

Another brilliant flash of lightning, this time in my rearview mirror.

One Mississippi.

Two Mississippi.

What do you think's at the end of the lightning bolt?

You're kidding. You don't actually trust him, do you?

Five Mississippi.

Six Mississippi.

The rain turned torrential. My wipers beat futilely against the onslaught of water. Gale force winds whipped the water sideways and tumbleweeds skittered down the road, fleeing the storm behind them.

Eight Mississippi.

Thunder, louder.

Another flash.

The rain let up, and then instantly stopped. An eerie silence followed, and then I heard something that sounded like a train, back toward the storm.

Five Mississippi.

Thunderclap.

A strong wind blew so fiercely that my car swayed. The door caught the wind like a sail, yanking it open and it felt like it would rip my doors from their hinges. My ears popped as the train sound grew louder. The air felt hollow, void of resistance, a vacuum.

I stepped out into the night, the car alert chiming as the wind continued to yank my door ajar. I turned toward the storm and ran. The lightning was more frequent now, bright piercing flashes that illuminated my steps every few seconds. Before me, revealed by the flashes of lightning, I could see the silhouette of a giant, swirling behemoth of cloud, something my mind could not quite comprehend. The blue explosions of power transformers appeared at its base, gobbled up by the unfathomable beast as it barreled down the road.

I was really going to run into the middle of a tornado, wasn't I? There didn't seem to be another option. I had to play by the rules. If I were to run in the opposite direction, I knew I wouldn't make it.

Just then, there was another bolt of lightning, a jagged and branching arc that shot down from the heavens. But what was strange about this bolt of lightning was that it didn't disappear as soon as it struck. It remained frozen in place, sprouting from the ground and jutting toward the sky, a great monument of light that filled the air with a bluish white haze. I'd say that it was about 500 yards away from me, this beacon of pure electricity. It wasn't completely blinding; I only had to squint to stare at it.

I could no longer hear the roaring train of the tornado as my ears now rang with a constant melodic hum. I continued to run forward.

Embrace the lightning.

The frozen lightning bolt illuminated the road and grass and fields with its brilliant light. As I neared, I could see that it ended at some sort of structure, a triangular tower that conducted energy and light all the way to the ground.

A radio tower.

I stopped and stood in awe at everything that I was seeing. It was just pure marvel and astonishment, the tallest thing ever jutting toward the heavens in an electric white that tinged the air in a light I had never seen.

I had read somewhere that a lightning bolt could reach temperatures greater than the surface of the sun. I had no idea if this was true, but I do know I didn't feel an immense heat radiating from the lightning. There was only a comforting warmth. Next to the radio tower was a squat and square one-story building, made of cinder blocks and painted white. There was a main entrance at its center. Above the entrance was a large sign that read: **ROTR RADIO.**

I approached the building. The door was open. I stepped inside.

I found myself in a waiting area of sorts. Chairs and little end tables with old magazines on them and a couple of fake potted plants. There was an empty receptionist window and a long hall that led past it. I thought I could hear music playing somewhere softly toward the back. The building had the lights on, but the lightning still provided a glare of light through the windows of the building. I made my way down the hall.

There was a sound booth with an open door. Above the door, an ON AIR sign flashed red. I couldn't tell you what kept me walking forward. It was like a dream where I didn't have any free will, like I was a passive observer in my own body. A calmness washed over me.

In the sound booth was a chair and a large microphone on a long swivel neck. A control panel was lit up. Needles danced in instrument meters. I sat, pulled the microphone toward me, and took a deep breath.

15
"GREATEST HITS"

A surge of electricity raced through my fingers and hand. There was a flash. A searing whiteness.
And then there was only darkness.

MY FACE IS PRESSED HARD on the ground, and drool is on my cheek. There is cotton in my brain. My eyes focus on the closeup view of the floor, the flat gray carpet that I lie upon. I become aware of my body contorted in space, a pain in my neck and shoulder. Legs still mobile.

I can hear a gentle and repetitive tapping, the shuffling of papers, a feminine voice singing softly. The scene slowly reveals itself to me, the minute details. A yard or two in front of my face there's a foot in a woman's loafer tapping out a rhythm on the floor, its counterpart dangling above it, the owner's crossed legs under a desk.

A ragged breath escapes my lips, and I roll onto my hands and knees and rise. I'm inside the radio station. But it's not the same radio station. It's alive now and in the here and now, fluorescent lights illuminated overhead. The woman sits at a desk with an adding machine, face buried in her work, punching the buttons of the machine and writing numbers in a ledger. There's a stack of checks and envelopes by her. To my left is the sound booth I had previously occupied. The ON AIR sign is shining red.

Before I can speak out to the woman, she's pushing away from the desk on her rolling chair, rising and leaving the room. Out the door and into the hall, skirt swishing.

"But . . ." I say, and my voice is hoarse and dry.

There's the faint sound of classic rock, a guitar solo. I look into the window of the booth and see a grungy-looking guy with headphones around his neck leaned back behind the microphone. A cigarette smokes like incense in the ashtray next to him. His hair is long and dandruff flakes are sprinkled throughout the shoulders of his black T-shirt and beard.

"Hey!" I yell and wave my arms. I'm a castaway on an island waving down a passing ship.

He can't hear me. Duh. It's a soundproof booth. But he should be able to *see* me. Is it a two-way mirror? No. That wouldn't make sense.

I hear a voice in the hallway, the woman's. Another voice responds. Kind of familiar. Twangy. My stomach turns. I hesitate to follow the voices into the hall. For an instant, I want to cower under the desk. But no, I push forward.

In the little waiting area at the end of the hall, he's there. At least I think it's him. All I can see is the back of his western plaid shirt, giant leather billfold sticking out of the back pocket of his jeans. He's going for the front door, his boots clomping on the floor, gray hair sticking out of the back of the cap on his head. He pushes the door open into daylight, steps outside. I rush after him, manage to catch the door right before it closes.

Outside, the sun is glaring. So bright, in fact, that I can

only squint into the blinding light, a halogen flashbulb filling my entire visual field.

I'm confused when my vision returns a few moments later. Somebody brushes past me. Then another. I'm no longer standing outside the radio station. I'm standing on a grassy incline in the middle of crowds of people. There are blankets on the ground, little ice chests. The buzzed chatter of people waiting excitedly for something. That's when I see the stage that the crowds congregate around. There are people pressed up close near the front of the stage, but the further back you get—where I am standing—people are more relaxed and spread out.

The people though, there's something not right about them. It's their clothes. It's their hairstyles. It's the old-school logos on the cans of beer they drink, and those glass bottles of soda. There are bell bottoms and cutoff denim shorts and men with mustaches and giant glasses. There are women in flowing summer dresses and tank tops and their hair is all feathery. I catch whiffs of cannabis in the sweltering air.

Nobody responds to me, no matter how loud I get or how hard I yell. I tap on shoulders and squeeze arms and am only ignored. I slap a man's face and the effect is a little more than a stiff breeze, his shaggy hair barely moving. It's like I'm not even here. Maybe I'm not.

Above the stage is a banner that reads 9th ANNUAL JUNEBUG JUBILEE and there are rock and roll instruments set up, waiting for a band to play them. Further behind the stage is a river, its sandy banks transitioning to the lush green grass, wherein the crowd lounges. I must be in some kind of park, a summer concert series, which doesn't make any sense because it was winter when I entered that radio station on those Texas panhandle plains.

What am I doing here?

What's going on?

All I can do is wait.

It's a shame I can't buy a beer, sit back and relax on the soft grass and listen to some tunes. The tunes are about to start, too, judging by the sudden increase in the crowd's volume, the hoots and hollers. But no band has appeared. There's just a lone figure in a loose paisley shirt and bellbottoms walking across the stage toward the center mic.

"How y'all doing tonight?" he asks. There's a drawl in his voice.

The crowd cheers.

"I don't think y'all heard me. I *said*, how y'all doing tonight?"

The crowd cheers even louder. A girl screams loudly right next to my ear, deafening me.

"I'm Buck Hensley, midnight voice of WLVD and we are so grateful that y'all have come out tonight. We're mighty happy to be sponsors for the JUNEBUG JUBILEE and we've got quite the show for you folks on this fine summer night. First up is a little group outta Jacksonville. Ladies and gents, I give you The One Percent!"

I can't believe it. It's really him. He's younger, and he has a full head of hair and a mustache. His voice differs from the one I heard through those car speakers, but it's really him.

I make my way through the roaring crowd, keeping my eyes glued to him. Bluesy chords and riffs fill the air, backed by a pounding drum beat while the crowd gets even louder. Bodies and shoulders and heads crowd my vision. I squirm through the throngs of people. He's disappearing from my sight.

I spot him to the left of the stage. Or is it stage right? No matter. I still have to cross the masses to get to him. He's a hundred yards away.

There's a scuffle of sorts in my path. A man shoves another man who loses his balance. A flailing hand slaps me right across the bridge of my nose. My eyes instantly water. My head swims. The world goes black.

A RADIO BOOTH hovers in the darkness, the viewing window bright with a figure behind it. I'm back at the station, perhaps the one I was in before. Perhaps not. I can't move, can't walk. A voice cuts through the dark, *his* voice.

"Howdy folks, Buck Hensley here and that was ZZ Top at the top of the hour. Stay tuned for more tunes here on KOTR radio after a quick break."

A chorus from nowhere sings the station identification, their voices echoing the call letters into the dark.

"K-O-T-R-r-r-r-r-r."

I CAN SEE, I can touch, I can smell, I can hear, but I cannot change. Can't alter the course of anything that's happened here. I can speak but cannot be heard. Doors move under my push when needed. Curtains flutter when I move past them. But that's it.

I am an observer.

I observe.

THEY RUN through fields of goldenrod in the golden hour of late evening. The slower of the two wields a stick, swings it at the tall stalks of the flowers as he passes, showering pollen into hazy clouds that hover in the air momentarily.

In their jeans and faded T-shirts and boots they dart toward the tree line. They are equal in stature and size. It's hard to keep up with them, the piss and vinegar and energy in their veins. Also, it's hard to keep them apart. They are almost like twins, yet if they are they're not identical. One's hair is shorter and lighter. There are subtle differences in their facial structure.

Finally, they stop at a muddy clearing in the forest, hands on their knees and sucking air. In the middle of the area is a wire basket of sorts, knee-high. It's a cage. At one end of the cage is a bloody and matted mitten made of fur. No, not a mitten. A dead rabbit. One of the boys inspects it.

"Ah, shoot. Nothing," he says, giving the cage a little kick. He looks down at the ground. "Ain't even any new tracks."

"Grandpa's gonna be pissed. You remember what he said?" the other boy says.

"That it's wrong to kill an animal for no reason."

"Yeah, and if we didn't trap nothing, then *we'd* have to eat it. So it wouldn't go to waste."

"Ah, Henry. He was just *joking*. There's rabbits a plenty. You ever hear the phrase screw like rabbits?"

"Yeah, yeah. I still wanna catch one, though. A real live bobcat. Heard you can make 'em your pet," Henry says.

"Well, we can check early in the morning before we gotta go back home. Unless you're just aching to have some rabbit stew," the other boy says and slides up alongside his brother and wraps him in a headlock.

"Dammit, Tucker. Let go, let go!"

"Say uncle!" Tucker laughs.

But Henry will not go down so easily. He grunts and shifts his weight, and with gravity on his side, they both collapse onto the muddy ground. They roll onto their backs, laughing together at the sky.

The two boys run rambunctiously through the countryside. They fish in ponds and catch crawdads with fish guts and bacon fat tied to string. They galivant through the creeks, up and down ravines, across pastures and meadows.

Bareback and barefoot, they ride together on a horse the color of the soil. One in front and one on back, they glide gently over rolling terrain, exploring the land around them and all it has to offer.

Even though the weekend is ending, and they have to go back home, it's okay. There's always next weekend and then the next.

It seems like they have all the time in the world to explore.

It seems like they'll have forever.

THE SUN REFLECTS off the blacktop, bouncing back shimmering waves of heat. There is a palpable excitement in the air. Crowds move toward a coliseum-like structure several hundred yards away. The attire of the individuals has advanced from the concert at the river, but a lot of it's the same. There's certainly more acid wash and some hairstyles are bigger, but this summer heat is a great equalizer for fashion. Shorts and tank tops and exposed skin never go out of style.

The cars in the parking lot are updated, too. Boxier and uglier. My guess is that we're in the 80s now. I hear music on the breeze and see a bright red van parked at an angle with big letters painted on its side, "102.7 WEBN." There's a table and a stack of speakers. Sitting behind the table with a microphone is a face that has grown more familiar with each passing vision.

He hands out T-shirts to passersby. His eyes are tired and bloodshot and there's gray in his goatee. I've never been this close to him and I see nothing intimidating. He's just a guy.

"Hey Buck!" I yell, walking towards him. But he doesn't respond. I'm still a ghost.

The music fades, and he takes the microphone. His chipper voice belies his appearance, and the worn-out expression on his face. It has a natural twang to it, but it's not the exaggerated version I've previously heard.

"Howdy folks, it's hot, hot, hot down here at The Riverfront. Shoulda known when they volunteered me for this gig that there was a catch. Oh well, guess 'Born in the USA' will be worth it. As hot as it is, I just ain't gonna be doing no 'Dancing in the Dark.' And for those that are, y'all best be bringing a boatload of talcum powder. Things are likely getting mighty sticky. Got some more tunes coming up after a word from our sponsors."

But I don't get to hear the word from the sponsors.

I'm gone before I even know it.

I'M LYING at the base of a thick tree trunk on a carpet of dead and brown needles. I hear voices coming from somewhere above me. Looking up toward their origin, I see the branches spiral outwards like spokes on a bicycle wheel. They jut out at just the right intervals to feel like this would make a perfect ladder. The two boys must've thought so too because I can see the soles of their shoes and their dangling shirttails, way up there.

"Tucker, I can't move. I can't reach the branch," Henry says. I can't tell which is which from down here.

"Look. It's right there, like a little drop," Tucker says, and points. He is lower than his brother, looking up at him.

"I can't look down. It's like I'm frozen," Henry says, his voice all shaky.

Tucker gives an exasperated sigh. "Guess that's why I'm the big brother."

He scrambles up the tree, pulling himself up on

branches with the ease of a squirrel. In the blink of an eye, he's alongside Henry.

"Damn, you really are shaking. Like dang ol' a cat. Alright, listen bubba. You're just gonna want to put your foot right there. I ain't gonna let you fall. I'll guide it down."

Henry lowers his foot to the branch below him, his brother's words guiding him.

Suddenly there's a loud crack. It's followed by more cracks as Tucker's body crashes through branches on his way down. He only gives out one yell of surprise, but Henry wails his name.

Bark and pieces of tree rain down. Tucker soon follows. He is unable to grab any tree limbs to stop his fall as he plummets to the ground. There is a final crack as he lands feet first and this time it's not a broken branch. His right leg is a crooked contradiction. There's a bulge in the thigh of his jeans, his ankle is bent at an awful angle. A groan escapes his throat, low and guttural as he tries to relax his diaphragm enough to inhale. I lean at his side and ask if he's okay, put my hand on his shoulder. Even though I know he can't hear me or feel me, I still do it anyway.

IN THE BLUE light of evening, there's a concrete canal stretching and bending to places far away. There's a trickle of stagnant water at its base. Trees grow alongside the wide bowl of cement, offering cover and if it wasn't for the cement and scummy water one could easily imagine this as a tranquil park; the ditch cuts through a vast swath of mowed lawn. Catalpa blooms litter sections of the canal like spilled popcorn. A couple sits amongst these spilled snowy flowers. Both are young and happy.

There's the far-off sound of music, the 4/4 time of a steady rock beat accompanied by bouncing bass lines. I hear the muddy vocals lost in the atmosphere, a guitar solo. Toward the noise and off in the distance I see the crowd and stage from earlier, the JUNEBUG JAM or whatever. I plop down a few feet away from the couple. They're close to each other but not touching.

"I saw you out there. A face in the crowd. I knew I had to try," he says.

"Oh, yeah? I'm sure you say that to all the girls at these things," she replies.

"Well, if that's true—which it ain't—I still picked you out of everyone else I saw tonight. Besides, I'm a midnight DJ. Not like I'm big-time or anything."

She smiles, looks away.

"So, do I get your name?"

"Carla."

"Nice to meetcha Carla. I'm Buck."

"I know *that*. I hear you on the radio," she says.

"Oh, but that's not really me. Actually, my name ain't really even Buck."

"What? It's not? You're kidding." A cute look of surprise crosses her face. Like any emotion she could ever express wouldn't look good on that face.

"Nah, it's a . . . what do you call it, a pseudonym? Like a stage name, except I'm not on the stage."

"Oh. Do I get to know your real name?" Carla asks.

"Maybe if I get to know you better. Everybody just calls me Buck. Hey, you still wanna go backstage?"

She shifts back on her palms, looks up at the tree branches overhead, the darkening sky. "I could take it or leave it. It's kinda nice over here with you. Besides, I'm feeling kinda stingy and don't wanna pass this around," she says, procuring a joint from out of nowhere.

Buck raises his eyebrows and grins. "I could kiss you right now."

Carla smiles and asks, "What are you waiting for?"

WE'RE in another radio sound booth. The equipment is more archaic than the ones I was previously in. The booth is a fishbowl of cigarette smoke. I sit in a chair at the corner of the room with Buck's back to me. His headphones are on and he is talking into the mic.

"That was Brian on the call with quite the addition to the list of rules. Always carry a roll of Charmin ultra-soft with you in your trunk. You never know when that convenience store hotdog might hit ya just wrong and you have to make an impromptu visit to the bar ditch. Lest you find yourself like ol' Brian here on the side of the road with a missing sock. Yessiree, it's always best to have a roll of toilet paper before you need a roll of toilet paper.

"Got some stories from the road out there? Got a little tip of your own? Call now to be featured on a future installment of 'The Rules of the Road'. Y'all stay safe out there. Buck Hensley, signing off. Molly Hatchet up next."

WOOD PANELING AND AN ORANGE LAMPSHADE. The room is cast in an ember-like glow. A painting of a woodland scene hangs on one wall. There's the faint smell of grass and cans of beer on the nightstand and dresser. I'm sitting in a wooden chair by a dresser with a rabbit-eared TV on it.

I see the smooth back of a woman, her head lying on the bare chest of a man. He's propped up on a couple of pillows and looks down at her while stroking her head and hair.

It's the woman from the concert.
Buck and Carla.
Carla and Buck.
"So, you gonna tell me your real name yet?" she asks.

"I reckon it's about time," he says. "If it's really that important to you. What's in a name, anyways? I've been Buck for so long I guess it's starting to stick."

"It is important to me. I wanna know all about you," she says.

Buck takes a deep breath and Carla props herself up on her elbow, attention rapt. "I had a twin brother," he says. "Tucker. Not identical. We were fraternal. Brothers in arms. Thick as thieves. Anyways, we were climbing this tree one day, this bald cypress out on my grandparents' land. Real tall sonuvabitch, but the branches were such that you could climb it real easy. We got up real high, and I froze up. I couldn't move. Couldn't climb back down. Tucker, he has to climb up to help me. And he does. I make it to where I need to go. But for some damn reason the next branch he steps on, just breaks right underneath him and he drops."

Carla lets out a little gasp.

"But he's fine for the most part. His femur is broken and his ankle's all torn up, but that's it. I carry him to the house on my back. Don't ask me how. They get him to the hospital. He has surgery. They set the bones. It seems like he's good to go. A couple days later he's dead," Buck says.

"Oh my God, Buck. I'm so sorry. What happened?"

"They didn't know at first. There was an autopsy. They determined he passed from a stroke. It was caused by a number of factors. There was a hole in his heart. Something he was born with. When he broke the femur it formed a clot of sorts, something from the fat in the bone. It traveled through his bloodstream and through that hole in his heart and into his brain.'

"Henry and Tucker. That's who we were. Then it was Hank and Tuck. From there, it turned into Buck and Tuck. Don't ask me how. Some uncle got to calling the both of us that. After Tucker died, I dropped the nickname for a long while. Buck just didn't make much sense when it was just me. Guess I brought it back as an homage to my long-lost brother. Add a maiden name from somewhere back—Hensley—and that's that."

"I can't imagine what that must've been like. Losing your twin brother like that."

"Yeah, it messed me up for a long while. Was just kinda numb for a while. I had a lotta guilt. If I had got down on my own, he wouldn't have stepped on that branch. If only I had just fallen, then it would've been me with the broken leg and still alive. I don't have no hole in *my* heart. It was just some fluke deal he was born with."

"I'm so sorry."

"Years down the road I'd try to reckon with it. I didn't want to be in a world without him. Felt like a piece of me was missing. Since before I was born he had been with me. Several times I tried to join him, I guess. Drinking and pills and a fender wrapped around a tree. None of it ever took. If it had been me on the other side and not him, I would want him to continue living. So that's what I do."

"All you can do. I'm glad you're still here," Carla says and leans in toward him. He lets her and they embrace.

I slip out the door to give them privacy.

I'M RIDING shotgun in an off-white Chevy Nova. We coast across a wet parking lot, the streetlamps off its surface like tinfoil. We park in the middle of the lot, the darkened town shuttered and sleeping all around us, but there's a diner open and full of business.

Sitting off by itself at the edge of the lot, the lone diner is a beacon in the damp night, the yellow lights shining from its windows homely and comforting. I can see the diners and patrons within, talking and raising drinks and utensils to their mouths. A waitress with curly hair bustles about. A neon sign reads I and mirrors off the slick surface of the parking lot.

That's when he spots her: a woman with a black apron around her waist leaning against an exterior wall, a leg bent at the knee and propping the place up. She smokes a cigarette and savors it, deep in thought.

Buck slips out of the car and ducks behind cars, sneaking up on her. When he gets at an approachable distance he bursts from his hiding place, taking her by surprise.

Carla lets out a playful scream as he embraces her and lifts her up off the pavement a few inches. He gives her a twirl and she squeals. I stroll up casually so I can hear what they're saying.

"Dammit, Hank! You scared the hell outta me." She gives him a little tap on his chest, still in his arms. "What are you doing here? Don't you have to go into work, soon?"

"Guess what?" he says, setting her down.

"You brought me a Nehi?"

"This is even better."

"Ooh, what?"

"You are currently looking at the new drive time voice of KMOD in Tulsa. Clear Channel called me up. Someone passed a tape of my show to one of the higher ups. They really dug it. Wants me to fill a slot and see how I do."

Carla smiles big and gives a little jump. "That's terrific Hank! I knew your break would come. I bet this is only the beginning."

"There's one other thing."

"Oh?"

"I want you to come with me."

She pauses and stares, processing what he just asked. This pause only lasts an instant before she leaps into his arms again, legs wrapping around his waist. They exchange a long deep kiss while he staggers backward, the patrons in the diner watching from the windows like an audience, dinner *and* a show.

I FOLLOW him in from the front yard, up the driveway. His gait is a little wobbly, and he fumbles with the keys at the front door but is able to slip into the house quietly. From the bedroom I can hear the canned laughter of a sitcom, see the flickering glow cast by a TV set dance across the bed.

Buck walks to the bedroom—veering into the wall on the way—and sinks down into an armchair. He reeks of booze and cigarettes. A woman lies in the bed, hair color the same as Carla's. He sits and watches her, gets up and hovers over her bedsheet entangled form, thinks to wake her, thinks better of it.

She senses his presence, stirs and reaches for him.

"Hey baby, how was the show?" she says through a sleepy haze.

"Oh, you know, another day at the office. Had to help break down the remote and then they needed me backstage to record some promo stuff. I'll try and use my pull to get you in next time. Wasn't the same without you."

"Seems like you managed," she says, more awake now, looking at him.

He doesn't respond.

"Sorry, I'm just jealous, I guess. Feel a little left out is all."

"Nah, you're right. Next time, babe," he says, patting her thigh. "Next time."

THERE'S two-handed handshakes and wooden smiles and a pair of suits. It all takes place in a boardroom. The suits sit on one end of the table. Call signs I can't remember are emblazoned in a flashy logo on the wall behind them. One of the suits is young and suave with slicked back hair, the other is bald and bloated with hair like a smoke ring. I sit at the table to the left of Buck, invisible and ignored.

I can never tell the year, only count the wrinkles around his eyes, the gray in his hair. There's a little more than the last time I had seen him.

The bald man talks in a jovial tone. "We just love what you bring to the table. The ratings are good, have been on a steady climb since Tulsa. That one segment you have, the uh one about misadventures callers have experienced on the road, that's a classic."

"The Rules of the Road?" Buck asks.

Slick points a finger. "That's it. And the other one you do about the stupid pet stories? You keep spinning gold with these bits. We think they have a broad-based appeal. Could go national with some of them, guest spots on all of our affiliates."

"Welp, I'm flattered fellas. But I've been in enough of these here meetings to know that this is about the time when you guys show me your 'but'. As in, here's some good news, *but*."

Baldy gives a forced lingering laugh, side eyes Slick. "It's just that we're looking to appeal to a different demographic. Broader. Younger. More urban, less rural."

"Yeah, hip," Slick chirps up. "What we're asking is if you could tone down the whole country schtick a bit."

Buck winces, starts to speak, but thinks better of it.

"Like we said. We think you have a lot of talent. We just want to put you in a position to succeed. I mean with the stuff I'm seeing, it's not outside the realm of possibility to see you in syndication."

"I'll see," Buck says and grits his teeth, "what I can do."

He would be syndicated, alright. Just not how any of us sitting in that room could ever foresee.

THERE ARE balloons on the floor of the gymnasium. Crepe paper streamers dangle from the rims of the basketball goals and banners that read SOMERSET PROM hang on the cinder block walls. An artificial fog snakes through the ankles of the students on the dance floor and Berlin's "Take My Breath Away" is playing loud while girls in big dresses and evening gowns and boys in tuxes and bow ties slow dance. They sway back and forth stiffly.

As my eyes adjust, I see there's the usual suspects as well, the wallflowers and slackers and jokers that can't be bothered with it all. They congregate along the walls and at tables, talking and joking.

At the corner of the gym, I see the setup with giant speakers and a table, the DJ of the night's festivities. I make my way over.

Buck leans back in a folding chair, boots on the table. He's sporting a bow tie and button-up shirt. He sneaks a pint bottle from his pocket, ducks behind a speaker and takes a long pull. After that he cues up the next song, an 80s dance tune I don't know of, and then gets up and sets out a side door.

He's fishing in his pocket for a light and there's a group of kids out there, four teenage boys that are too cool to be fooling around with no prom. Their shirts are unbuttoned, and jackets are slung over a metal TEACHER PARKING ONLY sign. A blue-green parking lot light casts their shadows onto the white cinderblock walls of the outside of the gymnasium. A couple of them smoke cigarettes.

"Hey dude," one boy says.

Buck gives a little nod, talks around the cigarette he's

lighting. "How y'all boys doing?"

"Oh, you know. Just rad," another boy says. "Was just getting a little lame in there. Gilly was gonna spike the punch but bitched out."

"I see," Buck says. "Best to keep the booze to yourself, though. Spike your own drinks as you go. Like this." He pulls out the near empty pint bottle and drains it, tosses it at a nearby dumpster.

"Ya know, if you wanted to really get this party going you could jam some heavy metal in there, man," the first boy says.

"Unless it's power ballads you're wanting, I'm a little short on that, I'm afraid," Buck says. "Say, you fellas are wasting your time out here. Where's your dates?"

"Fuck 'em," a skinny tall boy says.

"You wish! She's probably getting felt up on the dance floor by Tommy right as we speak," laughs the first boy. He turns to Buck, points a thumb back at his pal. "Gilly got ditched a week before this shindig. I talked him into coming. Now as for me, I just know my date's not gonna put out, so why waste my time in there listening to Debbie Gibson and all that teenybopper shit you're playing."

Buck holds up his hands defensively, shrugs. "Don't blame me, I gotta listen to them requests. It's what's popular at these things. On another note, I will say that you guys are going about this all wrong. You're gonna look back at nights like these when you were too proud or scared to have fun at a little ol' sock hop, and wonder what might've been."

"Whatever, dude," Gilly says.

"Of course, I don't guess I can tell y'all that. I reckon y'all know everything there is to know about everything and I'm just some old fogey. Why listen to me?" Buck says, waving his arm around. His words have a subtle slur to them. "There's only so much I could tell you that you might remember, but ultimately you won't know it 'til you've lived it. For instance, I could tell you that the first gal you lay down with here in bumfuck ain't the one you wanna end up with and you might understand all this in *theory*, but you won't know it. You won't know it until you're a decade in with a coupla kids and contemplating divorce."

"Um, dude. I think the song's over. You got another on deck?" the tall kid says.

And it is true that I can no longer hear the drumbeats from the gym. Buck waves his hands dismissively and continues talking. "What I'm saying is, you don't want to live your life by the dumpsters, waiting for the big dance, when the dance is taking place right next to you."

"Wow. Deep."

Another song has started. There must've been a system that allows for two records or tapes to play so not a beat is missed.

Buck sways a little. "Yeah, yeah, yeah. I thought I was smart once, too. Above it all. You see, my problem was I didn't listen. I had it all. She was a gem in this goddamn gutter we call life. Everything felt right with her. She was cool. She was beautiful. She was smart. She actually *liked* sex. That's some bullshit they teach you and let me impart you youngsters some wisdom. You don't have to be deceptive or trick 'em into doing it with you. Hell, if they like you, they'll *want* to. She liked to take me in her mouth and the way that it felt, my goodness … it was like kissing God."

The boys just stare at Buck, perplexed looks on their faces.

"Well, shoot. I gotta get back in there. Song's about to run out. You boys enjoy yourselves. It's closer than you think," Buck says and gives them a mock little bow. He turns and catches his foot on a broken chunk of concrete, staggers and almost busts his ass, but manages to right himself before entering the gymnasium again.

"That dude needs to get laid," one of the boys says.

I'M in the backseat of a car. The seat is vinyl and smooth and dark, color indistinguishable. There is plenty of room to stretch out and relax, which I do. Our headlights burrow through the night. White lines blur underneath our feet.

Up in the front seats are Buck and Carla. Or Hank and Carla, depending on who's asking. I don't know what year it is, what point in the chronology of their relationship I'm witnessing, but when I glimpse them under the lights of a passing town, they don't look too much different from the last time I saw them at the diner.

The radio plays softly between the two of them and there is little talking. The silence is not a comfortable one. There's tension in the air. I don't get the same warm and fuzzy feeling I used to in their presence. There's Carla rolling her eyes when Buck tries to be funny. There's the way he turns the radio back up when she turns it down. There's the cold shoulders and gritted teeth and sidewards glances.

I heard once that the best test of the durability of a relationship was a long road trip with your partner. If you didn't get on each other's nerves, if you didn't want to kill each other by the end, if you could still laugh at each other's jokes through it all, the person riding alongside you in that passenger seat just might be a keeper. I don't know if that's what I was witnessing here.

They vacillate between cold indifference and a lukewarm obligation toward one another. Sometimes, she gives a chuckle at his jokes. Sometimes, she lets him keep his hand on her thigh. Later on, he'll ask that age-old question many ask when it's already too late.

"What's wrong?"

"Nothing," she'll say.

Through the night we ride. Miles pass by like a dream.

We stop for gas somewhere in Tucumcari, New Mexico.

Stepping out to stretch my legs, I think about running off, escaping the uncomfortable scene. But what would that get me? I would just be stuck, waiting to transition to the next time period. What would I miss?

The desert air is cold and the wind brutal. Beyond us is just night and more night. Carla uses the facilities, one of those little side restrooms you need a key for. She comes back and stands by the car (another Chevy Nova, this one baby blue), stares off down the road. The wind whips her hair around and brings tears to her eyes. Or maybe it's something else. Buck is off paying and talking to the clerk, looking at a map.

I could sail a yacht through the gulf that's formed between Carla and Buck. Us out here near the Rockies, so close to the continental divide, it's hard not to think of the obvious metaphor of that continental distance between the two of them.

Buck finishes at the gas station and we get back in the car. They pull onto the highway, and he sings the opening lines to "Tulsa Time" for the fiftieth time and gets about the same response he's gotten every other time. It's the line about leaving Oklahoma in a Pontiac and heading to California.

"Gas station guy says we've got a little under two hours 'til Clines Corners. Then we'll turn north and be in Santa Fe before you know it."

"Groovy," she says flatly.

"You're gonna love Santa Fe. They've got these buildings made outta this stuff called adobe. One of the oldest cities in America."

She doesn't respond.

At Clines Corners we head north. Patches of snow clings to the bush scrub. The conditions aren't blizzard-like, but flurries fall and whip past the windshield.

And at a certain point as we drive north on 285 toward

Santa Fe, all of that tension that has built up breaks the wall of silence.

"What's your fucking problem, Carla?" Buck asks, calm but irritated. "I thought this was gonna be a good time. You. Me. Out on the road?"

She shakes her head no. "I don't want to do this right now. I need my space."

"It's eating me up over here, though. You owe me an explanation."

"I don't owe you shit," says Carla.

It's a quietly burning rage that has boiled over into this present outburst, something that's been simmering for miles, days, months.

Buck grits his teeth and clenches the steering wheel, shakes his head in disbelief. The wind has picked up. There's snow building up on the shoulders.

"You never really asked, did you? My dreams were your dreams. It was always about you. I was just along for the ride. You didn't even talk to me before you decided to move out here," Carla says. "I was never part of the decision. I simply didn't factor into it. I was happy with you in Tulsa. Was looking into classes. Had some friends I really liked. Still close enough to my parents."

"Wherever you go, that's where I'll go," Buck says. "We said that, remember?"

"I said it. You would be fine to leave me behind if I so much as threatened your precious radio career."

"Carla, you know that's not true. This is gonna be the next big break. Sacramento's a big market. I could really make a name for myself out there. Syndication. Everything I've—we've—wanted," Buck says. "Don't you think you're overreacting a little bit?"

"Overreacting? Don't tell me I'm overreacting, asshole!" Carla shouts. The volume and intensity are startling. "Did I overreact over all those late nights you came home? The nights you didn't? Did I overreact when I never asked questions about where you'd been or who you were with? You don't know how good you actually had it."

Buck responds in kind, fire with fire. He points at her and steers the car at the same time. "Carla, don't you fucking talk to me like that. What the hell's gotten into you?"

"Just shut up and be my cheerleader. Don't bitch. Do everything I say. That's what you want, isn't it?" She's still yelling.

"Listen. Let's just try and get to Sacramento in one piece and then we can discuss this further. I'm—sonuvabitch!"

The front end of the car shakes violently, and a loud knocking comes from the engine. The acceleration dies and steam rises from the hood. We coast to the side of the road, engine knocking and bleeding steam.

The horn honks twice in rapid succession as Buck slams his fist into the steering wheel. He buries his face in his hands for a bit and then pops the hood. It's like he's waiting for Carla to say something, offer some sort of reassurance, but she says nothing. She's not ready.

Buck lifts the hood and props it open, and now the Chevy Nova is a dragon with its jaws wide open, belching steam into the snowy desert night. He waves away the clouds of steam hissing from the radiator, hunches over the engine to investigate.

Somehow, it's like watching a movie scene I've seen many times before, knowing the outcome and desperately wanting it to change on this umpteenth viewing. How can I see the inevitable playing out so clearly? There's Carla slipping out the passenger side door and coming around to see what's the matter, sliding up and touching Buck's back and offering words of reassurance and encouragement. An olive branch of sorts.

But as that's happening, there's Buck stupidly getting too close to the overheated radiator, grabbing the cap as if he could just twist it off, a total lapse in thought or judgement. There's a slight delay before he jumps up from his burnt hand, his head banging against the trunk. It's all really one movement after he hits his head, how he slings his burnt hand out in an animalistic rage. The arc of this movement connects with Carl's stomach right as she leans toward him.

He didn't see her. There was steam in his eyes. There was steam.

That's what he'll say as he gets on his knees and begs her forgiveness.

It was an accident.

I didn't know you were there.

And headlights appear, driven by a knight in shining armor, or rather a good Samaritan in a pickup truck. He has a beard and trucker's cap and leans out the window, asks, "Y'all need some help?"

His eyes grow concerned when he processes the scene. A woman crying and in distress and the man that caused all this pleading with her as she pulls away.

"Name's Frank," he says as she hoists her bag into the truck and climbs inside. "Maybe we'll call someone for you when we get to town. If we can remember, that is," he yells out to Buck. "Might be best you just sit here a bit and think on whatever it is you did to this poor gal."

Buck watches their taillights fade into the desert night. He goes to the car, puts on his coat and gloves, pulls his hood down low, and grabs his large duffel bag. He sets off down the road. A hundred yards later he stops and drops his bag on the asphalt, unzips it and rifles through it. He finds the small object he's looking for.

He opens the small box and looks at the diamond ring inside. He clasps the lid shut and turns to the snowdrifts with the scrub grass sticking out, the barbed wire fences separating us from all of that desert. The jewelry box tosses and tumbles through the air. I can't even see where it lands.

Decades later I will pick up some facsimile of him walking this very highway, a ghost or an echo or maybe it really is him in the flesh, the piece of him that never made it off this highway, the pieces of himself he left behind.

THIS IS the nicest studio I've been to. The waiting areas are sleek and minimalist with a professional gleam. The framed posters of the radio personalities that line the halls are ginormous.

The sound booth itself is in the middle of an area with viewing windows on each side, easily accessible to the offices that lie off the hallways that encircle the booth. A song over the speakers fades out, and I can see Buck standing at a microphone. He speaks and his voice fills the hallways.

"Yeee-haw. That segment was brought to you by RV Central in Rancho Cordova, home of the 'no doc fees.' Buck Hensley here. Just a regular ol' country mouse in the big city. Was told earlier this morning by the man in the corner office to clean up my no good, cow tipping, hog wrastlin', squirrel eatin', tobacco spittin' act. Welp, I guess I owe it to you city folk to do so."

Buck's accent is more exaggerated than it has ever been. The bald man in the suit from the earlier meeting runs out of his office, eyes wide, waving his hands to try and get the attention of an audio engineer who sits adjacent to Buck's booth.

"I mean, I ain't that much of a hick am I? They say it's not incest to sleep with your third cousin, but maybe that's only cause I quit counting once I got to number three. There ain't no better place to pick up chicks than a family reunion, lemme tell ya. Ha! I'm just messing with you city slickers. I don't really do that. But I guess that's the vibe my accent puts off to you enlightened city folk. Like I'm just some goat fuckin' hayseed—"

His voice is cut off mid-sentence and "Burning For You" by Blue Oyster Cult starts playing over the speakers. Baldy bangs on the window of the booth, points a finger at Buck and yells "Out! Now!". Mouths it slowly so he can read. Buck shrugs and steps out of the booth.

"What the hell are you doing? The FCC is gonna fine the shit out of us," Baldy yells at Buck.

Buck smiles. "I just can't do it, good buddy. Can't tone it down. Sorry, but I don't think this is gonna work out between us."

"You bet your ass it's not. Get your things." He turns and yells down the hall for someone to call security.

AT THE EDGE of a parking lot, a phone booth floats in the dark. The phone rings and rings and then a man's voice answers.

He asks for her by name.

The voice asks who it is.

He tells him.

The voice says she's not around. Got married a while back. Who was he speaking to again?

He repeats his name. Both of them.

The voice at the other end says he really doesn't remember him. It sounds like he's lying.

It's a scene I'll see play out again and again.

A FOLDING TABLE and a control panel and a pop-up canopy tent. Speakers on a stand and an ice chest and several stacks of cardboard boxes full of beer koozies with radio station logos branded on them. People push shopping carts past and give awkward nods or smiles when they make eye contact with the man behind the table as he reports what songs he just played and says what he's doing in this Kroger grocery store parking lot, asks people to come out and see him and how Kroger is the "right store with the right price."

He's distracted as she approaches, but when he turns and sees her his mouth drops open slightly, morphs into an unrestrained and genuine smile.

"Hey there, stranger," she says.

"I . . . Carla? What are you doing here?" he stammers.

"I heard your voice on the radio. I couldn't stop thinking about it. I kept tuning in." She's older, yeah, but no less diminished. More confident, if anything.

"I just can't believe it. It's been so long. I'd love to catch up, apologize properly for how things went down."

She raises an eyebrow.

"I've never forgot," he says.

"I wouldn't have come here if I thought you had," she says, handing him her phone number.

Some say that forgiveness is our most unnatural act as a species.

Still, others will say that it's not so special, that it's a societal behavior that has developed to benefit the collective, a practice that has ultimately helped our species to survive.

I don't know where it comes from or why we do it, whether it's from a higher power or evolution or this or that. It's not important.

What's important is the power wielded by the wronged.

The effect it can have on the two people involved.

What's important is that it feels like a choice.

The universe may give second chances, but it doesn't *choose* to.

There's nothing more beautiful than a second chance.

IN A WAITING ROOM full of older women and women in various states of pregnancy, Buck sticks out like a sore thumb. He stares straight ahead and taps his foot quietly, takes glances up at the ceiling.

How do I know what year it is? I don't, but in his facial hair, there's more gray than not. Save for the cowboy hat, he looks roughly the same as he did in the Kroger parking lot.

A door opens. A woman in scrubs says his name and gives him a little smile, motions for him to come back.

I'm not privy to the goings on of what happens behind that door, but later on I'll find out that it's not a pregnancy they were there for. Later on, I'll find out how the universe treasures second chances. (Spoiler alert: It doesn't.)

HER HAIR never grows back the same after the chemo, the chemo that didn't quite seem to work the way the doctors had hoped. So, she keeps it cut short.

"Easier to manage out on the road. I'll be able to get ready almost as fast as you," she'll joke to him.

And that's what they decided they would do, take a final road trip. Once all the bargaining and sadness was exhausted, they planned it all out, right there on their bed with the afternoon light shining through the curtains. There was still so much she had wanted to see, so much she wouldn't get to, but they might as well die trying.

She was on her belly, hand propping her chin up as she wrote in a notebook while Buck stroked her ankle and leg.

"You wanna see Niagra? It's a total tourist trap out there," Buck says.

"What? I got this thing for waterfalls. It's like the top ten in the world and in our backyard practically. Ooh, I better not forget Yosemite," Carla says, adding it to her list.

"Now that I can jive with. Nothing like the West."

"Yawn. You and your wide-open spaces."

"I've got a thing for vastness."

Days and hours pass on the road like so many miles on the odometer, except with this engine there's no service that's due once it hits three thousand or whatever. There's just the inevitable. Maybe the salvage yard if she's an organ donor.

Still, it's not like you could tell at first glance. No signs of terminal illness rain on Carla's parade. She seems happy, if tired. Buck's a different case. Although he puts up a good show in front of Carla, bloody knuckles and a cracked bathroom mirror at a service station in Mississippi beg to differ. He wraps his hands in paper towels and saunters back to their vehicle, whistling a tune.

No road trip ever goes completely as planned, but when a terminal illness looms, more accommodations must be made. There are bouts of nausea and fatigue, plates of the best chicken fried steak in 3 counties that go untouched, days spent sleeping in and lounging in motel rooms, sights left unseen.

There are the other things that stick out to me as I ride in the backseat and witness it all, the country passing by through the windshield.

On I-20 outside of Shreveport, Carla leans out the window and cocks her arm and pumps it vigorously at a trucker. He returns the salute with a blast of his loud horn. In that moment, with her smile and short hair windblown by the interstate, she looks so full of life. If deceptive looks were enough to beat cancer, she would've done beat it. That's for certain.

Later that same day they stop at a roadside stand and buy a quart of boiled peanuts. Buck turns his nose up at them, says his grandpa made him eat them plenty of times and that he's never been a fan. He still eats a few for Carla.

Carla is full of other road trip games and superstitions. There's an ongoing game of punch buggy that's really just a love tap that she gives him whenever she spots a VW bug. There's the rule that they must hold their breath when they pass a graveyard. There are the panhandlers she tries to tip every time that they can. She says it's good luck.

At every hotel, they fill an ice bucket. She likes to chew on it when she's nauseous and can't seem to keep anything down. Keeps her from getting dehydrated.

Outside of Roanoke, Buck tries to change the radio station during a particular song, but Carla slaps his hand. She's having a good day and driving for once.

"Hey there, mister. What do you think you're doing?" Carla asks.

"Aw, c'mon Carla. This song is *so* long," Buck mock whines.

"It's 'Free Bird' though. You never change 'Free Bird'. It's supposed to be long."

"Do you realize how many times I've had to play this song on the air?"

"I'm sure a lot. But it's totally sacrilegious to skip it."

"Alright, alright," he concedes.

Full circle comes during a nighttime drive west of Des Moines, Iowa. They're trying to make it to Omaha. Out on the shoulder, their headlights cut across an object.

"You see that?" Buck asks.

"No," Carla says drowsily from the passenger seat. Her head is leaned back on the headrest.

"A single shoe on the side of the road."

"Hm."

"You ain't ever seen that? A shoe just sitting there? Why is it always just one shoe? How did it get there?"

"Maybe it's a dude with one leg that doesn't need it anymore," Carla replies, her eyes still closed.

"Maybe," Buck says.

ALL ROAD TRIPS must come to an end, and this one is no different. This one ends prematurely. We never have as much time as we think.

WOODEN RAFTERS and neon beer signs and rows and rows of bottles reflected in the mirror behind the bar. Lilting pedal steel wafts from a glowing jukebox in the corner. The longneck bottle is cold in my hand and the beer inside is like nectar; it's the first thing I've consumed since I started this trip. Thus far, I haven't thirsted, I've never hungered. But it's here and I don't remember how I got here, and I can interact with it, so why not?

It's finished before I know it, but there is a bartender at the ready, leaving me another on a cardboard coaster. To my left and further on down the bar are several patrons and to my right is Buck. He's got a cowboy hat on and his hair is gray.

He turns and looks at me.

Is this possible? Have I inhabited the memory of someone else's body?

"So yeah, I just don't see that there was ever any point, you know? It should've been me, it should've been me. The hurt I doled out. The life I lived. I deserved it," he says, like we've been in mid conversation.

"You've been through a lot," I find myself saying automatically.

"Others have been through worse. They all keep trucking. Hard-wired, I guess," he says and takes a drink of his glass, ice and bourbon.

"Are you thinking of checking out?" I ask.

He's a ghost, a vengeful spirit of the sound waves.

He chuckles. "No. Far from it. I'm checking *in*."

"I'm not sure I read you."

"This life is a rigged game. You can play by the rules and do everything right and it won't matter. I'm through with playing, but that don't mean I'm quitting. In fact, I'm just going to the other side of the table," he says and drains his glass, crunches his ice.

"How do you plan on doing that?" I ask.

He turns to the bartender and raises his index finger, turns back to me. "I already did," he says and gives me a wink. "You figuring it out yet?" he asks, his voice drenched in static.

He turns the dial, changes the station. I lose myself in a cacophony of white noise. The bar hisses and fades, crackles into nothing.

THE TOWN OF HOOPER, Montana, isn't a big one. At this point in time, you can tell its boomtown days have long since passed. Tourism from the surrounding mountains buoys it a little, keeps it on life support, but it slowly slips toward the inevitable.

These are the places that have been forgotten, places where you can go to be forgotten. Seemed like the kind of place that was tailor-made for Buck to end up after a long journey.

Even back before "The Rules of the Road" entered my life, I'd pass towns like these, these villages nestled in the most serene yet isolated places and daydream about what it would be like to live there. I'd wonder, how does one end up here? I guess I had an answer.

How you end up in a place like this is that you drift across the backroads and blue highways of these United States. You stop in one-church towns. Towns with a couple of stoplights and that's it. You pick up the local newspaper and scan the classifieds, look at the bulletin boards at the local I for HELP WANTED signs. When that doesn't yield anything, you just straight up visit the town's only radio station, tell them your credentials, ask if they're needing any help. Eventually you find the place.

It's a white brick building in the middle of a spacious and empty lot. It's bordered on one side by a row of identical senior living houses. A radio tower stands erect at the back of the property, a beacon flashing in the evening. There are faded and rusty letters that read KOTR.

This is KOTR Radio in Hooper, Montana. It's where Buck has landed after years of radio, years of travel, years of solitude. The station plays classic country year-round and has a minimal staff, spread thin and shorthanded. When Buck arrives, it is largely a one-man show, run by an old cowboy by the name of Rusty Miles. The two of them hit it off quite well.

"Now the pay ain't great, but I got a room you can rent free as part of the deal if you're interested. It ain't The Ritz or anything like that, but it keeps the rain out," Rusty says.

It's a guest house of sorts in the backyard of Rusty's house on the edge of town. It's a single room building, but it has a bathroom with a shower. Rusty's right that it isn't much, but to Buck it's all he needs.

It's really the only thing that's kept him going after all these years. A microphone and a soundproof room. A transmitter and a tower. A voice and a listener. It's his goal to die in the radio station. He wants his last words to be uttered over the airwaves. He wants his last words to be, "Buck Hensley, signing off."

The routine is simple, peaceful. He works days and some nights. They have an automated system that can broadcast pre-recorded taped playlists and advertisements, but he has gotten in the habit of working into the wee hours a few nights a week. It's a callback to his days as a small-time midnight man, back when he was starting out. Everything loops back around.

He reads the local news, the community bulletins, the obituaries and weather reports and high school football scores. There are announcements of church rummage sales and missing pets and Myrtle Mae Fletcher's 90th birthday celebration at the senior center. Snacks will be provided.

On the evenings he doesn't work, he sits on the back patio of Rusty's place. It's a routine and tradition Buck is fond of. Rusty will pour himself a single tallboy of Coor's Light in the same restaurant style red plastic tumbler, sit in his lawn chair and stare out at The Ruby Range. Buck will have a little more to drink and they will talk until the stars come out and the mountains turn into monstrous silhouettes.

One of these conversations stands out in particular. I guess that's why I get to see it.

"Sonuvabitch my knee's hurting something awful today," Rusty says one evening, rubbing his left knee. "Must be a front coming in. You ever hear of them radon mines up in Boulder?"

"No. Do tell," Buck replies.

"Place up in the mountains. Kind of a touristy place. These old mines that are supposed to give off a healing energy. Go in there and sit around for a while. Buy a bracelet after. I guess it's related to radiation 'cuz they don't let pregnant women and children in and you can only go a few times a year."

"You oughta go up there for your knee, eh?" Buck says.

"Thought of it. But it seems too good to be true. A cure for pain . . ." he trails off.

"Guess there's no escaping it," offers Buck as he takes a drink from his beer.

"If I was gonna mess with that, I'd try the place up at Buzzard's Roost not too far from here. They don't advertise it. It's a healing spring at the end of this old mining tunnel. They say you go into it and you will hurt no more forever."

"Wow."

"It's kind of a local legend. Although some teenager supposedly went up there one day. Got in the water. Went missing a couple days. They found them wandering the mountains out of their damn minds. They kept saying how they had seen something. One wouldn't talk for weeks. They ended up chalking the whole thing up to some bad shrooms."

"Damn, Rust. I can see why you wouldn't hurt no more messing around with something like that."

"If you're dead from uranium poisoning or crazy from a mercury spring, then I guess that's one way to do it," Rusty laughs and drains his cup.

MUCH FREE TIME is consumed in Rusty's garage. There's no room for vehicles here; it's been converted to a workshop full of radio equipment and parts. Shelves line the walls, and there are a couple tables in the middle of the room. A workbench with a transceiver sits along the back wall.

It is in this room where many hours are spent discussing all manners of electromagnetic radiation, particularly radio waves. There's talk of frequency modulation and amplitudes and ionospheres and ground wires. It all sounds like Greek to me. I failed my college physics class, and I can't help but zone out to their lengthy discussions.

They tinker with Rusty's HAM radio, the one on the workbench. They hear broadcasts in Portuguese and French, Russian and Chinese. Rusty tells Buck how you can bounce a signal from all the way down here off the surface of the moon, how he's even done it before way-back-when.

Buck hauls around a book titled *Radio Wave Propagation Theory*, fills its margins with notes. He tinkers with a military surplus high frequency antenna, a portable job that he sets up in the backyard one afternoon. It sets up on a tripod and wires run from a central mast. A battery pack serves as a power source and there's a radio handset connected to that.

He fires it up. He's transmitting. He whispers into the receiver. It's a prayer to whoever's out there, whoever's listening. But the power source will not reach his intended listener. There's just not enough power.

He says, "Carla, are you out there? It's me, Hank."

"You ever hear of WLW? What they did in the '30s?" Rusty asks one evening during another back-patio session.

"Yep. Actually did a spell in Cinci. Awful chili. I know all about the superstation. 500,000 watts," Buck replies.

"Ha. Yeah. Whole Lotta Watts. They said that's what the letters stood for. You ever hear the effects of all of that power on the folks that lived near the tower?"

"I don't think I heard that."

"The radio waves were so powerful in the surrounding area that a gas station couldn't turn its lights off. Neon signs stayed on. It rattled gutters. Strangest of all was that people reported hearing the station from the strangest places: water faucets, radiators, and barbed wire fences!" Rusty stamps his foot and laughs.

"Wonder if there's a limit to it all?" Buck wonders out loud.

UP A GRAVEL SWITCHBACK ROAD, the jeep bumps along and kicks up yellow dust. The road runs across a flat stretch that's interspersed with pines and then a meadow before climbing upward once again. The road stops at a clearing and a flat patch of gravel. There's graffitied initials on some large boulders, some empty beer cans and broken bottles. A rugged trail leads up through the pines.

After a brief but strenuous hike, an opening appears on the mountainside. There it was: the long tunnel that felt like forever and the headlamp illuminating the passage. There were the glowing crystals embedded in the wall that breathed and sighed as we passed. A sonorous, salient drone could be heard. The smooth surfaces of the glowing purple rocks that burned with such brilliance that the headlamp was no longer needed. All of that fluorescence. The pulsing stalactites like coral.

At the end of it all was the cavernous chamber with a large hole in the center of its cathedral ceiling, an opening to the sky, and the wind blew through the hole in an incessant caterwaul.

There it was: the great transcendence, the years of tears and the days that followed. The antenna at the center of the room, the limitless energy, the water dripping into an ankle-deep pool that glowed in an ultraviolet hue. He kneeled at the rocky shelf in the center of the room where the tripod was installed, and the antenna jutted up and was welcomed by the wide opening above. The purple glow grew brighter and the lights and static and warmth enveloped us. And it was there that I saw you and there that I knew.

EPILOGUE

I awoke in a saline haze amongst the fragmented vision of a hospital room. Images faded in and out. A blurry nonsequence: the TV mounted on the wall, the sunlight filtering through the vertical blinds, the whiteboard with the nurse's name on it, the bed's side rails, the weakness of my legs. From there, a feeling of waking up over several days.

It seems I had been found in a vacant radio station in Nebraska. A landscape worker was mowing the property and had heard someone within the building. The worker went to investigate and there I was found in a state of significant starvation and dehydration, speaking hoarsely into a dead microphone. I collapsed after encountering the landscaper. I had no recollection of any of this.

I had no identification on me and for over three weeks I was a John Doe at a university hospital in Omaha. I was kept in the ICU for eight days, my blood acidic and my kidneys shutting down. From there, I was in a non-responsive state and breathing on my own, a coma of sorts, until I slowly came to.

Voices waxed and waned around me. It was the talk of nurses and physical therapists and dieticians and doctors and social workers as they visited. I couldn't commit these conversations to memory just yet. They were simply fleeting moments as my brain ascended from its fog.

Yet through all of this, I could finally give them the personal details of my life and I remembered how the business administrator's face lit up when I told her I had insurance. My next of kin was contacted, my sister in New York. We had never been very close, and distance had only made it worse. I spoke with her on the phone several times, told her there was no reason for her to drop everything to come visit. They were taking good care of me.

My muscles had severely atrophied, and I required daily physical therapy for strengthening. When I wasn't doing that, I was lying in bed, zoning out to marathons of *American Pickers* on the TV.

I had difficulty sleeping most nights. Dreams were mistaken for reality, and I was never sure what I had lived or simply witnessed in another world. I asked a nurse if there was a small radio I could borrow. I could tune to the static. Maybe the white noise would help me sleep, the knowledge that all of those invisible waves floating through the air would have a conduit nearby, proof of their existence.

I had advanced in my abilities enough to ambulate to and from the restroom on my own with a walker when I received something in the mail. It was a letter with no return address. Had the hospital and my room number and everything. I kept it in my lap and stared at it for hours before getting enough gumption to open the envelope.

It was a single piece of notebook paper with a message written in sharpie. "Check your spam folder," was all that it said.

I got my assigned social worker to loan me a laptop. She handled my discharge, and I discussed how I needed to access my banking account and email in order to secure my place to stay after I got out of here. This wasn't a lie. I was going to need to do these things. The letter had just expedited the process.

There's no need to delve into the minute details of the hundreds of emails I discovered in my spam folder. So many of them were similar and had collected there over the months that they all blurred together. The gist of each one in the folder was this:

"HEY THERE, *saw your website after some Googling and just want you to know that I heard this broadcast one night while heading to Moab and I did hear the rule. I didn't end up following it because it was inconvenient, but I'm fine and I didn't experience anything after. Not sure if this helps you any, but I guess sometimes spooky stuff has happened. Guess I'm lucky.*"

WHAT WAS I to make of this revelation? The broadcast had reached numerous people and left them unscathed. It sent me into a depression. What was going on here?

Later, during my slumber with the static, he visited me. There was bouncy pop music that appeared on the radio, but it was in the background, a soundtrack to his voice.

"Howdy folks, Buck Hensley here interrupting your good night's slumber with a special call-in episode. We're taking your calls late into the night. Give us a ring at (555) 867-5309. Operators are standing by. Just don't ask for Jenny. Ask for Hensley!"

I shot straight up in bed and scrambled for the bedside phone. My bleary eyes in the dark finding the numbers. The phone rang.

"How we doing? You're on the air," Buck said over the line and on the radio with a slight delay.

"Why, Buck? Why? Just tell me ..." I stammered and trailed off.

I was greeted with hysterical laughter on his end. "Why? Why? That's a good one. You just kill me sonny."

"But the rules. Now I find out that people have ignored them without consequence? And why did you show me that stuff?"

"Show you what stuff, buddy? I will say that I've enjoyed your so-called quest. Helped break up the monotony a bit. As for the other, all I can say is this: good things happen to bad people, bad things happen to good people, but most of the time, nothing happens at all. As to why? Even ol' Buck can't tell you *that*."

"But there's . . ." my heart was racing. The words wouldn't come.

"You have a good night, ya hear?"

And he was gone.

I'M LEAVING "THE RULES" behind. But not before one final interaction.

Up in McCurtain County there's a bridge over the Kiamichi River, a one lane bridge way out in the middle of nowhere. It doesn't get much traffic at all. At its highest point, you're 80 feet over the water.

I've mapped out my routes. I have signs in my trunk and traffic cones. The signs read "DANGER: BRIDGE OUT." I don't want to risk any innocent lives.

Would it be a test of my faith to keep driving past the next shoe on the side of the road? To do nothing and simply let it lie?

Or is it the opposite? That continuing to perform the rule is the safe way out, the blind choice of a coward? If I keep doing what I've always done, I'll continue to get what I've always gotten.

I guess we'll see.

ACKNOWLEDGMENTS

Many folks out there were vital in the creation of this book. Without their help and inspiration, this novel would not be here today. I'd like to take this next page or two to call them out, to thank them for their talents and assistance and love and generosity.

For Christopher O'Halloran, Derek Walker, Ryan Tinker and Alex Wolfgang, thanks for taking the time to beta-read this book in its early stages. There are only so many hours in a day and our choices for media are practically infinite, so for y'all to take the time to read a book from an unproven and unpublished author is huge. Also, Rafael Marmol for beta-reading as well and offering valuable input (and for saving me a huge headache from BMI and their lawyers).

Shane Hawk, I'd like to thank you for not only beta-reading, but for the hours of editing you graciously offered. I know the hours were long and you really helped push this to the next level and if only the readers could know how much easier you made it on them. Keep up the hustle.

Kyle Goldtooth, thanks for the awesome covers and for putting up with my countless revision requests.

I'd like to thank The NoSleep Community, both authors and readers, and those that have been Buck fans since day one. If you've made it this far, I sincerely hope you've enjoyed the journey. This creation was organic because of you. I tried to read every comment and every theory, keeping them all in mind as I went down the road.

To all those pseudonymous denizens of the dark corners of the internet, those Rotsoils and Undead Gorillas that took me in during the early days. To the recurring voice, Mercury Rev who killed it on numerous occasions and to anyone else who brought these characters to life; there have been so many. Extra special thanks to The Baron for the life he breathed into this, the guy who "really gives a fuck about Buck."

Thanks to Daniel Kabon for some input and insight into some of these singular stories and keeping me motivated.

Thanks to the HOWL Society. Hope to continue to work with y'all for years to come.

Lola for the inspiration for "Cold As Ice."

Addie for the continued interest, even though you'll have to be a little older to read this.

Kyle for the reads and support over the years. Love ya, brother.

To the rest of my siblings and their spouses who offered their reading times and answered questions (particularly the ones providing me with their legal expertise).

For my parents for making sure I grew up a reader, for instilling in me the love of empty highways and wide open spaces.

Finally, I'd like to thank my wife. I had put writing on the backburner years ago. You brought me back to this place. This would not be here without your support and encouragement.

This one's for you.

Made in the USA
Monee, IL
23 May 2022